The

Training

The Training

TARA SUE ME

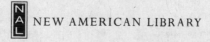
NEW AMERICAN LIBRARY

New American Library
Published by the Penguin Group
Penguin Group (USA) LLC, 375 Hudson Street,
New York, New York 10014

USA | Canada | UK | Ireland | Australia | New Zealand | India | South Africa | China
penguin.com
A Penguin Random House Company

Published by New American Library,
a division of Penguin Group (USA) LLC

First Printing, October 2013

NAL REGISTERED TRADEMARK—MARCA REGISTRADA

LIBRARY OF CONGRESS CATALOGING-IN-PUBLICATION DATA:
Me, Tara Sue.
The training: the Submissive trilogy/Tara Sue Me.
p. cm.—(The Submissive trilogy)
ISBN 978-0-451-46624-2 (pbk.)
I. Title.
PS3613.E123T73 2013
813'.6—dc23   2013017841

Printed in the United States of America
1 3 5 7 9 10 8 6 4 2

Set in Perpetua
Designed by Sabrina Bowers

To Cyndy, Danielle, and Kathy.
So much of this story wouldn't be what it is without you.
Thank you will never be enough.

Acknowledgments

First and foremost, many thanks to my husband, Mr. Sue Me. I'm not sure what he expected when he married me seventeen years ago (we were five when we got married, just in case you were wondering), but I have a strong suspicion it wasn't what he got. Thank you for your support. I know it hasn't always been easy, but you've been by my side through it all. Or at least you were when I finally confessed what I like to write . . .

Hugs, kisses, and love forever to my two children. My most fervent hope is that you aren't scarred for life by all the takeout, paper plates, and, "Yes, Mommy is editing. Yes, again."

Much love and thanks to Danielle and Cyndy. The story wouldn't have been the same without you (the blindfold was all you, Danielle, and it was perfect!). Without you, I hate to think of what it would have been.

Thank you, Ccchellesss, for the envelopes.

To Amy, who never gave up and to Gereurd for carrying on.

My deepest thanks, respect, and awe for everyone at Penguin for being the most amazing group of people to work with.

Jhanteigh, I'll never forget getting your e-mail in the car and pulling into the nearest parking lot so I could read it. I'm forever grateful you saw something in me (and I'll never pass a Burger King without smiling).

Claire, you're an anchor in this crazy world. Thank you for your patience, guidance, and direction.

To everyone who has in any way, shape, or form supported me, I wish my memory was good enough to remember you all. There is a piece of you in everything I do.

And to Ms. K, once again, there are no words. Thank you for being a true friend. I am blessed to have you in my life, and you're stuck with me forever.

The
Training

Chapter One

—ABBY—

The drive back to Nathaniel's house took longer than it should have. Or maybe it just felt like it took longer. Maybe it was nerves.

I tipped my head in thought.

Maybe not nerves exactly. Maybe anticipation.

Anticipation that after weeks of talking, weeks of waiting, and weeks of planning, we were finally here.

Finally back.

I lifted my hand and touched the collar—Nathaniel's collar. My fingertips danced over the familiar lines and traced along the diamonds. I moved my head from side to side, reacquainting myself with the collar's feel.

There were no words to describe how I felt wearing Nathaniel's collar again. The closest I could come was to compare it to a puzzle. A puzzle with the last piece finally in place. Yes, for the last few weeks, Nathaniel and I had been living as lovers, but we both felt incomplete. His recollaring of me—his reclaiming of me—had been what was missing. It sounded odd even to me, but I finally felt like I was his again.

The hired car eventually reached Nathaniel's house and pulled into his long drive. Lights flickered from the windows. He had set the timer, anticipating my arrival in the dark. Such a small gesture, but a touching one. One that showed, like much he did, how he kept me firmly at the forefront of his mind.

I jingled my keys as I walked up the drive to his front door. My keys. To his house. He'd given me a set of keys a week ago. I didn't live with him, but I spent a fair amount of time at his house. He said it only made sense for me to be able to let myself in or to lock up when I left.

Apollo, Nathaniel's golden retriever, rushed me when I opened the door. I rubbed his head and let him outside for a few minutes. I didn't keep him out for too long—I wasn't sure if Nathaniel would arrive home early, but if he did, I wanted to be in place. I wanted this weekend to be perfect.

"Stay," I told Apollo after stopping in the kitchen to refill his water bowl. Apollo obeyed all of Nathaniel's orders, but thankfully, he listened to me this time. Normally, he would follow me up the stairs, and tonight that would be odd.

I quickly left the kitchen and made my way upstairs to my old room. The room that would be mine on weekends.

I undressed, placing my clothes in a neat pile on the edge of the twin bed. On this, Nathaniel and I had been in agreement. I would share his bed Sunday through Thursday nights, anytime I stayed over, but on Friday and Saturday nights, I would sleep in the room he reserved for his submissives.

Now that we had a more traditional relationship during the week, we both wanted to make sure we remained in the proper mind-set on weekends. That mind-set would be easier to maintain for both of us if we slept separately. For both of us, yes, but perhaps more so for Nathaniel. He rarely shared a bed with his submissives, and having a romantic relationship with one was completely new to him.

I stepped naked into the playroom. Nathaniel had led me around the room last weekend—explaining, discussing, and showing me things I'd never seen and several items I'd never heard of.

At its core, it was an unassuming room—hardwood floors, deep, dark brown paint, handsome cherry armoires, even a long table carved of rich wood. However, the chains and shackles, the padded leather bench and table, and the wooden whipping bench gave away the room's purpose.

A lone pillow waited for me below the hanging chains. I dropped to my knees on it, situating myself into the position Nathaniel explained I was to be in whenever I waited for him in the playroom—butt resting on my heels, back straight, right hand on top of my left in my lap, fingers not intertwined, and head down.

I got into position and waited.

Time inched forward.

I finally heard him enter through the front door.

"Apollo," he called, and while I knew he spoke Apollo's name so he could take him outside again, another reason was to alert me who it was that entered the house. To give me time to prepare myself. Perhaps for him to listen for footsteps from overhead. Footsteps that would tell him I wasn't prepared for his arrival. I felt proud he would hear nothing.

I closed my eyes. It wouldn't be long now. I imagined what Nathaniel was doing—taking Apollo outside, feeding him maybe. Would he undress downstairs? In his bedroom? Or would he enter the playroom wearing his suit and tie?

Doesn't matter, I told myself. *Whatever Nathaniel has planned will be perfect.*

I strained my ears——he was walking up the stairs now. Alone. No dog followed.

Somehow, the atmosphere of the room changed when he walked in. The air became charged, and the space between us nearly hummed. In that moment, I understood——I was his, yes. I had been correct with that assumption. But even more so, even more important, perhaps, he was mine.

My heart raced.

"Very nice, Abigail," he said, and walked to stand in front of me. His feet were bare. I noted he had changed out of his suit and into a pair of black jeans.

I closed my eyes again. Cleared my mind. Focused inwardly. Forced myself to remain still under his scrutiny.

He walked to the table, and I heard a drawer open. For a minute, I tried to remember everything in the drawers, but I stopped myself and once again forced my mind to quiet itself.

He came back to stand at my side. Something firm and leather trailed down my spine.

Riding crop.

"Perfect posture," he said as the crop ran up my spine. "I expect you to be in this position whenever I tell you to enter this room."

I felt relieved he was satisfied with my posture. I wanted so much to please him tonight. To show him I was ready for this. That we were ready. He had been so worried.

Of course, not a bit of worry or doubt could be discerned now. Not in his voice. Not in his stance. His demeanor in the playroom was utter and complete control and confidence.

He dragged the riding crop down my stomach and then back up. Teasing.

Damn. I loved the riding crop.

I kept my head down even though I wanted to see his face. To meet his eyes. But I knew the best gift I could give him was my absolute trust and obedience, so I kept my head down with my eyes focused on the floor.

"Stand up."

I rose slowly to my feet, knowing I stood directly under the chains. Normally, he kept them up for storage, but they were lowered tonight.

"Friday night through Sunday afternoon, your body is mine," he said. "As we agreed, the kitchen table and library are still yours. There, and only there, are you to speak your mind. Respectfully, of course."

Both of his hands traced across my shoulders, down my arms. One hand slipped between my breasts and dropped to where I was wet and aching.

"This," he said, rubbing my outer lips, "is your responsibility. I want you waxed bare as often as possible. If I decide you have neglected this responsibility, you will be punished."

And again, we had agreed to this.

"In addition, it is your responsibility to ensure your waxer does an acceptable job. I will allow no excuses. Is that understood?"

I didn't say anything.

"You may answer," he said. I heard the smile in his voice.

"Yes, Master."

He slipped a finger between my folds and I felt his breath in my ear. "I like you bare." His finger swirled around my clit. "Slick and smooth. Nothing between your pussy and whatever I decide to do to it."

Fuck.

Then he moved behind me and cupped my ass. "Have you been using your plug?"

I waited.

"You may answer."

"Yes, Master."

His finger made its way back to the front of me, and I bit the inside of my cheek to keep from moaning.

"I won't ask you that again," he said. "From now on, it is your responsibility to prepare your body to accept my cock in any manner I decide to give it to you." He ran a finger around the rim of my ear. "If I want to fuck your ear, I expect your ear to be ready." He hooked his finger in my ear and pulled. I kept my head down. "Do you understand? Answer me."

"Yes, Master."

He lifted my arms above my head, buckling first one wrist and then the other to the chains at my side. "Do you remember this?" he asked, his warm breath tickling my hair. "From our first weekend?"

Again, I said nothing.

"Very nice, Abigail," he said. "Just so there's no misunderstanding, for the rest of the evening, or until I tell you differently, you may not speak or vocalize in any way. There are two exceptions— the first being the use of your safe words. You are to use them at any point you feel the need. No repercussions or consequences will ever follow the use of your safe words. Second, when I ask if you are okay, I expect an immediate and honest answer."

He didn't wait for a response, of course. I wasn't to give one. Without warning, his hands slipped back down to where I ached for him. Since my head was lowered, I watched one of his fingers slide inside me, and I bit the inside of my cheek again to keep from moaning.

Shit, his hands felt good.

"How wet you are already." He pushed deeper and twisted his wrist. *Fuck.* "Usually, I would taste you myself, but tonight, I feel like sharing."

He removed himself, and the emptiness was immediate. Before I could think much about it, I felt his slippery finger at my mouth. "Open, Abigail, and taste how ready you are for me." He trailed his finger around my open lips before easing it inside my mouth.

I'd tasted myself before, out of curiosity, but never so much at one time and never off of Nathaniel's finger. It felt so depraved, so feral.

Damn, it turned me on.

"Taste how sweet you are," he said as I licked myself off his finger.

I treated his finger as if it were his cock——running my tongue along it, sucking gently at first. I wanted him. Wanted him inside me. I sucked harder, imagining his cock in my mouth.

You will not release until I give you permission, and I will be very stingy with my permission. His words from the office floated through my mind, and I choked back a moan before it left my mouth. It would be a long night.

"I changed my mind," he said when I finished cleaning his finger. "I want a taste after all." He crushed his lips to mine and forced my mouth open. His lips were brutal——powerful and demanding in their quest to taste me.

Damn, I'd have a stroke if he kept that up.

He pulled back and lifted my chin. "Look at me."

For the first time since he entered the room, I met his eyes——they were steady and green. His tongue ran over his lips, and he smiled. "Every time sweeter than the last."

I forced my eyes to remain on his even though I wanted to see his chest, to enjoy the sight of his perfect body. But his body was not mine to enjoy, so I kept my eyes locked with his.

He broke our connection first by turning and walking to the table. He put something in his pocket, and I dropped my head as he turned around.

He walked five steps to me; then darkness cloaked my vision.

"Totally at my mercy," he said in a voice as smooth as the silk scarf covering my eyes.

He stroked my breasts. Long fingers took my nipples and rolled them, pulling and twisting.

Fuck.

"I thought about bringing out the clamps tonight," he said, flicking the tip of a nipple.

Double fuck.

We had talked about the clamps, though I'd never felt or used them. A small bubble of anticipation swelled in my belly. Nathaniel promised I would like the clamps, that the brief pain would be worth the pleasure they brought.

"Thought about it," he continued, "but decided on something else."

Cold metal made its way across my chest. It felt like a prickly pizza cutter. He ran it slowly around one breast and then the other. The sensation felt incredible. He didn't go near either nipple. Instead he rolled the wheel closer and closer before moving away. Then there were two, each one mirroring the other in its movements. Teasing and taunting, but never hitting exactly where I needed. Closer and closer they went, then retreated once again. They went even closer on the next pass, and I knew I'd combust if he didn't touch me soon.

And then he did—the wheels ran over my nipples right where I needed relief. It felt so good, I forgot where I was, what we were doing, and I moaned out in pleasure.

"Ahhh."

He immediately pulled back. "Damn it, Abigail," he said, taking the scarf from around my eyes. "That's twice in less than two hours. Now and earlier in my office." He pulled my hair back so hard I had no choice but to meet his eyes. "You're making me believe you don't really want this."

Tears prickled my eyes. I'd wanted so badly to do everything perfectly this weekend. Instead, I'd already messed up twice—once in his office and once again in his playroom. But the worst, the absolute worst, was knowing I'd disappointed Nathaniel.

I wanted to apologize. To tell him I was sorry and I'd do better. But he'd told me not to speak, and the best thing I could do was obey that command.

"Let's see," he said, still looking me in the eyes. "What was the penalty for disobedience during a scene?"

He knew the penalty as well as I did. Probably better. He dragged it out only to make me sweat.

"Ah, yes," he said, as if remembering. "Number of strokes for disobedience during a scene is at dom's discretion."

Dom's discretion.

Fuck.

What would he decide?

"I could give you twenty." He ran his hands over my backside. "But that would end all play for tonight, and I don't think either of us want that."

Hell, no.

He wouldn't do twenty, would he?

I dropped my eyes and tried hard not to give in to the temptation to look at the whipping bench.

"I gave you three earlier in my office, though," he mused, "and they obviously did no good."

My heart beat through the skin of my chest. I felt certain he saw it as well.

"Eight," he finally said. "I'll redo the prior three and add five." He leaned over and whispered, "Next time, I'll add five more for a total of thirteen. After that it goes to eighteen." He gave my hair a hard tug. "Trust me. You don't want eighteen."

Hell, no, I didn't want eighteen. I didn't want the eight I had coming.

He unbuckled my wrists. The tin of salve on the table, ignored. There would be no soothing rubdown for now. "To the bench, Abigail."

Fuck.

Fuck. Fuck. Fuck. Fuck. Fuck.

I could do this, I told myself as I walked to the bench. *We* could do this. This was nothing like the last time. He'd explained his negligence in the lack of aftercare last time. And there would be only eight strokes tonight.

I'd make damn sure there weren't any more.

But as bad as last time had been, it wasn't the thought of pain that made my steps slow. It was disappointment in myself. Disappointment in my disobedience, but even more so, guilt that my actions forced him to punish me on our first weekend of play. The very first hour of our first weekend.

I settled my body into the smooth groove of the bench, wanting it to be over so we could continue on to more enjoyable pursuits.

He didn't make me wait. Almost immediately after I dropped into position, he started spanking me with his hand.

Warm-up.

He swiftly smacked my backside with slaps that were harder than his erotic spankings.

"How very disappointed I am to be doing this so soon," he said.

Yes. That was what hurt the most.

"I had you count in my office." He picked something up from beside the bench. "But since I told you not to speak or vocalize, *I'll* have to count this time."

The sting of the leather strap came down across my backside. "One," he said, voice strong and firm.

Again it came.

"Two."

Ow.

By five, silent tears ran down my face. I sucked my bottom lip into my mouth to keep from saying anything.

"Three more," he said, rubbing where he struck.

"Six," he said after the next one. I could tell he wasn't putting as much strength behind the strokes.

Two more. Only two more and we could move on.

"Seven."

And finally, "Eight."

I heard him breathing hard behind me, and I blinked furiously to get the tears out of my eyes. He set the strap down, and I listened to his footsteps as he walked away.

Moments later, his hands came back, rubbing something cool and wet over me. "Are you okay?" he whispered.

I let out my breath in a shuddering sigh of relief. "Yes, Master."

His hands continued caressing as he talked. "We discussed this. I hate having to punish you, but I can't let broken commands slide. You know that."

Yes, I did. I'd try harder next time.

He moved to the side of the bench and leaned down so his face was level with mine. Ever so gently, he kissed first one cheek and then the other. My heart pounded frantically as his lips drew closer to mine. And then, finally, he kissed my mouth—slow and soft and long.

I sighed.

He pulled back, and his eyes danced with a wicked gleam. "Come, my lovely." He held his hand out. "I want to taste that sweet pussy."

Chapter Two

—NATHANIEL—

She took my hand and I squeezed it once before letting go. She didn't stumble as she stepped off the bench and moved to the table.

"Paragraph two," I said.

I'd thought a chastisement might be necessary this weekend—our first weekend back into our roles. We'd lived the last few weeks as lovers and, while we both enjoyed our relationship, there was something missing for both of us. Yet this pivotal weekend would also be the most difficult.

Chastising her would never be my favorite act, but I felt relieved. I now knew I could do it. There had never been a question in my mind *she* could handle it.

I watched her and felt myself slip deeper into the needed mind frame. I hadn't done this for several months, but was surprised at how comfortable I felt reestablishing myself. As always, she had been right—we were ready.

I returned my focus to Abigail. She was positioned on her

back, arms to her sides, knees bent and spread wide. An exact description of paragraph two.

"How pleased I am you remembered," I said. While she didn't move or in any way acknowledge my words, I knew my praise would encourage her.

My eyes traveled over her body. I took in the long line of her limbs, the trusting way she offered herself to me. *Sheer perfection.*

I placed my hands on her hip bones and traced her torso up to her arms, capturing her hands and bringing them above her head. Our eyes met briefly. "Close your eyes," I told her.

I bent her arms at the elbows and secured her to the table. I trailed my fingers across her stomach and hip bones, careful of her backside, and bound her ankles to the table. Her skin broke out in gooseflesh. When finished, I stepped back.

Fuck.

What the sight of her did to me . . .

"Take a minute and feel, Abigail," I said. "Feel how exposed you are." Her nipples pebbled at my words. *Excellent.* "How vulnerable."

I let the weight of what I said sink in, knowing just how defenseless she would feel in her current position.

"I can do anything I want to you," I said, still not touching her. Still letting my words alone stroke and excite her. "And I plan to do so much."

I took a pillow and slipped it under her butt. Her backside would still be sore. Plus this position gave me better access. I thought briefly about reminding her she couldn't climax until I granted permission, but decided against it. She needed to learn. I felt certain she would remember, and on the off chance she didn't, it would be part of her training. Although thirteen strokes on top of the eight I just gave her would end all play.

"So beautiful," I murmured.

I started at her neck and worked my way down. Running my hands over the delicate bones of her shoulders, my thumbs grazed the edge of the collar near the hollow of her throat. I stroked her body gently for a few minutes, allowing her to grow accustomed to her bound and defenseless state. Allowing her time to focus on my touch and me. Gradually, my hands grew rougher, but she remained silent.

I positioned myself between her legs and drew a finger across her slick folds. She startled slightly, but otherwise remained still and silent.

"Mmmmm," I said, palming her sex, my thumb against her clit and my middle finger barely inside. "Serving me like this excites you. Doesn't it, my naughty girl?" I pushed deeper. "Being bound turns you on." My thumb stroked her. "Is it knowing you belong to me or knowing I will do anything to you I want?" I slipped a second finger inside. "Maybe both?" I asked in a whisper.

Both, I knew. Definitely both.

I removed my fingers and dropped my head to place a tender kiss on her bare skin. She shivered under me. I spread her gently before running my tongue over her slit. Again she shivered, but she still remained quiet. I licked her again, enjoying her sweet taste, feeling the faint quiver of her skin as she worked to remain motionless and silent for me. My tongue pushed deeper inside, and I dragged the tip up to her clit, ending with a little swirl. On the next pass, I added my teeth, grazing her just a bit.

I stroked her thighs as I licked and nibbled, tickling her skin with featherlight touches. Then I pulled myself to her, nibbling harder, stretching out her pleasure and bringing her precariously close to the edge.

I knew exactly when she started working to hold off her climax—her breathing became ragged and her legs started to shake. I blew once, sending a long, steady stream of warm air across her swollen clit. She tensed as she held her release at bay.

I didn't want her to fail in her efforts, and I knew if I touched her sensitive flesh again, she would be unable to contain her climax. I pulled back, stroking from her upper thighs down to her lower legs. Bringing her back from the ledge. Bringing her down.

She exhaled deeply, and her body relaxed.

"You did well, Abigail," I said. "I'm very pleased."

A small smile flitted across her face.

Yes, my lovely. Find your joy in my pleasure.

She had been bound in one position long enough. I untied her arms first. Starting with her wrists and working down to her shoulders, I gently caressed away any potential kinks, placing her arms at her sides when I finished. Next I dropped down to her legs and repeated my actions on her lower body, untying her ankles and tenderly massaging her calves. When I finished, I placed them so they hung off the end of the table, her knees still spread.

I left her side, walking to the cabinet on the far side of the room. I opened a door, placed a vibrator in my pocket, and took out the rabbit fur flogger. I walked back to the table, my bare feet padding softly on the hardwood floor. I stepped heavier than normal, wanting her to hear and know where I was.

Her eyes were still closed.

Excellent.

"Guess what I have," I said, even though I knew she wouldn't answer. Her body remained relaxed. Very gently, I dragged the strands of the flogger across her chest. "A flogger." I snaked the ends farther down her body, letting them tickle her stomach. "Tell me, Abigail, would you like for me to flog you?"

Her breath hitched.

"I'm being, perhaps, a bit unkind," I said. "Commanding you to remain silent while I use a new toy." I flicked the strands of the flogger over her belly. "But you'll do as I ask, won't you?" I questioned. "You'll do anything I want you to." That would be the state I'd eventually get her to—where she would trust me completely with her body. When she would give me all she had and more. She wasn't there yet, though. She might think she was, but I knew better—it would take time.

I took my time, once again, and slowly worked her body. Using the flogger not only to pleasure her, but also to remind her I was in control. I would use her, yes, but I would never harm her. I would show her she could trust me. She was safe.

I switched my stroke. The flogger landed softly across her chest, first one way and then the other, the tips brushing her sensitive nipples. I brought the soft strands lower down her body, gradually picking up speed. The rabbit fur was soft. I had planned to work up to the suede, but that had been before the chastisement. I wanted to work her slowly and softly, and feared the suede would be too much for her after the spanking.

I moved the flogger to my left hand and ran the fingers of my right between her legs, lightly grazing her clit, then dipping slightly into her obvious wetness.

Perfect.

I switched the flogger back to my right hand and struck her upper thigh. The tips of the flogger strands ran across her entrance. I lifted my hand to strike again.

"Does it tickle, Abigail?" I asked. "Enough friction to make you ache, but too soft to bring relief?"

I continued for a few more minutes, changing my position and alternating where the tips landed. I immediately noticed when her body became too tense. "Relax, Abigail," I said, brushing the fur across her belly. "I won't be using anything harder on you tonight and, at this point in our play, I would tell you before I did."

She exhaled, and the tension left her body.

"That's it," I said, using the flogger once more across her chest. "Just feel." I dragged the strands down her body and flicked them against her clit. "Trust me."

I took the vibrator from my pocket and turned it on, letting her hear it before I used it on her. "Can you handle more?" I asked, knowing she could.

With one hand, I continued using the flogger and, with the other, I slowly pushed the vibrator into her. I knew if I pushed too hard and fast, I'd make her climax, so I pressed slowly, allowing her to grow accustomed to the low buzz.

My cock grew harder within the confines of my jeans, but I pushed my needs and desires to the back of my mind and made myself focus on her. Tonight was about her, getting her accustomed to our new arrangement, working to regain her trust. Introducing her to a new type of control, one I had never pushed too far before.

I slowly worked the vibrator in and out of her while continuing to tease with the flogger. The fur strands landed on her breasts at the same time I pushed the vibrator deeper. I started a rhythm and then changed it a bit to keep her guessing.

When I noticed her struggle to keep orgasm at bay, I removed the vibrator and set it and the flogger on the table. I walked to her side and gently stroked her face. "Open your eyes, my lovely."

She blinked a few times before focusing on me.

The trust and love I saw in her eyes nearly took my breath, but I collected myself. "Are you okay?" I asked.

"Yes, Master," she whispered.

I leaned over and brushed her lips with mine. "You're doing

great," I said against them before pulling back. "You may leave your eyes open."

I moved to her side and unzipped my jeans. Standing close enough for her to hear, but out of her peripheral vision, so she couldn't see, I pushed my jeans down and swallowed hard when my erection sprang free.

Fuck.

I wasn't sure how much longer *I* could hold out. I stood still for a few minutes, trying to decide how to proceed, and absent-mindedly stroked my cock a few times.

I stepped out of my jeans and moved to the table. She lay still, blinking every so often, breathing steadily. My eyes wandered over her—from her pebbled, hard nipples, down to the soft skin of her belly I could taste from memory—she would have a faint salty flavor by now. It took all of my control not to rush the table and bury myself deep within her.

But how could I expect her to learn control if I couldn't show I had mastered it myself?

I tweaked one of her nipples. "The clamps tomorrow, I think," I said, giving her other nipple a hard squeeze. She sucked in a deep breath. "But for now," I said, "get on your hands and knees and put that beautiful ass in the air for me."

She moved at once, rolling to her side and scrambling to her hands and knees.

"Keep your stance wide," I instructed.

When she had positioned herself, I stepped back and slowly lowered the table. My padded table was custom-made, with an automatic lowering and raising mechanism. Once I had it lowered at the height I wanted, I moved to stand behind her. "Scoot back until I tell you to stop."

She backed toward me, and I placed a hand on her backside. "Far enough," I said.

I ran my hands across her ass. "What do you think, Abigail?" I asked. "Have I tormented you long enough?" I pushed my hips against her so she could feel me. "Should I let you have my cock?"

She dropped her upper body so she rested on her elbows and waited.

"Mmmmmmm," I hummed, enjoying the sight of her spread and waiting for me. Spread and ready. I gave her ass a light slap. By this time, pain from her spanking would have subsided slightly. The slap I gave served only to excite her further.

I placed my hands on either side of her hips and slowly eased my way inside.

Fuck.

I'd taken her in the shower that morning. Had taken her twice the night before. Why did it always feel so fucking good, every single time? My head fell back as I pushed deeper.

So good. So right.

Fuck.

Focus.

I pulled out slightly and teased her clit with my fingertips. "You've done so well tonight, I might let you come." I pulled out farther. "Or I might make you wait until tomorrow."

And with that, I started a slow, teasing rhythm. Pulling almost all the way out. Waiting for what seemed an inordinate amount of time. Easing my way back inside.

I slowed even further. Enjoying the sensation of being within her. Making sure she felt every inch of me. Feeling her stretch as I filled her once again.

Then, finally, I started moving faster. But only slightly. With each push, I swirled my finger around her clit, purposely avoiding any direct contact.

"Move with me," I commanded. On my next thrust, she pushed back, drawing me deeper.

Yes.

I kept our pace steady. Her breasts fit easily in my hands as I moved within her. I pinched a nipple, imagining the clamps I would put on her the next day—her head thrown back in ecstasy as I brought her to the edge of pleasure again.

I flicked one and rolled the hard tip between my fingers. She pushed back in to me harder, showing me without words or sounds how she felt. My hands ran down her sides, and under my fingertips, her breathing became ragged. Shorter. Neither one of us could hold out much longer.

I increased my rhythm, pounding strong and steady as she breathed even harder.

"I love being inside you," I said, digging my fingers into her hips in a vain effort to get closer. Deeper. Anything. "The way your body stretches." My words came in pants as I moved faster. "How it accepts me." My hips rocked and I shifted deeper. "Fuck."

My words dissolved into grunts, and I wasn't sure what I said. The world disappeared. Time slowed. Only we existed.

Her body trembled under me.

"Should I let you come?" I teased. Her only answer was another thrust back into me. "Or should I be really cruel?" I stopped talking for a second as she took me deeper. "Make you wait until tomorrow? Keep you aching all night?"

I moved faster, my thrusts long and hard. She stilled; her body was taut and tense from the strain of withholding her climax. My balls ached with the need to release.

I leaned over her back and whispered, "Come hard for me, baby." My finger swirled around her clit and my voice dropped even lower. "Let me hear you." I grazed her clit with the tip of my finger.

Her scream echoed in the quiet room.

Fuck.

I thrust into her again.

"Holy. Fucking. Hell," she yelled as her body clamped around me. Her orgasm triggered my own, and I came just as hard as she did.

Completely spent, her body dropped to the table, limp. I leaned forward and rested on my elbows, placing soft kisses along the small of her back as I struggled to bring my breathing back to normal. She didn't move.

"Are you okay?" I asked.

"Y-yes." She took a deep breath. "Master."

I moved up her body, caressing and kissing as I went, climbing up the table to get closer before finally moving off of her. "Sit up when you're ready," I said. "Feel free to talk."

She lay still for a few minutes more, so I took my time—rubbing her muscles, nibbling and brushing her skin lightly with my lips. "You did so well," I said into the nape of her neck. "I'm so very pleased."

She rolled over, a faint smile of pride on her lips, and I couldn't help but kiss her softly. *Why did I ever think not kissing was a good rule?* "Take some time," I said. "Take a shower, get some water—whatever you feel like—and meet me in the library in thirty minutes."

Chapter Three

—ABBY—

It was, hands down, without question, no need to even think about it, the most amazing orgasm of my life. Somehow, not being able to speak, or even moan, *and* having to wait for permission, made everything so much more intense. Then, as I walked out of the playroom, I remembered his husky whisper. *Come hard for me, baby. Let me hear you.* I almost came again.

Baby.

I shivered just thinking about it.

The first thing I noticed when I entered my room was the bucket of ice on the dresser. Funny, it wasn't until I saw the bottle of water in the bucket that I realized how thirsty I was. Of course, Nathaniel would have thought of it, though. He thought of everything.

I swallowed half the bottle before noticing the unassuming nightgown waiting for me at the foot of the bed. I smiled. Nathaniel had been quite busy setting up before entering the playroom. I put my water down and picked up the gown. It was a delicate green and not overly sexy or revealing; I'd feel like a queen wearing it.

Since I had plenty of time before I needed to be in the library, I took a quick shower, allowing the warm water to run over my still sensitive skin. After slipping the gown on, I discovered even more of a surprise: the cool satin swept against the warmth of my skin. It gently brushed the slight sting left by our evening, so that even from the opposite side of the house, I felt my master's touch.

I stopped just outside the door of my room.

My master.

It was the first time I thought of him as *my master* instead of *Nathaniel.* I didn't dwell on it for too long, but hurried down the stairs, anxious to be near him again.

He waited for me in the library, standing near the table of decanters. His eyes traveled over me as I entered.

"The gown looks beautiful on you, Abigail," he said.

Abigail. A reminder that, even though this was my library, it was still a weekend, I still wore his collar, and I was to behave as such.

He wore his tan cotton drawstring pants and didn't look half bad himself. I dropped my gaze to the tops of my toes. Watched them wiggle. "Thank you, sir."

"Look at me when we're in the library," he said.

I looked up and met his eyes. They shone darkly with emotion.

"Remember," he said softly. "This is your space."

"Yes, sir," I said. Last week, he told me I could use *sir* in the library or at the kitchen table. Any other place during our weekends, he expected me to call him *master.*

"How does it feel?" he asked, and then quickly added, "The gown, I mean."

"Delightful." I swung my hips, and the satin brushed once again across the dull ache of my backside.

He smiled as if he knew exactly what I felt. Who knew? He probably did. Everything he did was calculated.

"Come on in," he said, waving me farther into the library. He held up a wineglass. "Red?"

"Yes, please."

He motioned to the floor in front of the empty fireplace. Piles of pillows lay scattered about with fluffy blankets among them, forming an inviting place to sit down. I took a tentative seat on a large pillow.

He joined me seconds later and passed me a glass of red wine. I noticed he didn't have one. Not too much of a shock, considering what he'd told me days earlier.

"You probably thought I was being melodramatic the night of Jackson and Felicia's party," he said, as we sat on his leather couch on Tuesday night after dinner. "When I told you that your leaving almost killed me."

"I did," I admitted. "I never thought of you as being one for dramatics."

"I was bad after you left," he said. "It started as soon as I returned from following you home."

I wasn't sure where he was going with this. Talking about that time in our lives wasn't something I enjoyed. Certainly, he felt the same.

He frowned. "I'm not sure how much I drank that day, but when Jackson found me, I was trying to burn down the library."

"You what?" I asked.

His eyes closed. "I don't remember it very well. Don't remember parts of it at all. I just . . ." He trailed off momentarily. "I just needed to tell you. It felt important, somehow."

"You could have died," I said, shocked at the nonchalant way he talked about burning his house down.

"*Probably not,*" he said. "*I was too drunk to do much of anything. At least, that's what I tell myself. It's not like I had a death wish. I didn't want to die. I just wanted . . .*"

"*To burn your house down?*" I volunteered.

"*No.*" He shook his head. "*Just the library.*"

"*That doesn't make sense,*" I argued. "*You can't burn just the library. The entire house would go up.*"

"*I know,*" he said. "*I'm sure it made sense to me at the time. All I really remember is pain, emptiness, and despair.*"

I took his hand and stroked it. "*No wonder.*"

He kissed my knuckles. "*No wonder what?*"

"*No wonder Jackson felt the way he did.*"

His lips stopped their kissing. "*Did he say something to you? I swear, if he did, I'll kick his ass.*"

I hushed him with a finger. "*No. He never said anything. Now, Felicia . . .*" I laughed, remembering her outburst the day she came home with a ring. "*Felicia ripped into me something awful. It makes sense now. She'd heard Jackson talk about how my leaving affected you.*"

"*He came by my house every day for a long time,*" he mused. "*I worried the entire family sick. I told him, eventually, that your leaving was my fault. That it wasn't you.*"

My hand rested on his knee, and I squeezed him gently. "*Must be why he hugged me the night of the party. I noticed a change in him that night.*"

"*I'm sorry if he ever treated you like our breakup was your fault.*" He sighed, a sad, regretful sound. "*So much I should have told you.*"

"*Which is why from now on, we're going to talk,*" I said. "*A lot. And about everything.*"

Talk a lot about everything. Probably what he had in mind for the library.

He held out a plate. "I know you had an early dinner. Are you hungry?"

My stomach let out a growl in reply, and he smiled. Why hadn't I realized I was hungry before?

Cheese and crackers, almonds, grapes, and dried cherries covered the plate. He set it down between us, and I took a block of cheddar cheese. When that was gone, I grabbed a handful of almonds and ate those as well. He munched on a few grapes and a cube of Gruyère cheese.

The snack was nice and welcome, but surely he had another reason for asking me to the library. We could have gone on to bed. He could have told me to grab a snack in the kitchen. Why would he want to meet in the library?

You could ask him, I told myself. Even though I knew this was my library, it still felt odd to just address him like I would during the week.

I was beginning to see what he meant about talking.

We hadn't done a lot of it the last time I was collared.

But what should I say? *Thank you for the amazing orgasm?*

He cleared his throat. "I won't do this every night, but I thought it would be a good idea to come together and talk about how the evening went." He smiled at me. "Since it was our first night. And only your second time in the playroom."

I traced the golden filigree design on the plate.

"I need for this to be a two-way conversation," he said.

"I know," I said finally. "It's just . . . odd."

"Maybe talking about the oddness will help."

We both reached for a grape at the same time and our fingers touched. I jerked mine back.

"See?" he asked, voice heavy with emotion. "What was that for?"

I took a deep breath. "Just trying to keep the weekday Nat . . . I mean, man, separate from the weekend one." I glanced down at the plate. "It's harder than I thought it would be."

He lifted my head so our eyes met. "Why?"

"I don't want to mess up," I admitted. "I don't want to over-step."

"I think it's highly doubtful you would overstep." He gave a small laugh. "You may have difficulties in other areas, but I don't think showing respect in the library or at the kitchen table will ever be a problem for you."

"You say that because this"—I pointed from him to me and back again—"is easy for you. *This* you're used to."

"I would argue that *this*"—he indicated the space between us—"is new to me." He looked up at the ceiling and frowned. "But, on second thought, perhaps you're right in other regards."

I know I am.

"The fact remains," he continued, "that we can't talk honestly about the scene if you're not open and relaxed with me."

I sighed deeply.

"Now, just what—" He pushed the plate of food out of the way, took my wineglass and set it aside. "Just what are we going to do about that?"

My heart started to thump faster. "Beats me."

The corner of his mouth lifted. "Beating you wasn't quite what I had in mind."

My head shot up. "Sign?" I asked, using my old way to deter-mine if he was joking.

"Yes," he said. "It was a joke, and not a very good one. I'm just trying to lighten the mood a bit." His voice dropped to a low whisper and his eyes darkened. "Come here."

I scooted closer, and he took my face in his hands.

"How am I ever going to get you to relax?" He kissed my cheek. "To talk openly?" He kissed the other. "To tell me how you feel?"

His touch was the connection I craved, what I unknowingly

needed, and I felt myself melt under his hands. His lips traveled from my cheek to my ear. "Yes," he said, feeling my body react.

I turned my face toward his, and our lips brushed softly. I unconsciously moved closer to him, and his arms came around my shoulders. He held me close to his chest and leaned us back so we reclined against the pillows.

"Better?" he asked in a whisper.

"Much," I said, closing my eyes. "Thank you."

He stroked my hair for a few minutes, and I listened to the steady *thump, thump, thump* of his heart.

"Okay," he said. "Let's do it this way—you tell me what you liked."

We'd talked about our checklists for hours. About what we enjoyed and wanted to try. Why did talking about something we'd done make me embarrassed? I told myself it was crazy. Nathaniel had seen all of me. Touched all of me. There was nothing to be embarrassed about.

"Not being able to vocalize was very intense," I said.

"Very intense meaning, *I loved it; let's do it again?*" he asked. "Or very intense meaning, *I hated it; never try that again?*"

I took a deep breath and inhaled the deep woodsy scent of him. Someone else had taken a shower recently. "Mmmmm. I loved it; let's do it again," I said.

"I think you can handle more," he said. "Next time we'll see if you can go a bit longer."

My body tingled with anticipation. *Longer next time.* I could only imagine what he meant. I was glad he thought I could handle more. Frankly, I thought I had reached the end of my control there at the end.

"I liked the flogger," I said, wanting to switch subjects. "It wasn't what I was expecting."

His hand ran down my side. "I've decided to use only the rabbit fur this weekend." The press of his fingers grew rough against my backside. "But I meant what I said about the clamps. I'll use them tomorrow." He leaned down and spoke softly in my ear. "And it's a good thing you've been using your plug."

I nodded, suddenly unable to speak. The tingle in my body became stronger and moved lower, coming to rest right between my legs.

Gah.

"The eight strokes?" he asked.

"Hurt like the devil," I finished.

"They were meant to."

"I know," I said. "I completely understand that part." I lifted my head. "You didn't seem surprised. Did you know I'd mess up so soon?"

"I thought you might," he said. "It made sense to me you would. I didn't want to say anything before it happened, though. How would that have sounded?"

I laid my head back on his chest. "I probably wouldn't have believed you anyway."

"Probably not," he said.

"What hurt most was knowing I'd disappointed you," I said.

"That was my least favorite part of the night," he said. "Having to punish you. But you learned. You didn't make the same mistake twice."

I didn't want to dwell on my failure. "Your turn," I said. "What was your favorite part?"

"Look at me," he said, and I tilted my head to catch his gaze. "My favorite part was you. The trust you have in me. Your obedience. The joy you find in pleasing me."

I shook my head. "That's not what I meant. I meant——"

"Shhhhh," he hushed. "I'm not finished."

I pursed my lips together.

"You are," he said slowly, "*exquisite* in your service to me. And that, my lovely, was my favorite part. *Is* my favorite part."

I found I couldn't help myself. I brought my head up and kissed him, our lips merely grazing.

I love you, I wanted to say, but wasn't sure it was allowed. Didn't know if it would be wise. Perhaps some things were best left unsaid during the weekends. At least for now, anyway. We had plenty of other days to murmur our love.

He didn't often tell me he loved me. Mentioning it, perhaps, only a handful of times. It didn't bother me that he wasn't very vocal with his feelings. Somehow, the rarity of his words made them all the more special.

He didn't attempt to deepen the kiss, and neither did I. Both of us feeling that, for right then, the simple touch of our lips spoke loud enough. We fell into a comfortable silence while I listened to the steady beat of his heart again and enjoyed the security of his arms.

"Anything you didn't like?" he asked.

"No," I said. "Nothing I'd change." I knew in time the talking would become easier. I wondered how the conversation would go if or when he did something I didn't like. "You?"

"Nothing."

I'm not sure how long we stayed in the library. It wasn't until the mantel clock chimed midnight that he spoke again. "You should go on to bed if you're finished eating."

"I know," I said. As I extracted myself from his arms, I felt the absence of his touch immediately.

He stood with me and touched my shoulder as I turned to leave. "Breakfast in the dining room at eight. We'll head into the playroom shortly thereafter. I don't mind if you do it tonight or tomorrow morning, but I want the playroom cleaned before breakfast."

A fresh wave of desire washed over me at the way he commanded me so unobtrusively. "Yes, Master."

He gave me a light kiss. "Good night, Abigail."

I tossed and turned for a long time, the reason why escaping me. I'd slept in the small bed plenty of nights before. Slept in it more times than I'd slept in his bed, truth be told. Why would I have trouble sleeping? He was right down the hall. We'd decided together to sleep separately on weekends. It was the arrangement I wanted. The one he wanted. The one *we* wanted.

I wondered if sleep shunned him as well.

Right when I decided to give up and walk to the library to pour myself some brandy, I heard it: the soft, haunting sounds of a piano. The melody both delicate and comforting in its simplicity.

I sighed in pleasure and closed my eyes.

I tossed no more.

Chapter Four

—NATHANIEL—

I'd anticipated not being able to sleep. I somehow knew having her back in my house as my submissive, even though it was what we wanted—what we needed—would be difficult. That she wanted to spend Friday and Saturday nights in her old room brought me a certain measure of relief. Her indication in the library that our relationship was easy because I was used to it could not have been further from the truth. Our entire relationship was uncharted territory.

I left the library after playing the piano and walked back upstairs. Her bedroom door was closed, causing me to wonder if she slept yet or if she still tossed restlessly. I didn't anticipate sleep coming quickly to her, either. Something in my mind whispered I should have made her sleep on the floor in my bedroom.

I stopped outside my own bedroom door.

I'd made her sleep on my floor once before. Would have made any other submissive sleep on my floor the first night after I collared her.

Does that mean I won't be able to be both dom and lover to her?

I didn't allow myself to dwell on those thoughts. Instead, my mind drifted to the image of her wearing my collar. My collar and nothing else. I thought back to our conversation in the library—how badly I'd wanted to take her. To slip the gown from her shoulders and run my hands down the curves of her body . . .

My cock grew uncomfortably hard and I slipped my hand past the waistband of my pants to grasp it. I remembered scenes from earlier in the day:

On her knees in my office.

Waiting for me in the playroom.

Holding back a moan as I informed her of my plans with the clamps.

My eyes fell again on her bedroom door.

She might not be sleeping on my floor, but she was still my submissive. She was to serve me however I decided.

I pushed her door open and saw her sleeping.

"Wake up," I said.

She mumbled something in her sleep and rolled away from me.

"Now, Abigail."

Eyes heavy with sleep, she slowly sat up. Her hair fell around her shoulders in disarray—sleep had not come quickly to her. She ran her hand up to her collarbone to straighten the strap of her gown.

"You sleep on Friday and Saturday nights when it is convenient for me." I slipped my pants down over my hips and stepped out of them. "And right now, your sleeping *is not* convenient."

Her eyes fell on my erection. Yes. She knew exactly what I was talking about now.

"I'm feeling cordial tonight, though, so I'll let you decide how you want it," I said.

She blinked a few times. "However it pleases you, Master."

"I believe, Abigail"—I ambled over to her bed—"I just told you what would please me." I leaned over her. "I want you to decide how you'll take my cock."

Her eyes dropped again. Was she embarrassed? Was that it? She needed to get over any embarrassment. Embarrassment had no place in our relationship.

I hooked my fingers under the straps of her gown and slipped it over her head. "Whatever you decide," I told her, "I want this off."

When the gown was off and she was naked, I raised an eyebrow at her. She still hadn't said anything.

"Time's up," I said. "You didn't tell me quickly enough, so I'll choose for you." I turned her on the bed and pushed on her shoulders so she lay down on her back with her head hanging over the edge. "Since you chose not to talk when I asked you a question, I'll put that mouth to a better use."

I had to bend slightly, but I put my hands on either side of her hips and pressed forward so my cock brushed her lips. "Do a good job and I might let you go back to sleep."

I closed my eyes as she enveloped me. Her warmth felt so good, my erection grew even harder as I worked my way into her mouth. I brought a hand to her belly to check on her breathing and started thrusting, pushing myself deeper.

She took all of me, relaxing her throat and sucking as I slowly fucked her mouth. Her tongue wrapped around and stroked me when I pulled out, only to run back down my length as I reentered.

I knew that, once more, she had disobeyed. I had asked a question, asked for an answer, and she had not given me one. I needed to address it.

"I'm getting ready to come," I warned when my release grew

imminent. I thrust harder into her mouth. "You are not to swallow. Hold my come in your mouth until I command otherwise."

I held motionless as my release shot through me, digging my fingers into the soft skin of her waist.

Fuck.

She lay still as I stepped away to retrieve my pants, and she hadn't moved when I turned to face her once more.

"Sit up."

She sat up, breathing through her nose, cheeks slightly puffed. I walked over and took her jaw in my hand.

"When I tell you I want an answer, I want an answer," I said. "Swallowing my come is an honor I do not bestow upon you lightly. Do you understand?" She nodded and I squeezed her cheeks. "Savor the taste of me in your mouth, because you're the only person in the world able to do so. The only submissive allowed to serve me." I jerked her chin up. "The one I selected to wear my collar."

Her eyes teared up, and I felt a slight tinge of discomfort but pushed it away. I needed to make a strong impression this weekend—to remind her I had not been lying when I told her the last time was easy.

I ran my free thumb under her eyelashes and gathered the wetness there. My point had been made and was understood. "I see the disappointment in your eyes. Swallow, Abigail." I kept my hand on her jaw and watched her throat as she obeyed.

While I had known this weekend would not be easy, it had not struck me just how hard it would be for both of us.

I wanted to reestablish my connection with her somehow, to let her know we were okay, but felt at a complete loss as to how to go about doing it. I had never struggled with anything like this before.

She sat before me with her eyes downcast, disappointment

still etched on her features. I searched for the right words to say. Anything that would reassure her we were okay. That this was a tiny blip on our journey and she should not feel overly upset. Yet I felt uneasy whispering accolades of love after the reprimand I gave her.

Then inspiration seized me. I leaned over and whispered:

" 'For I must love because I live.

And life in me is what you give.' "

Surely she would remember those were the last two lines of "Because She Would Ask Me Why I Loved Her" by Christopher Brennan, one of the last poems recited as part of the poetry reading series held by the library where she worked.

She gasped in recognition, and I smiled. Yes. She remembered.

I pulled back, my lips brushing her cheek as I did so. "Good night, my lovely."

I heard her rustling around the house after I went back to my room and crawled into bed. She was cleaning the playroom, probably unable to get back to sleep after I'd woken her.

I rolled over and glanced at the clock. It was two a.m. Fuck, it was late. I wondered idly how Paul and Christine's first weekend had gone years ago, when they'd first set up their arrangement. He was probably still awake. The last time we talked, he mentioned their son, Sam, was going through a nasty bout of colic. Still, even if he was, I doubted he'd be pleased to hear from me. I'd call him sometime after breakfast. Or lunch.

I rolled away from the alarm clock and waited until I heard her go back to her room before I allowed sleep to overtake me.

She waited for me in the playroom shortly after breakfast. She sat on her knees, hands folded in her lap, head down. Exactly the way I had instructed her to wait for me in the playroom. The sight of her, in position and wearing only my collar, caused my cock to jump to life.

"Perfection," I said. "I expected nothing less." I felt pride radiate from her body. "Stand up, Abigail," I said. "Let me see what belongs to me."

Fucking beautiful, I thought when she stood.

Her eyes were downcast, but I could feel her anticipation and excitement. The room nearly buzzed with it.

I stood behind her and ran a hand down her side, noting the increased rate of her breathing. I bent slightly to whisper in her ear, "I'm going to push you a bit today." She shivered under me. I continued. "Remember, I can push because I trust you to use your safe words if you need." I cupped a breast. "I'm going to allow you to vocalize and climax as needed. I still require your complete honesty when I ask how you're doing."

I walked to the cabinets and took out two nipple clamps connected with a chain. Her eyes followed me as I returned to stand in front of her. "I'm also leaving your eyes uncovered. I want you to see what I'm doing."

I bent my head down and sucked a nipple into my mouth. I ran my tongue around its tip, making her moan in the process. I took her deeper and reached out my hand to stroke her other nipple. When she started shivering under my touch, I switched places and paid the same amount of attention to her other breast.

Finally, I straightened up and took her left breast in my hands. I fondled her   rolling and pinching, watching as her skin broke out in gooseflesh. This next part would hurt a bit; I needed to make sure she was ready.

"Take a deep breath, my lovely," I said, pinching her nipple with one hand as I opened the clamp with the other. Once she inhaled, I gently slipped the clamp onto her.

She let out her breath in a short gasp.

I slipped my hand down her body and stroked between her legs. "Very good."

I repeated the procedure with her other nipple—going slowly, gauging her reaction. I watched her carefully. She closed her eyes briefly and shivered, but she was fine.

"Are you okay?" I asked when I had finished.

She smiled. "Yes, Master."

I returned her smile with one of my own. "Look down, Abigail," I said. "Look and see just what a naughty girl you are."

My eyes followed hers, and I took in the sight of her perky nipples—decorated with my clamps, the chain hanging slightly.

"We're going to play a little game," I said. "I want you to undress me." She was still looking at her breasts. "Look at me." When she looked up, I continued. "The catch is, each time you touch my cock, I earn the right to pull that chain." I took a step back. "Start now."

I closed my eyes and waited for her to start. I wore only pants. It would be difficult, but not impossible, for her to undress me without touching my cock. The clamps were new to her. If she hated them, feared them, or was in too much pain, I knew my cock would go untouched during the next few minutes.

By the time my pants were on the floor, I'd counted four touches of her hand. The last was a brazen upward stroke of my cock as she moved to her feet.

Four.

I hid my smile.

"How many pulls do I get?" I asked.

"Four, Master."

"Mmmmmm. Four." I took the chain and gave a slow tug. She let out a guttural moan that shot straight to my cock.

Fucking love this woman.

"You owe me three more," I said. "I'll collect later."

I walked back to my cabinets and took out a silken rope. Once I returned behind her, I took both her arms and pulled them to her back. Taking my time and tying the rope with the utmost care, I gently but securely bound her arms.

"I like you in this position," I said, moving to stand in front of her again. "Your breasts pushed out in silent offering to me." I slid a finger under the chain, caught her eyes, and gave a slow, upward tug on the chain.

Her eyes fluttered. "Oh, God."

"Like that, do you?"

She let out another moan. "Yes, Master."

I lifted the corner of my mouth in a smile, pleased she had taken to the clamps so well.

"Spread your legs." I slipped a hand between them; she was slick and ready.

Almost.

I needed her more heightened. More sensitive.

I knelt between her legs and placed a kiss on her clit, then leaned back and blew gently. I stuck my tongue out and licked her slit from bottom to top, still focusing my attention on her clit. I placed soft kisses on her inner thighs and trailed a line to end between them, where I nibbled on her clit more. Sucked it into my mouth. I reached up, grabbed the chain, and pulled. She yelped, and I worked her clit even harder, bringing the pleasure and pain closer together in her mind. I grazed her with my teeth and gave the chain another hard tug. She jerked against me.

I dropped the chain then and slid two fingers into her, reaching to the place—*right there*—I knew would make her totally unhinged. I swirled my tongue around her clit and pushed my fingers into her again.

She gasped and climaxed around me.

Fuck.

I heard her heavy breaths as I stood and noted the faint flush coloring her skin. Her breasts looked fine, but she'd had the clamps on long enough for the first time.

"Deep breath, my lovely," I said, taking a clamp in one hand and gently cupping her breasts with the other. Her warm breath floated across my shoulders and chest. "Another one," I said. "Exhale slowly."

This time when she exhaled, I released the clamp as slowly as possible. She gave a sharp intake of breath as the blood returned.

"Are you okay?" I asked.

Her voice was tight. "Yes, Master."

"Very good."

I reached between her legs again and stroked her still sensitive flesh. She jerked her hips toward me.

"Another deep breath," I said when I felt her relax. "Exhale slowly." Again, I removed the clamp, dropping them both to the floor. I slipped a finger into her, lightly brushing her clit with my thumb, hoping to alleviate some of the pain. Her hair tickled my cheek as I murmured how pleased I was with her. How proud. She sighed.

"Spread your legs wide," I said, backing away.

I left her there for a few minutes, knowing she felt the warm air between her legs. Knowing her every nerve stood on end. She looked beautiful.

Fucking lucky-ass bastard.

I took the warming lubricant from the top of the table and returned to stand behind her. I reached around and swept my fingertips lightly across her delicate nipples. She groaned in reply, backing her hips toward me.

I merely chuckled. Within minutes I'd spread the lube onto my cock and fingers.

"You told me recently that having my cock in your ass made you feel completely consumed," I said.

She jumped when I applied the lube to her backside.

"Ready to be consumed again, Abigail?"

Chapter Five

—NATHANIEL—

She mumbled something under her breath I couldn't make out.

"Either stay quiet or speak so I can hear," I said, giving her ass a sharp smack. "Understand?"

"Yes, Master."

"Very good." I took hold of her bound hands. "Now bend over."

She moved slowly, getting her bearings. I kept a firm grasp on her hands with my left hand, wanting her to realize she could let go and trust me. Her legs were spread wide, giving her a steady stance and giving me an incredible view.

"Very nice, Abigail," I said. "I love how open your ass is in this position." The lubed finger of my right hand circled her. "Let's see if you were telling the truth about using your plug." I pushed into her a little. "I can't wait to take you here."

She groaned and pushed herself back against me. My finger slipped deeper.

Fuck.

I slowly fucked her with my finger, making sure I kept a firm grasp on her hands to ensure she wouldn't fall. Her head fell between her knees, hair trailing over the floor and sweeping against the hardwood with each thrust of my finger.

I slipped another finger into her. Pushing slowly. Stretching her. Preparing her. She was still so tight.

As she grew accustomed to my fingers, I started rethinking my plan. Taking her here, in the middle of the floor, wouldn't work. I couldn't hold on to her, work her body, and thrust without putting unnecessary strain on her arms and shoulders.

Glancing around the room, my eyes fell on the whipping bench.

Perfect.

"Have you missed this?" I asked. "Missed me preparing your ass for my cock?" I pushed deeper. My cock ached for friction, and as much as I wanted nothing more than to remove my fingers and thrust into her, I knew I couldn't. She trusted me to make this good for her, and I treasured that trust.

I stilled my fingers, and she stopped moving as well. When I was certain she was steady, I let go of her arms. Keeping my fingers inside, I slipped my other hand between her legs and stroked her slickness.

"Very good, Abigail," I said. "You *have* been using your plug. Missed my cock, have you?" I brushed her clit.

"Oh, God," she moaned. "Yes, Master."

I continued teasing her clit with one hand while slowly stretching her with the fingers of the other. Every so often, she'd let out a soft whimper of pleasure.

"I'm going to remove my fingers," I said. "When I do, I want you to move to the whipping bench."

I use it for chastisement, I'd told her once. *But it serves other pur-*

poses as well. Would she remember? Dare I hope I'd gotten her to a place inside her head where she trusted me implicitly?

I slipped my fingers from her, slowly removing them, and gave her clit one last swirl.

"Stand up for me," I said, with a tug on her hands.

She stood slowly, her hair falling softly into place around her face.

"To the bench, my lovely."

She didn't hesitate. Knowing, hopefully, she had done nothing requiring punishment.

"I'm so proud of you," I told her, when she had positioned herself. "The way you trust me."

She was bent over the bench with her backside to me—her arms were behind her back and she'd kept a wide stance with her legs. I moved behind her and leaned over.

"You can feel it in this position, can't you?" I asked, slipping a prepared finger inside her again, causing her upper body to move against the bench. "Your nipples." I pulled out a bit and her body moved slightly. "How they scrape the bench with every push of my hand?"

Again I worked to stretch her with my fingers and slid a hand between her legs to graze her pussy. I wanted her to ache for me. Wanted to get her to where she hungered for my cock. The movement of her body against the bench, the gentle stretch of my fingers, the play of my fingers against her clit—they all worked to get her there.

She moaned.

"What is it?" I asked. "What do you need?"

"Oh, God," she said as I pushed deeper.

"What do you need?" I smacked her across the ass, and she gave another moan. "Tell me."

"You," she panted. "Me."

"Ready for me?" I removed my fingers and placed the head of my cock against her.

"Please," she said.

I had to go slowly. This was only her second time. It would still hurt.

"Easy," I said, more to myself than her. I pressed gently into her, gritting my teeth against the burning need to plunge forward.

I stilled my hips and dipped two fingers into her wetness. "What you do to me," I whispered. "Is it the same for you?"

Her only answer was a groan as my fingers circled her clit. I pushed my hips forward and stopped suddenly at her sharp intake of breath. "Are you okay?" I asked.

"Yes, Master," she said in a tight voice. "More. Please."

I slid farther into her. Backed out. Slid deeper. I hooked my fingers and, when I pressed inside her, felt the push and pull of my cock.

Fucking hell.

I thrust even deeper on my next pass, pushed her harder against the bench, and slipped all the way in. Her muscles tightened around my fingers.

"Let it go." My voice was strained. "Whenever you want."

She arched her back, and my fingers hit deep within her. I started a slow rhythm—my cock pushing in as my fingers came out and brushed her clit. Then I pulled out, with my fingers sliding inside.

She might have thought I consumed her when I took her this way, but the opposite was true—she totally consumed me. Every breath, every heartbeat, every nerve of my body pulsed with her name. Pulsed with a need for her. She swallowed me whole. Consumed *me.*

I threw my head back and increased my pace. Her body scraped harder against the bench.

"Ah," she moaned, tightening around me again.

Yes.

I pushed my fingers deeper.

"Oh, God," she whispered. "I can't . . . I can't . . ."

"Then don't," I whispered back, pushing deeper.

She climaxed around me with a soft yelp.

I thrust again, allowed the need to wash over me, and released into her.

We lay for several seconds, our pants and thumping hearts the only noticeable sounds. My head finally cleared, and I gently pulled away from her.

"Are you okay?" I asked.

"Oh, God, yes."

I smiled. "I'll be right back. Don't move."

I walked into the bathroom adjoining the playroom and washed my hands, keeping my eyes on her. From my heated towel rack, I took some large towels, then ran hot water over several washcloths, knowing they'd cool by the time I needed them.

I spread the towels on the floor. When I made it back to her, I gently unbound her arms—kissing her wrists, letting the rope drop as I made my way up her arms, continuing a soothing massage to her shoulders. I took one arm and kissed inside her elbow before placing it beside her and doing the same to the other arm. I moved beside her and knelt so we were eye level. Her eyes were deep and dark with pleasure.

"You amaze me," I said. "Every time." I kissed her softly. "Can you stand?"

She nodded and stood up.

"Come lie on the towels." I took her arm. "They're warm."

Once she was situated, I washed her body with the washcloths and finished by wrapping her in more fluffy towels. She nearly hummed in pleasure.

"I'd ask if it was good for you, but I really don't think I need to," I teased. She responded with a low, sultry giggle. I brushed my lips against hers. "Are you tired?"

"Mmmm." She closed her eyes. "I feel like a jellyfish. All rubbery." She yawned. "Maybe a little tired."

A little tired?

I stifled my laugh. She'd had maybe four hours of sleep. Probably less. A little tired, indeed.

"I want you to rest for the next few hours. Make yourself some lunch if you want. I'll take care of myself." I kissed her again. "You nap."

After I made myself a sandwich and checked to make sure she was sleeping comfortably, I went into the living room and called Paul.

He picked up on the second ring. "Nathaniel?"

"Hey, Paul," I replied.

"How's it going with Abby?" he asked.

He knew how important this weekend was, knew how hard it would be for both Abby and me. I was fortunate to have a friend like him to talk with. I knew how lost I'd be if I didn't have someone to talk to.

What about Abby?

"Oh, no," I said as the realization struck me.

Who did Abby have to talk with?

"No one," I mumbled.

She has no one.

"Nathaniel?" Paul said, worry replacing his previous casygoing tone. "Is everything okay with Abby?"

She had me and no one else. As her dom, did I really count? Who else would she go to? Felicia barely accepted our relationship. Things with her were easier, but I knew she didn't approve of our lifestyle. Abby spoke frequently with Elaina, but while my best friend's wife knew of our lifestyle, and accepted it, she wouldn't be a good support person for a new submissive.

"Fucking hell." I slumped against the chair. "Failed again."

"Nathaniel," Paul snapped, bringing me back to the issue at hand. "How's Abby?"

"What?" I said, realizing I was still on the phone. "Abby? She's sleeping."

"Okay," he said. "So tell me, how did you fail?"

"I was just thinking how nice it was to have you as a support person, someone to talk things over with, and how hard it would be without that." I took a deep breath. "Abby doesn't have anyone." I squinted my eyes, remembering. "She had a dabbler friend who used to live in the area, but I don't think they're still in contact."

"I see."

"I mean, she has me. We talk." I thought back to the library, how hard it still was to get her to speak freely while she wore my collar. "Sometimes."

"But outside of you, she doesn't have any friends in the lifestyle?" he asked. "Another submissive to talk with?"

"No, not that she's mentioned." She would have mentioned them, right?

"Have you thought about taking her to a party? Somewhere she could meet people?"

I had, actually. It was on my list to call a few community members once Jackson and Felicia's wedding was over.

"Yes," I said. "But we've got this wedding, and we just started back this weekend. I thought . . . Fuck." No matter how busy we were, I should have made certain she had the support she needed.

"Remember what I told you when I visited?"

"Visited?" I asked. "Is that what you call it? You mean when you called me out for being a sorry lump of shit?"

"Yes, that."

"You said a lot of things." My face heated with shame at the reminder that Paul had had to leave his newborn son to save me from myself. "Which one in particular?"

"How I wanted the two of you to visit when you got back together."

Okay, truthfully, I'd forgotten that bit. Likely as not, when he said it, I never thought Abby and I *would* get back together.

"I know Jackson's getting married in two weeks," he said. "But is there any way possible? Maybe next weekend?"

"Oh?" I asked, trying to work out the timeline in my head . . . It just might work. *"Oh."*

"I'll talk to Christine, see if her mom can watch Sam for a few hours on Saturday." He stopped, thinking. "Talk to Abby. Send me your checklists; maybe we can play together. Or do you still not share your collared submissives?"

Share Abby?

I tried to imagine another man putting his hands on her. Another man sliding his fingers into her hair. Another man's lips on hers.

Never.

"I don't share," I said in an almost growl.

"Pity," he said. "The four of us—"

"Regardless," I interrupted. "It's a hard limit for Abby." I knew sharing had never been a problem for Paul or Christine. I was fine with that. It just didn't work for me.

"In that case, maybe we can play for the two of you?" he asked. "Maybe something Abby has listed as a soft limit? Christine gets off on being watched, and we both need some playroom time."

I thought for a few seconds. "Sounds good. Let me talk with Abby."

We spoke about the weekend so far.

"How did the punishments go?" he asked, when I brought up their necessity.

"Hard," I answered honestly. "For both of us. She was upset, and seeing that upset me and . . ."

"You questioned whether you were doing the right thing," he finished.

"I don't remember it being as hard with the others."

"Your previous submissives?" he asked.

"Right," I said. "I don't remember feeling this way."

"I remember," he said, a hint of tease in his voice.

"What?"

"When you called me after you punished Beth for the first time."

"Beth?" I tried to remember. "That was ages ago."

"And you were upset then, much as you are now," he said. "Maybe even more."

I wished I remembered. Beth seemed like such a long time ago, so very far removed from where I was now.

"Since you don't remember the incident, you probably don't remember what I told you," he said.

"Hell, Paul," I said. "Just get on with it."

"It's completely normal for you to have a hard time causing someone pain, even in the type of relationship you're in," he said. "If you found it easy, that's when I'd be worried."

"I know, but—" I started.

"No buts," he said. "Most doms I know experience the same thing."

"How did it go for you and Christine?" I asked. "On your first weekend after you started seeing each other romantically?"

"Christine and I were different from you and Abby," he said. "We went into a twenty-four-hour, seven-days-a-week relationship."

"I thought that was before you started dating," I said.

"No, it was after."

"Huh," I said, trying to imagine living that kind of lifestyle with Abby. "How long did that last?"

"A few months," he answered. "It didn't work for us. Too difficult." I heard the smile in his voice. "So you see, Nathaniel, everyone has struggles."

"Still?"

"Yes," he said. "Still. Granted, they're different now."

I sighed, more from relief than anything. What I was experiencing was normal. Abby and I were going to be fine. It would just take time to work through everything.

"What are your plans for tomorrow?" he asked.

"I'm trying to decide if I should ask her to sleep over tomorrow night," I said, mulling the idea over in my head. Abby had spent Thursday night with me, and I wasn't sure she'd want to stay over until Monday.

"I don't know if that's such a good idea," he said.

"Why?"

"You're new to this dual relationship," he explained. "And, to be honest, I see Abby being able to handle it better than you will. But you." He hesitated. "I think you may have some emotions to work through tomorrow night. I don't know if having her in the house when you come down from this weekend would be the best idea."

I hadn't thought about that, but he was probably right. I'd need time to work through for myself how the weekend had gone, even after I discussed it with her. Maybe it would be better for me to work it out alone.

After all, we still had Monday night. And Tuesday night. And Wednesday night . . .

Sam's cries broke through my concentration.

"Ugh. He never sleeps," Paul said. "Let me go."

"I'm reconsidering this weekend already," I teased.

"I wouldn't blame you."

We said our good-byes after I promised to talk with Abby and call him later in the week.

I hadn't set the phone down for two minutes before it rang again.

Jackson.

"Hey there," I said. "What's going on?"

"Felicia and I wanted to invite you and Abby over for a cookout tomorrow night," he said. "Break the house in."

Jackson and Felicia had recently bought a new house outside the city after Jackson decided his penthouse wouldn't do for a newly married couple. They had started moving the previous weekend, even though I knew Felicia still *technically* lived next to Abby.

Another conversation that needs to happen sooner rather than later.

"A cookout?" I asked.

"You know," he said. "Steaks. Potatoes. Man food. Although I might throw some fish on the grill if you want."

"Steaks are fine," I said, thinking frantically. "What time?" I wanted to uncollar Abby and have a discussion about the weekend before we did anything Sunday night.

"I don't know," he said. "Does it matter? You catching a plane?"

"How about five?" I asked. That would give us two hours. Not optimal for our first weekend, but it would work.

"Five sounds great," he said. "Ah, no, baby," I heard him say to someone, Felicia probably. "That has to be there. It's a football thing."

I coughed discreetly.

"Sorry, Nathaniel," he said. "Chicks, you know? Love her, but leave my shit where I put it."

As we got off the phone, I looked around my living room.

Chicks, you know?

I really didn't.

Chapter Six

——ABBY——

"Thank you for serving me this weekend," he said after taking the collar off on Sunday afternoon at three. His fingers stroked my bare neck and my skin delighted in the love I felt in his touch.

"Thank you for allowing me to serve you," I said. I never wanted him to think I didn't get just as much out of our weekend time as he did. Especially considering the mistakes I made.

It was crazy, but I felt different after the collar was off. It was difficult to describe. I wouldn't call it a weight. It wasn't a burden, but once it was off, I knew exactly what Nathaniel had meant when he said it put me in a certain frame of mind.

I peeked up at him and felt a smile tug at the edges of my lips.

"Will you sit with me?" he asked. "So we can talk?"

Something about him had changed as well. He looked different. Acted differently. Less certain of himself.

I wondered if it was my imagination.

The weekday me would tease him. The me of last week would answer with a snappy comeback.

But I'd spent the last two and a half days giving in to my more primitive desires, and those desires didn't include the voicing of snappy comebacks.

He knew that, of course.

"I had hoped you would be more"—he paused, looking for the word—"*uninhibited* once the collar came off."

Okay, that was too much.

"You think I was inhibited this weekend?" I asked. "What part would that have been? When I was bent naked over the whipping bench? Or was tied to your padded table?" I tapped my finger to my forehead. "Oh, I know. It was the nipple clamps, wasn't it? Definitely the nipple clamps."

I didn't have a chance to get to my next sassy comeback. I took a deep breath, gearing up for a nice teasing launch into Saturday night's activities, when his hands took my face and he pulled me close for a long, passionate kiss.

"There you are," he said when our lips parted, his hands still on either side of my face. His eyes gazed steadily into mine. "I knew you were in there somewhere."

I ran my hands through his hair, tugging at the tousled strands. "I never left."

"I know," he said. "I just feared you wouldn't talk. That this would be awkward."

"Give me a few minutes. I just need to"—I wrinkled my eyebrows—"is *adjust* the right word?"

"'Adjust' is just as good as any," he said, pointing to the couch. "Sit with me? It seemed to help Friday night."

He sat down first, patting the spot next to him. "Put your feet in my lap. I'll give you a foot rub."

"I'm tempted to say you've given me far too much already." I settled myself onto the couch, placing my bare feet in his lap. "But I'm a sucker for a foot massage."

He smiled and took my left foot, his long fingers magical as they stroked between my toes and tugged them. "I've given you far too much? How is that?"

"By letting us be us," I said. "However we choose *us* to be."

"Does that mean you're not going to throw your hands up and tell me you don't want my collar anymore?"

"Of course not. Why would you think that?" I asked.

He worked silently for a few minutes, a frown marring his expression. "I wondered if I was too rough, too hard. That you would decide you didn't want me. Not *every* part."

"That's what you wondered?"

"Yes."

I had to tell him my fears. I had to be honest. He was working so hard to be honest with me. "I feared you wouldn't want me. That you'd decide training me was too much work. Not worth it." I swallowed the lump in my throat. "I messed up so much."

His hands stopped. "It was our first weekend. I was harder and more demanding than I'd been before. I'd have been more surprised if you hadn't messed up."

"Really?" I felt better for some reason.

"I told you that Friday night," he said.

"Right, and an hour or so later, I messed up again."

"I need you to be honest with me," he said, restarting with the rubbing. "Not letting you swallow, how did you feel?"

"Honest?"

His only answer was a raised eyebrow.

"I was so afraid I was going to gag and spit everything out on you," I said, remembering. "And I felt so bad for not answering and knowing I'd disappointed you. I hate that feeling." My voice dropped a notch. "But then there's a certain power in knowing how strongly I affect you. Knowing you wanted to wake me up. Had to wake me up."

"Yes."

"But to turn that power back over to you, to give you free rein . . ."

He smiled and waited for my response.

"I love that part," I finished.

"The actual punishment, though?"

"I didn't love *that* part," I said, then noticed his mouth start to open. "I know it's punishment. I'm not supposed to."

"Was it effective?"

"Yes."

"Then it served its purpose," he said. Then he added, "Why didn't you answer?"

"My brain thinks too much," I said. "I kept thinking about how I should answer, how you wanted me to answer. What would happen if I said the wrong thing?"

"The only wrong thing was what happened." His thumbs swirled over the bottom of my foot, pressing and rubbing the spot right under my big toe. "It's not often I'll give you a choice on the weekends, but when I do, I expect you to make a decision. You could have picked anything—even your hand."

"If I'd said I wanted to ride you?"

"Did I give you any stipulations?" His eyes were dark. "I simply wanted you to choose."

An image of us moving together floated to my mind. "And if I'd asked you to make love to me?" The way he'd burst into my room didn't mesh with the image. I doubted I would have asked him to make love to me, but I still wanted to know what he'd have done.

He lifted my foot to his mouth and kissed the underside. "It would have been a very different ending."

"You would have done it?"

"Yes," he said. "If that was your choice."

"Oh," I said, disappointed in myself once again.

"Abby," he said, as if sensing my sadness. "Don't let one mistake weigh you down. It's a learning experience."

"But it was a rare occasion, and I blew it."

"And you'll blow it again. I'll blow it sometimes. We learn. We move on."

He switched to my other foot, slowly working his way from the top to the bottom.

"Thank you for the poem," I said. His reciting of "Because She Would Ask Me Why I Loved Her" had been just what I needed to calm my fears early Saturday morning.

"You're welcome."

Felicia and Jackson's new house was beautiful. It had five bedrooms, five full bathrooms, three half baths, and a large rooftop deck. I spent most of my lunch hours and many of my evenings going to furniture stores, antique dealers, and designer fabric makers. Felicia was an astute decorator. She knew what she wanted and, most of the time, got it. Of course, being engaged to one of the country's most well-known football players helped.

Yet there was a certain sadness overshadowing my time with Felicia. We had been neighbors for years, and it was hard to believe that in less than two weeks, she'd be gone. When I wasn't with Nathaniel, I'd be all alone.

Unless . . .

No, I wouldn't even think that. It was much too soon to even think about moving in with Nathaniel. Even if he wanted to.

Right?

What's the big deal? I asked myself. *I mean, you will probably be at his house most of the time after the wedding anyway.*

Still . . .

Best not to push it, I decided. Everything was still too new for both of us.

"What has you thinking so intently?" he asked as he opened the passenger's-side door. "Abby?" he asked again, holding out a hand for me.

"Just thinking," I said. His hand was warm and firm around mine. "Nothing in particular."

"Remind me to ask you something about next weekend," he said as we climbed the steps to the front door.

"Next weekend?" I looked up at him. He didn't usually tell me his plans for the weekend. "What about it?"

His hand squeezed mine. "Later."

"There you are," Jackson said as the door swung open. "Come on in. I was just getting ready to light the grill." He leaned over and gave me a one-armed hug. "Felicia needs your opinion in the kitchen."

"No," I said, returning the hug. "She just wants me to smile and nod in agreement with her opinion."

He laughed. "Yeah, you're probably right."

We walked into the kitchen, where Felicia was busy setting out salad ingredients. Once the men gathered the steaks and left the kitchen to go outside, she cocked an eyebrow.

"No collar?" she asked.

"I thought you didn't want the details." I hadn't told her about our new arrangement. Still, she knew I had spent the weekend with him and probably guessed the rest. I sat down at one of the new barstools we'd picked out early last week. "I knew these would look good."

"Yes, they do look good." She took a head of lettuce and washed it in the sink. "And no, I don't want the details. I just thought you'd have it on. You *did* spend the entire weekend with him. And you *didn't* take an overnight bag with you."

Damn girl was too observant for her own good. "You either want the details or you don't. You can't have it both ways." I took a knife. "Need help?" She passed me a cucumber and I started chopping. "Since you asked, yes, I did wear his collar this weekend. But I wear it only on weekends."

"You can do that?"

"Honestly, Felicia," I said, dicing the cucumber into smaller pieces.

"Sorry," she said. "I just worry about you. Especially since the last time—"

"You're sweet to worry," I said. "But don't. This is nothing like the last time."

"He better be careful," she said. "It'd look really bad if I had to murder my cousin-in-law."

The realization that Nathaniel would become Felicia's cousin-in-law always left me with an ache in my heart. It was as if she would have some kind of connection with him I didn't.

"At least it's got diamonds," she said. "It'll look good with the dress."

Her comment caught me off guard. I hadn't thought about wearing the collar to the wedding. But it would be held on a weekend. Per our arrangement, I would wear it. I chewed my lip as I threw the diced cucumber into the salad bowl. It was no big deal. I'd worn the collar around Nathaniel's family before. I could do it again.

But this is Felicia's wedding.

But again, no big deal. It wasn't as if Nathaniel would pull me into a darkened closet and spank me with a coat hanger.

Of course, on the other hand, that could be fun.

My face heated at the thought.

No. Must. Not. Think. That. Way.

Or maybe he would command me to crawl under the table and suck him off.

No, he'd never do that.

Salad, Abby, I told myself. *You're making salad.*

But the more I tried not to think about serving Nathaniel at Jackson and Felicia's wedding, the more I thought about serving Nathaniel at Jackson and Felicia's wedding, and the more my imagination ran away with me. By the time the salad was finished, I'd concocted scenario after scenario of wedding possibilities. Each one dirtier and more exciting than the last.

Laughing voices came from down the hall, and I looked up from washing my knife just in time to see Nathaniel and Jackson walk into the kitchen.

Jackson would probably be the man most eyes would be drawn to. Not only was he handsome, but he had a build that just screamed for attention. And because he was always laughing and smiling, one just had a natural tendency to want to be with him.

But it was his quieter, unassuming cousin I focused on. Even from the doorway, his presence called to me. Nathaniel walked with an understated elegance and confidence that totally mesmerized me. My eyes caught his, and our gazes held as he walked into the room. He set down a plate of steaks, his eyes burning into mine. My gaze dropped to his full lips, and it was as if I felt his kiss again, along my back after he'd taken me over the whipping bench the previous day. The way he'd commanded me to look at myself after he put the clamps on.

You naughty girl.

My face heated, and I focused my attention on the knife I was still washing.

"You okay, Abby?" Jackson asked. "Do I need to turn the air on?"

"No." I shook my head. "I'm fine. Just got a little overheated." I nodded to the water in the sink. "Dishes."

Nathaniel, of course, knew exactly what I was thinking. He walked up behind me, took the knife from my hands, and gently set it on the countertop. "I think this is clean enough." He turned me so I faced him. "Are you okay?"

Are you okay?

The three-word question he'd whispered over and over the last few days to ensure I was fine and safe and able to continue. My mind automatically checked each part of my body and mind to verify and ensure my answer was truthful.

"Yes, Mas——" I stopped short at his intake of breath. "I mean, yes, Nathaniel." I lifted up on my toes and brushed his cheek with my lips. "Yes, I'm fine." I whispered in his ear, "I just slipped a little there."

His expression was unreadable, almost as if he was gauging whether to say something or not. "I did wonder," he mumbled to himself, but didn't finish what he wondered.

"Hey, you two," Jackson said. "Knock it off and let's eat."

I noticed then that Nathaniel's arms were around me, and to anyone else, we probably looked like a couple in a lover's embrace. My gaze shot over to Felicia, but she just gave a short nod of approval and went about pulling plates from the cabinets.

"Come on," she said to Jackson. "Let's take the plates and steaks outside. I'm not sure why you two brought them back inside in the first place." She smiled at Nathaniel and me. "Bring the salad with you when you come."

"Will do," I told her, my arms still around Nathaniel.

Felicia and Jackson left, discussing the potatoes left on the grill and whether or not they'd be ready.

"Sorry," I said to Nathaniel, when they were out of earshot.

"Whatever for?" he asked.

"I didn't mean to slip there. When I said——"

"I want you to do something for me," he interrupted. "I want you to stop apologizing for everything. Matter of fact, I want you to go the rest of the evening without apologizing for anything." His eyes sparkled. "Can you do it?"

"I'll try. I don't know what happened there," I said. "Hearing you ask if I was okay just triggered something, I guess."

"It was me," he said. "I need to find new words." He pulled away and took two bottles of dressing from the refrigerator. "She has only Italian and ranch? No bleu cheese?"

I shrugged. "Hasn't stocked up the refrigerator yet, I guess. Think you can do Italian for one night?"

He didn't answer, but instead went back to our previous conversation. "When I walked into the kitchen and saw you at the sink, you just looked"—he wrinkled his brow—"perplexed or confused or something." He took a cucumber from the salad bowl and chewed it thoughtfully. "I wonder if we should have stayed at my house tonight."

I wondered the same thing. It was just odd being a "regular" couple after such an intense weekend.

"I know," I said. "But I think it'll be good. Jackson's such fun and I want"—I took the salad bowl and moved toward the door—"I want to show Felicia we're fine."

We had gone out with Felicia and Jackson a few times since getting back together. While part of me wondered if Nathaniel and I should have stayed at his house for the night, a larger part of me wanted to be back around Jackson and Felicia. To prove, somehow, that we were able to do the dual relationship.

Nathaniel and I made it to the rooftop deck right as Jackson took the potatoes from the grill.

"Right on time," Felicia said.

Nathaniel placed the dressings on the table and took the bowl from me. Then he came behind my chair and pulled it out for me.

"You don't have to do that, you know," I told him, taking a seat as he pushed the chair under the table.

"Humor me?" He trailed his fingers down my back and then back up, coming to rest at the nape of my neck with a soft squeeze. It was as if he felt more comfortable touching me. Needed a physical connection with me.

I glanced over to Felicia and Jackson. They stood by the grill, talking. Felicia balanced a plateful of potatoes.

"I like taking care of you," Nathaniel said, taking his own seat.

"You took care of me all weekend," I countered.

"No." He smiled. "You took care of me."

I placed a napkin in my lap. "How about we just agree that we both took care of each other?"

"I'll go with that," he said. "But you need to accept the fact that I will always pull your chair out, open your car door, and stand when you leave the table." He leaned over to whisper, "It's the way I was raised. My dad and uncle did the same things for mom and Linda, and they never served them the way you serve me."

"That you know of," I shot back.

He laughed. "I'm not even going to think about that."

Jackson and Felicia walked to the table.

"So," Jackson said, sitting down. "What have you two been up to this weekend?"

Felicia's eyes bugged out. I almost giggled, it was so comical.

What did she think I was going to do? Launch into a running commentary on the ins and outs of what we had done?

"Abby treated me to her delicious French toast," Nathaniel said, speaking of the breakfast I'd made for him that morning. He raised his glass to me. "Superb, as always." He looked over to Felicia. "Has she shared her recipe with you? Jackson loves French toast."

Felicia shook her head. "I'm not much of a cook. I'm afraid Jackson will have to do without that particular delicacy."

And just like that, the conversation drifted away from our weekend. I placed a hand on Nathaniel's knee and he reached down to intertwine our fingers.

I squeezed his knee. *Thank you.*

He returned the squeeze. *You're welcome.*

"I'd better head home," Felicia said two hours later, when the last dish had been put in the dishwasher, following the high-spirited dinner. "Abby promised to help me finish the table seating arrangements."

Jackson leaned against the countertop. "Explain to me again why we care where people sit?"

Felicia huffed and picked her purse up from beside the refrigerator. "We just do."

"But, baby, you've gone over the table arrangements five times already." He winked at me, obviously enjoying pushing this particular button of Felicia's. "We'll be just as married if the Tompkinses sit beside the McDonalds or not."

She ignored him. "When did you say your dad was getting into town?" she asked me.

"Thursday before," I answered, slipping my hand inside Nathaniel's. He had mentioned how much he was looking forward to meeting my dad. A thought flitted through my head: *will he mention the collar if I have it on?*

She put her hands on her hips. "Think he'd like to sit with the Tompkinses?"

"Even I don't think that would be a good idea," Nathaniel said. Of course he wouldn't think that would be a good idea. Who wanted his current girlfriend's parent to sit next to and have dinner with his ex-girlfriend's parents?

"In that case, I guess Abby and I have a lot of work to do," Felicia said.

Nathaniel pulled me to the door. "I'll take you home." He nodded to Jackson. "We still on for dinner tomorrow night?"

His cousin had eyes only for his fiancée. "If I make it to tomorrow. I'll make you a deal," he said to Felicia. "I won't say another word about table arrangements if you let me keep the trophies in the living room."

Her hands were still on her hips as her lips curled. "As long as you know I still think they would look better in your office."

He moved to her, a twin smile covering his face. "And as long as you know I still don't know why we care where everyone sits."

He'd made it to her. Their arms came around each other. He leaned down and whispered something in her ear. She giggled and pressed closer to him.

Nathaniel and I walked out of the kitchen, still holding hands, and left through the front door.

"Meet me for lunch tomorrow?" he asked.

"Sushi?"

"I can always do sushi," he said. "Though I do prefer when you and I make it."

We'd made it to his car. "Then how about we do sushi Tuesday night and do something else for lunch tomorrow?"

"Tuesday night sounds great," he said. "Do you have plans for tomorrow night?"

I picked at an imaginary piece of lint on his shirt, just because I wanted to touch him. "Final dress fitting."

"Fun."

"Not really, but I'll survive. Especially if I have Tuesday to look forward to."

He smiled. "Tuesday night we make sushi." His voice dropped. "Will you stay the night?"

I leaned toward him. "Yes," I said, and I felt his breath on my cheek.

His lips grazed mine. "Thank you."

"If I can't apologize"—I put my arms around him—"you can't thank me."

His laugh was warm and deep in my ear. I pulled back and smiled. "Deal?"

"Deal."

As he, once more, moved close to me, I shut my eyes and breathed in the scent of him. He smelled dark and woodsy.

Our lips touched, gentle at first. I sighed and ran my fingers through his hair. He moaned and parted his lips, deepening the kiss. Then what was gentle grew passionate and what was soft became laced with need. But we both knew we could not give in to our need. It wouldn't progress beyond the kiss.

When our lips parted, he sighed against my cheek. "I love you."

Chapter Seven

——ABBY——

I turned the rice cooker on and walked to where Nathaniel stood cutting cucumbers, carrots, and avocados. I reached under his arm and grabbed a peeled carrot.

"Hey." He spun around. "I was just getting ready to use that one."

"You have plenty." I took a small bite, enjoying the satisfying crunch.

He narrowed his eyes and watched me with mock ire as I chewed and swallowed.

"FYI," I said, shaking the carrot at him. "I will never pick peas over carrots on a Tuesday night. Unless they're cooked. I hate cooked carrots."

His eye crinkled up at the edges and his mouth gave way to a beautiful smile. "Point taken."

"Now." I reached for the peeler and took another carrot. "Since I've deprived you of your peeled carrot, the least I can do is peel another one for you."

"Oh, yes," he said, his hand brushing my shoulder just slightly before moving away from me. "The very least."

I knew he was working hard, trying to let me dictate our weekday time. He had been hesitant at lunch the previous day, a change from the cookout with Felicia and Jackson when he'd touched me almost constantly.

I turned to him and stroked his hand. "I like it when you touch me. Don't stop just because you're afraid I'll take it the wrong way or will feel obligated."

His smile grew even larger. "You know me so well."

I lifted to my toes and gave him a small kiss. "Sometimes."

The look in his eyes told me he didn't believe me. I decided not to pursue it further. Besides, there was something else I wanted to talk about. I turned back to the counter and began peeling the carrot.

"You wanted to ask me something about this weekend?" I asked.

He took another carrot and we worked side by side.

"You've heard me talk about Paul?" he asked.

Paul was Nathaniel's mentor. I knew that. The man who had been his instructor. Nathaniel told me once that Paul was the only person he'd ever subbed for. My mind still couldn't wrap itself around that—Nathaniel subbing for someone. Even if there wasn't any sex involved, it still confused me.

"And Christine?" he asked.

Paul's wife. And submissive. They had a three-month-old son, Sam. Paul had e-mailed Nathaniel pictures of the pudgy baby. Sam was cute as a button and had a precious toothless grin.

"Of course I remember you talking about Paul," I said. "Hard to forget that one."

The image of Nathaniel willingly submitting himself to anyone wasn't anything I could easily forget.

"I spoke to him," he said. "He's invited us to New Hanover this weekend."

This weekend?

"I told him I'd talk to you about it, get your thoughts," he said. "You could talk with Christine some. She's a submissive, and I think it would be a good idea for you to talk with someone you can relate to like that."

I kept peeling the carrot. Someone to talk to? Someone who wasn't Nathaniel? Would that be weird? How did one start that conversation, anyway? *Hi, I'm Abby and I crave domination?*

"He also mentioned the two of them playing for us," Nathaniel said. "Perhaps something on your soft limit list."

Watch people have sex?

The peeler slipped from my hand and clattered to the floor.

He dropped down and picked it up. When he stood, he gently cupped my face. "You have 'watching others' listed as *willing* on your checklist. I would never violate your hard limits. Ever."

My mind spun in a hundred directions. Would we be in Paul's playroom? How did that work? Would Christine care?

"You have 'forced nudity around others' and 'exhibitionism among friends' listed as soft limits." He didn't move his hand. "I won't push those limits this weekend. You will remain clothed, and I will not ask you to play in front of anyone."

We were both silent for several seconds, and his unspoken words rang in my head. A reminder he *would* push my limits at some point.

He smiled. "And it's Tuesday, Abby."

Tuesday. Abby.

He waited until Tuesday to bring the weekend up because he wanted my honest opinion. I understood immediately why he hadn't asked me on Sunday, not when I'd very nearly called him *master* in front of Jackson and Felicia. He knew my answer might be hindered by wearing his collar so recently if he'd asked any earlier.

"Wow," I said. "When I marked that down, I guess I wasn't thinking anything would happen this fast."

"Do you not want to go?"

I tilted my head. "No. It's not that. I just have to think a minute."

I went back to the vegetables, making sure everything was ready for when the rice came out. He walked to the refrigerator and pulled out the tuna and eel—giving me space, allowing me time to think through my answer.

"Have you ever had sex with Christine?" I asked.

"What?" He looked up from unwrapping the fish. "No."

"Have you ever played with her?" I asked, rethinking my question.

"No." He took a knife and cut the tuna into strips. "I have watched them before."

"That would have been my next question."

"I thought as much."

I separated the vegetables into little piles—my pile and his—and thought more about his question. Would it be odd to sit down for dinner with a couple after seeing them in a playroom?

"Abby?" he asked, washing his hands. "Paul and Christine are highly regarded in the community, and they're quite used to dealing with jitters. It may be slightly uncomfortable at times, but this is something they're both used to. He told me Christine gets turned on by being watched."

I thought about that. Remembered back to when Nathaniel and I had sex at the Super Bowl. There was still an undercurrent of excitement that ran through me whenever I thought about it.

"Christine would be a good person for you to talk with," he said. "She would understand and help you with any questions you have but aren't comfortable talking to me about." He walked to me and stroked my cheekbone. His expressive eyes betrayed the even tone of his voice. "And she married her dominant."

Married her dominant.

Would Nathaniel and I one day be at that point? Would he want that? Would I?

I thought about how close I was to Felicia and pondered how nice it would be to have a girlfriend in the lifestyle I could talk with. Then I thought about my checklists and the items I had marked as soft limits. Would I be willing to modify my checklist afterward? Would watching one of my soft limits play out before me change my interest?

"Let's go." I smiled. "Let's do it."

I thought he would ask me if I was sure, but instead he kissed me softly. "I'll call Paul tomorrow."

After dinner, we took Apollo outside to play a bit of catch. He knew what we were going to do and ran out before us, practically dancing in his excitement.

Nathaniel and I walked outside, our arms brushing every so often. He threw a tennis ball to Apollo when we'd made it out to the cherry trees. Apollo growled low in his throat and took off at a run to catch the ball and bring it back for another round.

I giggled when Apollo nearly tripped over his feet as he turned back to us. He looked as if he were laughing when he returned.

"What a ham," I said.

"He likes to show off for you," Nathaniel said, throwing the ball again.

The three of us played fetch for a few more minutes. The weather had finally turned warm, and even though it was still more than a week away, it looked as if Felicia and Jackson would have nice weather for the wedding. I wasn't sure how Felicia did it; I'd never be able to handle planning an outdoor wedding. Too much uncertainty.

"When does the lease on your apartment run out?" he asked.

His question rattled me, and I messed up on my throw of the ball. Fortunately, Apollo didn't care.

"Mid-June," I said.

"Are you going to renew?"

"I haven't decided yet."

I heard him take a deep breath from where he stood beside me.

"I've been thinking," he said.

I steeled myself. Was he going to ask me to move in with him? What would I say? How would I answer? I threw the ball to Apollo again, and I noticed my hand shook.

"Will it bother you to be alone once Felicia's not next door?" he asked.

I'd asked myself that same question numerous times. "I don't know."

"I'm not sure I like you being there by yourself."

"Because Felicia offered me so much protection? I am a big girl, you know."

"I know you are. I just worry."

"Maybe I'll get a dog or take Apollo with me or get a really big can of Mace or——"

"Or you could move in with me."

My breath caught, and I shifted my gaze to follow Apollo. "I suppose that depends."

"On?"

"On if you want me to move in because you want me or because you're worried about me."

His eyes were soft and pleading. "You doubt I want you?"

"It didn't seem like that was your primary motive in asking me to move in."

"I messed up," he confessed. "Let me try this a different way." He took my face in his hands and lifted my chin so our gazes met. "I want you in the morning when your hair's a mess and you're grumpy until you've had your coffee. I want you in the evening so you can tell me about your day while we make dinner together. And I want you at night because I love nothing more than to fall asleep knowing you're closer than my next breath." His lips lightly brushed mine. "Will you move in with me?"

My mouth was dry. I couldn't speak.

"Abby?"

"Yes."

Smiling once more, he took my hand and we walked back inside the house.

Hours later, I stood in his room, watching as he took Apollo out one last time. Through the large picture window in his bedroom, I could see Apollo roaming the yard, nose to the grass. Nathaniel stood at his side, looking up at the moon, deep in thought.

I scanned the expanse of his yard, following the long path of his driveway until trees obscured it. It didn't seem real that in about three weeks, this would be my new home. This house. This yard. This room.

"What has you thinking so intently?"

My eyes flew back to the yard. I'd missed seeing and hearing Nathaniel return to the house. I turned to face him.

He still wore his suit pants from work and, though he'd taken off his tie, he hadn't changed out of his white dress shirt. His lips turned up at the corners at catching me off guard, and he walked closer.

"I was thinking how, in less than a month, this will be our room," I said.

"Our room." He made it to me and placed a hand on either one of my shoulders. "I like the way that sounds."

"Do you?" I asked. "You've lived alone for so long, I worry I'll be in your way. Somehow invade your privacy."

"I've lived my entire adult life thinking there was something wrong with me. Feeling like less than a man because of who I am." He brought a hand to my cheek, and one long finger traced my collarbone. "To have found you. To have you with me like this? And to have you want me?" His finger moved to skim my lips. "I don't want to be alone anymore. I want you. Here with me."

I closed my eyes as he drew me close for a soft kiss.

He pulled back. "You look beautiful, by the way. I meant to say that before you distracted me with the talk of *our* room."

I felt positively delighted he noticed the gown. I'd picked it out just for our first night together after the weekend. It wasn't anything outrageously expensive, but it was the silver color he liked on me and its cut showed off my curves to my advantage.

"Did you see the back?" I teased. The back dipped low, with tiny straps crossing this way and that.

"When you were by the window. I very nearly didn't say anything, just so I could stand and admire you."

He wasn't the only one doing some admiring. I started at the top of his shirt and worked my way down, unbuttoning one button at a time.

"As much as I enjoy admiring you in your white shirt," I said, "I'd much rather admire you with it off."

I took my time undressing him, enjoying the thought that we

had the entire night before us. Hours of time to enjoy each other, to love each other, to reconnect with slow, sweet touches. I felt heady with the knowledge that very soon, we could be like this every weeknight. Would I ever look at this room, with him in it, and find it familiar?

His hands caressed me. With leisurely tenderness, he took the gown and pulled it over my head.

"You in the moonlight," he said, his hands moving on me. "So beautiful."

It was him. He made me beautiful. His words. His touch. His love.

Before I could say anything, his lips were on mine and he was kissing me.

We were both naked by the time he pulled back the covers and we climbed into bed. Then he was over me, kissing the hollow of my neck and tasting me. I ran my hands down his back and felt him shiver as my nails grazed his skin.

Feeling bold, I pushed on his shoulder and sat up. When he turned to his back, I straddled his body, brushing his nipples, first with my fingertips, then with my lips. I'd nearly forgotten how sweet he tasted—all male combined with a hint of the deep woods.

I kissed my way down his stomach while my hands stroked lower. I avoided all contact with his cock, focusing instead on the other parts of him—the dip of his navel, the dusting of hair on his lower belly, the sensitive skin right above his groin.

"Fuck, Abby," he said as I nipped the skin of his inner thigh. I was so close to his erection, I knew he could feel my breath. He lifted his hips in a vain attempt to find friction, but I wasn't finished exploring him yet.

"Look at *you* in the moonlight," I said, pulling back and watching how the pale light played against his skin. I sat up and trailed a finger from his shoulder to upper leg, once more skirting where he was most needy. I ran my hand low and cupped his balls. "The shadows here." My fingers danced along his thigh. "The brightness here."

"Come here," he said, reaching for me.

"Not yet."

"I want you." His hands brushed my upper arm.

"Wait."

I dropped lower on the bed and licked his knee. Picked it up and kissed the underside.

"Now you're just being cruel," he said.

"Mmm," I said, concentrating on memorizing the muscular curve of his calf. I ran my hands down his leg and lifted his foot. I was after the spot right under his anklebone. I found it and kissed the soft skin there.

He sighed.

"What?" I asked.

"I don't think anyone's ever kissed me there before."

I kissed the spot again, running my tongue over it. "How very negligent."

I paid the same amount of attention to his other leg and ankle, finally working my way back up his body. Somehow, enjoying him had heightened my arousal. He sat up, and when he brushed the tips of my nipples with his thumbs, I very nearly came on the spot.

He watched my response with a sly grin. "Eager?" He lowered his head and sucked a nipple into his mouth.

I tightened my grip on his hair. "Oh, God, yes."

"Too damn bad," he said, switching to the other side.

He lowered me to the bed, his mouth never leaving my skin. I was under him, and his touch was soft and light, his mouth and lips skimming the valley between my breasts, tongue flicking out occasionally to tease me.

When he made it to my belly, I let out a moan. He moved lower and licked the skin right above my clit. Then he blew a soft stream of warm air across the wetness, laughing softly at my muttered curse.

I tugged at his shoulders, wanting him to cover me, wanting to feel his weight on me. He didn't make me wait, but crawled up, gently spreading my legs with his knees. I wrapped my arms around him and he dropped his head to my neck.

He entered me slowly, letting me feel every inch of him. Or perhaps feeling every inch of me. When he was fully seated inside me, I slid my hands to his backside. His hips flexed just a bit, in preparation for his thrust.

"Wait," I said, stilling him with my hands.

"Fuck," he grunted in my ear. "Why?"

"I want to feel you for a minute," I said, enjoying the slight stretch of having him so deep inside.

He mumbled something under his breath, but held still.

Soon it became too much—having him so close but not giving in to the urge to move and find relief. His breathing grew ragged; his body tense.

"Okay," I said, when I couldn't bear it anymore. I moved my hands up to his shoulders.

"Thank God."

He pulled out almost all the way and thrust back inside me with a long, slow stroke. We moved in unison—my legs came around his waist and I lifted myself to him with each thrust. Even then, our joining was unhurried. Neither one of us wanted to rush; instead we took our time, enjoying the way we fit together, the way we moved with and against each other.

My release slowly built, starting as a low ache deep in my belly and spreading lower. He must have felt the same, because he picked up his pace and entered me deeper. Harder.

I tried to hold on to the feeling, wanting to draw it out, make it last longer, but I couldn't. I tightened once around him and allowed my climax to overtake me. He followed shortly after, coming inside me with a soft groan.

For several long minutes, we were still. Then he lifted his head and kissed me, long and deep. I rolled us so I lay on his chest, his arms wrapped around me.

I wanted to stay awake, to lie in bed and talk about nothing and everything. But the emotions of the day had taken their toll, and I felt my eyes grow heavier with each second that passed.

I didn't realize I'd spoken out loud until I felt his chest vibrate under me with laugher.

"Go on to sleep," he whispered, stroking my hair. "There'll be plenty of time later."

Chapter Eight

——NATHANIEL——

Taped moving boxes lay scattered around the apartment when I met Abby for dinner at her place on Wednesday night.

"Someone's been busy," I said. We sat at the kitchen table, enjoying grilled chicken and corn.

"Jackson has a moving van coming this weekend to pick up most of Felicia's stuff. She had a few extra boxes."

"Will you be lonely after she leaves?"

Her eyes danced as her fork stopped its upward path. "I don't plan on spending a lot of time here after the wedding."

My breath caught. I knew she wanted to live with me. Knew it was more than just a matter of convenience, but to hear her say it . . . It got me every time.

"Is she upset you won't be here to help move this weekend?"

"No," she said. "She knows better than to try and dictate our weekends."

Our weekends.

"That's good," I said, teasing her slightly. "I'm the only one allowed to dictate our weekends."

"She's so much better," she said. "More supportive this time."

"I'm glad. I'd hate to think she was harassing you about us."

"Don't get me wrong. I wouldn't say she's understanding, but she's accepting." She pushed her corn around her plate. "She even said the diamonds in my collar would go well with the dress."

The diamonds and the dress?

"Why would she say that?" I asked.

She stopped pushing the corn and looked at me. "It's a weekend."

"What is?"

"Their wedding day, Nathaniel," she said, as if what she was talking about made complete sense.

"I know that. I'm just trying to decide what . . ." I started, and then it hit me. "She thought you'd wear the collar to the wedding?"

Her eyebrows crinkled. "Won't I?"

Fucking hell. I'd done it again. Assumed she knew.

"I didn't plan to have you wear the collar next weekend," I said.

"You didn't?" she asked. "Why?"

We should have had this conversation weeks ago, maybe even when we first discussed how often she would be collared.

"Do you remember why I didn't want you to wear the collar all week in the first place?"

She nodded. "You said it put me in a certain mind frame."

I reached across the table and took her hand. "And now that you've worn it for a weekend and removed it on a Sunday afternoon, would you agree with me?"

I could practically see her mind work as she thought. I imagined her replaying Sunday night—the almost slip at Jackson and Felicia's.

"Yes," she said.

"And do you think I'd want you in that mind frame at your best friend's wedding? When you're the maid of honor?"

"Oh," she said simply.

"Conversely," I said. "Do you think I want to be in the mind frame I'm in when you wear my collar? When my cousin is getting married and I'm the best man?"

"*Oh*," she said, as the reality of both sides hit her.

"I should have brought this up sooner." I shook my head. "It just never occurred to me you might think you'd wear it."

"So it's like a weekend off?"

"It's a give-and-take relationship." I stroked her knuckles with my thumb. "We make it work for us. Rearrange it as needed."

A sly smile covered her face. "There goes my fantasy of you spanking me with a coat hanger in the closet."

I blinked.

Twice.

"You had a fantasy of me spanking you with a coat hanger?" I asked.

She nodded, clearly enjoying her upper hand. "And going down on you at the reception."

"You know, it's not just kinky people who enjoy closet time at wedding receptions."

"Or engage in a little under-the-table action?" she asked with a wicked gleam in her eyes.

"You are so, so evil."

She slipped her hand out of mine and coolly took a sip of white wine. "So I've been led to believe."

"Whatever will I do with you?"

She lifted the damn wineglass to her lips and took another sip. I couldn't look away. "I'm sure I have no idea," she said.

"On the contrary," I said, watching her lips and imagining them wrapped around my cock. "I'm sure you have several."

"Maybe."

"Perhaps we should discuss these ideas of yours?" I nodded toward her bedroom. "In a more . . . *comfortable* location?"

"Perhaps." She slowly stood up. "But clear the table first. I hate leaving dishes in the sink overnight."

I took both our plates and walked toward the kitchen. Before leaving the room, I looked over my shoulder. "And, Abby? Just so there's no misunderstanding, if it were anyone else's wedding?"

She stopped, halfway to her bedroom.

"The collar would be on," I finished.

She met me at the airport on Friday afternoon at five thirty. I waited for her outside the jet.

"How was your day?" I asked, kissing her cheek and taking her hand.

"Long."

Yes, my lovely. I know exactly what you mean. Her collar was waiting inside. I planned to collar her after we reached a comfortable cruising altitude.

Once we were seated and on our way, I turned to her. "I want to talk for a few minutes before we do anything else."

"Is everything okay?"

"Of course," I said. "I just wanted to set expectations before I collared you."

"Give me an opportunity to voice any concerns?"

I couldn't help but smile. "You're a fast learner."

"I try."

I knew she did and I wanted to help her in any way possible.

"I want you to feel comfortable this weekend," I said. "I want you to feel free to talk with Paul and Christine. I want you to feel free to talk to me."

"Really?"

I nodded. "Look at Paul and Christine's house as one big library or kitchen table. You are still to address me as 'Sir' or 'Master' since there's nothing to keep from Paul or Christine. There will be additional expectations for his playroom, but we can go over those tomorrow. Okay so far?"

"Yes."

"If I decide to make changes, I'll let you know."

"I'm not sure I understand."

I was glad she questioned me. I'd intentionally made the statement vague, simply to see if she'd ask for clarification.

"If I decide library time is over, that I don't want you acting freely for whatever reason—that I want to play—I'll let you know." I watched her face for understanding. "Is that more clear?"

"If you decide you want to spank me with a coat hanger?"

"Yes." I laughed. "If I decide I want to spank you with a coat hanger."

"Got it."

I glanced down at my watch and then looked out the window. We were flying smoothly and our ascent had leveled off. I unbuckled my seat belt and stood.

Her collar rested on the table near my wet bar. I lifted it from the box. Her eyes followed my every move.

I held it out. "Come here, Abigail," I said. "And show me how much you want to wear my collar."

Paul and Christine lived in a modest two-story house. As I pulled into their driveway, I thought back, trying to remember how long it had been since I'd last visited them—two years maybe?

I looked out the corner of my eye to Abigail. She sat rigid and unmoving beside me. She'd been that way since leaving the car rental agency.

"Relax," I said, stroking her knee. "They're two normal people who happen to enjoy the same interests we do. I promise there is nothing to be scared of."

She nodded and took a deep breath, but didn't talk.

"Remember what I told you on the jet," I said. "I want you to feel comfortable speaking this weekend, not only to me, but to them as well."

"I'm sorry," she said. "I've really been looking forward to this. It's just that now that it's here . . ."

I patted her knee. "Everything will be fine."

"Yes, Master," she said, but unconvincingly.

"I don't want a cookie cutter reply," I warned her. "I want you to believe me."

She didn't say anything as I parked the car and got out to open her door. I knew there was little I could say to convince her. She'd have to learn herself that Paul and Christine's house held nothing to fear.

Lights blazed throughout the house even though it was well after nine o'clock. Didn't they have the baby? I thought I remembered Paul saying his mother-in-law wouldn't keep Sam until the next day.

Then, as we approached the house, I heard it—the unmistakable sound of a baby's high-pitched wailing.

"Looks like it may be a long night," I said.

She opened her mouth to say something, but closed it before speaking.

I raised an eyebrow at her and turned to ring the doorbell.

Paul opened the door, and the screams got louder. "Nathaniel," he said, pulling me into a hug. "I'm so glad you're here." He waved us into the house.

Once we were inside, he faced us again. "You must be Abby." He reached out a hand to her. "I've heard so much about you. It's good to finally meet you."

Her cheeks flushed just a bit. "I've heard a lot about you, as well."

"Don't believe any of it," he said in a low, joking whisper. "Well, don't believe all of it. Some of it's probably true."

"Believe every word of it," Christine said, stepping into the foyer. "Every word of it and then some." She laughed and hugged me. "How's it going, Nathaniel?" Then she held out her hands. "Abby, welcome to our home. As you can see, Sam didn't want to miss your arrival."

"Consider it birth control," Paul said.

Christine shot a dirty look at her husband before turning her attention back to us. "Come on inside. Need some help with your bags?"

"Nathaniel?" Paul said, jerking his head to the door. "I'll help you get the bags inside."

"And Abby and I will be waiting in the den," Christine said. "Can I get you something to drink?" she asked as the two of them left the room.

"She's lovely," Paul said, once they left and we were outside alone.

"She is, isn't she?"

"Little jittery about this weekend?"

"Of course. But I have all faith in Christine. She'll have her calmed down in no time."

"Mmm," he agreed. "She does have that effect."

"I hope so. Abby didn't talk the entire way from the airport."

We collected the bags and started back inside.

"I'm putting the two of you in the guest room down the hall from our room," he said. "I hope Sam doesn't keep you up all night."

"We'll be fine."

We made it back inside, and he set Abby's suitcase by the door, excusing himself to step inside the den, where Abby and Christine talked quietly. He placed a hand on Christine's shoulder, leaned down, and whispered something to her. Christine said something I couldn't hear and got up to walk into the kitchen after placing a kiss on Paul's cheek.

Paul motioned for me to join him in the den.

"Nathaniel and I are going to step into my office for a bit," he told Abby. "I won't keep him long."

She nodded.

"We'll be back shortly," I told her. I knew Christine would make her feel at home, but I didn't want to be gone from her side for long.

"Yes, sir," she said with a quick glance to the floor.

It was the first time she'd called me 'sir' in the presence of someone else, and I wasn't prepared for the fire that pounded through me. I fought the urge to jerk my head to the guest room and command her to meet me there. To take her hard and fast . . .

"Nathaniel?" Paul said.

Paul's office hadn't changed much since I'd last seen it. I noticed our checklists on his desk.

"Little light reading?" I asked, sitting down in a spare chair.

"Just in between bouts of colic."

"What have you decided for tomorrow?"

"Well." He picked up one list. "She looks to be rather adventuresome, even though she has limited experience. The thing that stood out to me, though, was her hard limit on canes."

I nodded.

"I taught you about canes," he said. "You're an expert with them."

Yes.

"I think I'll use the cane on Christine tomorrow, show Abby they aren't to be feared."

Part of me thought it was a good idea, to show her how a cane could be wielded when not used for punishment. Paul could use the cane; then Abby and I could discuss it. Abby and Christine could discuss it.

But I remembered a conversation just weeks before, the fear in her eyes as she spoke about the case in Singapore, and I knew now was not the time to introduce her to canes. Not our second weekend of play.

"No," I said.

He raised an eyebrow.

"It's one of her hard limits," I said. "And since we're starting what will hopefully be a long-term, if not permanent, relationship, I want to move slowly."

"Long-term, if not permanent," he repeated.

"What?"

"It's just hard to believe you're the same man I flew to New York to help months ago."

"I've had a lot of help," I said. "A lot of forgiveness and a lot more love than I deserve."

"Everyone deserves love. I'm glad you finally realized that. I'm glad Abby didn't give up on you."

"Right," I said. "So I'm not going to repay her by making her watch a caning scene the second weekend she's wearing my collar."

"Good point," he said. "Someone's taught you well."

"Fucking hell. Don't go getting a big head."

He laughed. "Remember one thing for me."

"What's that?"

"This is new to you," he said. "New to Abby. Don't try to make it exactly like your previous relationships. It's not. It's okay to change the rules or make new ones."

"Thanks. I needed to hear that."

He smiled. "I know you did."

His words rang in my head an hour later as Abigail walked into the bedroom from the adjoining bathroom.

She looked around the room and then dropped her eyes to scan the floor, probably looking for where she was to sleep.

I'd thought many times over the last week how the night would go. What we would do as far as sleeping arrangements.

I turned the corner of the bed down. "I'd like for you to share my bed tonight, Abigail."

Her eyes grew large.

"You're free to turn me down, of course," I said. "I did tell you to speak freely this weekend, and Paul gave me an air mattress for you to use."

She swallowed audibly.

"I said I only rarely invited submissives to share my bed," I said softly. "Not that I never did."

That got her attention.

She walked to me and took my hand. "I'll gladly share your bed tonight, Master."

Chapter Nine

——ABBY——

I couldn't get my mind to settle and go to sleep.

Christine and Paul were nothing like I imagined them to be, not that I ever pictured exactly what I thought they would look like. I just envisioned something scarier.

With that in mind, I was woefully unprepared for the average-looking couple that welcomed me into their average-looking home. Paul was a few years older than us, was tall and well built, with dirty blond hair and beautiful blue eyes. Christine, on the other hand, was shorter, with shoulder-length brown hair and friendly-looking eyes that danced when she laughed.

I kept watching, searching in their demeanor for something, anything, to betray their relationship. Surely there would be a touch, a look, an action, and I would think, *Yes, now I can tell. Now it's obvious.*

Except there was nothing.

Nothing but Christine teasing her husband and giving him a

nasty look when he referenced their crying son as birth control. No subtle glance. No small but meaningful touch.

Just your average, everyday couple.

When the men left the den, Christine talked naturally—asking questions about how Nathaniel and I met. She knew about the wedding, and we talked, not only of Felicia and Jackson's wedding, but of hers as well. Not surprisingly, our conversation eventually turned to Sam and the ups and downs of new motherhood. Not once did we talk about . . . well, what I thought we'd talk about.

The men eventually returned to the den, and Nathaniel and I went on to the guest room.

I rolled to my side, careful not to disturb Nathaniel. I was still surprised he'd asked me to share his bed and felt honored he'd done so. I knew, based on our prior conversations, that when he said he rarely shared his bed with a submissive, he meant fewer than four times.

Ever.

We hadn't talked about the next day. How the day would go or what we'd do. I kept trying to think about how our time in the playroom would go—would it be strange to see Paul and Christine naked?

Paul and Christine's guest room had a queen bed. For some reason, it felt odd. I wasn't sure why—I had a queen bed in my apartment, and while we slept together more frequently in his king-sized bed, we did on occasion share my queen.

To keep my mind off the next day, I decided to think about beds. I wondered why beds were sized the way they were. Twin, queen, and king. Why not small, medium, and large? And why was twin the smallest?

I curled my knees up to my chest, and suddenly two arms came around me.

"You're uncharacteristically restless tonight," Nathaniel said, pulling me close.

"I'm sorry to disturb your sleep, sir."

"Do you want to talk about something?"

"Not if it'll keep you from sleep."

He kissed the back of my neck. "I wouldn't have asked if I was worried about losing sleep. Right now, my focus is you—making sure you're comfortable. That you're able to rest. I want you in the best frame of mind possible for tomorrow."

I knew what his focus was. Knew how much time and attention went into planning our weekends. We were setting aside precious time for this visit. Time that would normally be ours, we were sharing.

He planned down to the tiniest detail how to best get me in the proper frame of mind, to help me relax and feel comfortable around his friends. He'd even invited me to his bed.

Since he told me to look at this weekend as library time, I ran my hands over his arms and enjoyed the strength in them, how comforting they felt around me.

"I feel better now," I said.

"How so?"

"With you touching me. I know it sounds strange, but you're always able to relax me with your touch."

His arms tightened briefly. "I'm learning just as much as you. You looked a bit surprised when I invited you to bed. I feared maybe you wanted to sleep on the floor but didn't want to disappoint me."

I turned so I faced him. "I never want to disappoint you, but my reasons for sharing your bed tonight were completely selfish. I just felt more at ease sleeping with you tonight."

"I'm glad," he said. "What do you think of Paul and Christine?"

"They're not at all what I thought."

"Dare I ask what you thought?"

"Someone big and burly for Paul. Lots of body hair. Lots of black leather." I yawned. "Maybe a mask."

"You have the strangest imagination."

"Someone reserved and quiet for Christine," I said. "Mousy."

"Christine is anything but mousy." He traced the edge of my collar. "This does not leave you without free will. It does not make you a doormat. You know that here." He tapped my head. "You need to get it here." He laid his hand over my heart. "You are brave and strong and fierce."

"It's you," I whispered, glad for the cover of darkness. "You let me be brave and strong and fierce."

"You've only scratched the surface, my lovely." His lips brushed my cheek. "I can't wait for you to actually see it."

"I'm nervous."

"I know you are," he said. "And tomorrow, even with your nerves, you will continue to be brave and strong and fierce. Because that's what you are. It's what I need from you, and it's what you will give me."

All of me. I would give him all of me. Anything he asked for was his.

"Will it help you sleep if I hold you?" he asked.

"It always helps when you hold me, sir."

He turned me so my back was to his chest once more, and I pressed close to his warmth. His arms came around me, and I fell asleep within minutes.

After Paul cooked a huge breakfast of sausage and pancakes, Christine and I made our way to the den. She held Sam, preparing to feed him.

"You don't mind, do you?" she asked.

I thought it was nice of her to ask, even considering what she was going to be doing in front of me in a few hours. "No," I said. "I don't mind."

I hadn't been around many babies before, much less watched a woman breastfeed. She deftly situated Sam and flipped a thin blanket over her shoulder, hiding most of the feeding infant.

She sighed and leaned back in her chair. "He's a big eater," she said after a few minutes. "Gets it from his father."

I nodded, but seeing no point in waiting, launched into one of the questions I wanted to ask. "How do you and Paul still play with a baby?"

"Not as often as we used to. That's for sure."

"You don't do the weekend thing anymore?"

"No," she said. "It hasn't really worked with a baby. For now we use the playroom when we have time—which hasn't been a lot lately."

"With good reason, though," I said, nodding toward Sam.

"Oh, yes. I wouldn't change anything." She thought for a moment. "Well, not much. I might change the amount of sleep I get. And the constant leaking." She dropped her voice to a whisper. "Do you know how strange it is to wear a bra in the playroom?"

"We only started playing again last weekend," I said. "But yes, I can see that."

"Listen," she said. "I'm a very open and honest person. Do me a favor and tell me to knock it off if I give out too much information."

"You're fine."

"The first time we played after Sam was born, about four weeks ago, I didn't wear a bra and, well . . . leakage. I've very rarely seen Paul look taken aback." She giggled. "But the expression on his face was priceless."

I tried to picture the unflappable Paul looking taken aback and failed.

"What did he do?" I asked.

"He cleaned it up," she said. I pictured washcloths and paper towels. "Afterward, he said it tasted almost sweet."

I felt myself blush.

"I'm sorry," she said. "That was too much."

"No," I said, wanting to hear more about her and Paul. "Just unexpected, although maybe we should start with something easier. I want to hear about how the two of you work. Tell me how you met."

"Paul's very well-known," she said, and I got the impression she told this story often. "His reputation preceded him. Probably much the same as Nathaniel."

I nodded.

"I met him for the first time, here actually, at a meeting," she said. "I'd been a submissive for a good number of years, but I was between relationships at the time. He asked for my help with a demonstration a few weeks later. I know Nathaniel is your first dom, but trust me, when you play with someone experienced"—she shook her head—"it's amazing."

I doubted anyone else could make me feel the way Nathaniel did, but I refrained from saying so.

"We played casually for a few months," she said. "And eventually moved to a weekend arrangement. We started dating, and well, the rest is history."

"Nathaniel said you had a twenty-four-seven Dom/sub relationship once."

She nodded. "After we started dating. There were some parts I really enjoyed, but I don't think Paul liked it very much."

"I don't think Nathaniel would either."

"Would you?"

I thought about that. How would it be to go an entire week as his submissive? To expand our weekend play? Seven days . . . My mind wandered, thinking. So much time. So much we could do.

"Maybe," I said. "Just for a week or so. To try."

"Like I said, there were parts I liked. It was a different kind of experience." She took a minute, switched Sam to the opposite breast and then covered herself again. "I don't want to see the look on Nathaniel's face if you decide to tell him you want to try a twenty-four-seven relationship." She laughed. "Probably not what he had in mind when he said he'd like for us to talk."

I laughed along with her. "Probably not."

"The thing you need to remember about Nathaniel," she said, once more all serious, "is that he's in love for the first time ever. He's going slower with you than he has with previous submissives. I know part of that is because of your inexperience, but part of it is he's afraid of coming on too strongly."

I definitely believed that. "I know, and I can tell there'll be times I'll want him to push harder and further."

"You need to tell him. It's your job to tell him when you want things to happen differently."

"I just can't get to that point in my head. Not during a weekend."

"He needs that feedback," she said. "Although, if it's more comfortable for you, tell him on a weekday. There's no rule you can't talk about your weekend time on a Wednesday night."

"That's what I need to remember. It's feedback. Not telling him what to do."

"Right. The ultimate decision is still his, but he can make more informed decisions if you're giving him all the information he needs."

There were other questions I wanted to ask, but just one I really needed to talk to someone about. Someone who wasn't Nathaniel.

"Can I ask you something?" I asked.

"I'm an open book," she said with a smile. "Very little is off-limits for me."

"Canes," I said, almost shivering at the word. "Tell me about them."

"That's rather random."

I picked at a fingernail. "I marked them down as a hard limit, because I was scared. But Nathaniel really likes them."

"And you want a submissive's view on canes?"

"Yes."

"I'd be surprised if Paul hadn't used a cane or two on Nathaniel during his mentorship," she said. "But I suppose his view is different from mine."

"So you'll tell me?" I asked, very interested to hear what she thought about the scary-sounding items.

She nodded. "Now, Paul's punished me with a cane before, and that's something completely and totally different. I don't like *that* use of the cane at all."

"You can use canes for reasons other than punishment?"

"I know several people who enjoy it when a cane's used on them. I'm one of them."

"Really?"

"It's all in the technique, and Paul has the most amazing technique. And Nathaniel learned from Paul."

I didn't say anything.

"I won't lie to you. It hurts," she said. "But so do spankings, right?"

"Right. But I like the spankings."

"In that case, when and if you ever feel comfortable with

canes, you'll probably like Nathaniel using them," she said. "If he builds up to it properly, that is."

"Builds up? Like a warm-up spanking?"

"Yes, like that."

"Mmmm," I said, by way of reply. I'd put that aside to think about later. Canes for pleasure? Who would have thought?

The doorbell sounded right as Christine took Sam out from under the blanket and straightened her shirt.

"That must be Mom," she said. "What perfect timing."

After Christine's mom left with Sam, Nathaniel and I went back to the guest room. He told me he had an outfit laid out for me, but stopped me before I could put it on.

"Before you change," he said. "Until further notice, library time is over. Understood?"

A twinge of desire, lust, and yearning shot straight through me.

"Yes, Master."

"Paul has certain rules for his playroom," he said. "You are to wear your hair up. The only jewelry allowed inside is wedding rings. He made an exception for your collar. I don't want your head down. I want you watching both Christine and Paul. And as an observer, you are to remain silent." He smiled. "Unless you become overwhelmed, in a negative way, and need to use your safe word. Understood?"

"Yes, Master."

He leaned forward and kissed me. "Meet me outside our room in fifteen minutes."

When we entered the playroom downstairs, Christine was already in position. Nathaniel walked over to the straight-backed chair at the edge of the room, and I followed behind him. After he sat down, I sat on the pillow at his feet and tentatively placed a hand on his knee. Christine didn't move. As I expected, she wore a bra, but was naked otherwise.

I watched her for a minute, letting myself grow accustomed to the sight.

She's naked, I told myself. *She's naked and it's okay.*

I took a minute to glance around the room—it was twice as large as Nathaniel's and held more equipment. Much of the room was the same—a refrigerator, a sink, and a large first-aid kit. One shelf held a baby monitor, though, and the realities of playing with a child hit me. I became even more thankful Christine's mom had taken Sam for a few hours.

I wasn't sure how many times Christine and Paul had played since Sam's birth, but I assumed it hadn't been many. Between the late-night feedings and colic, who would have time? It occurred to me then that maybe Christine and Paul were just as happy as we were to have someone else watch their son for a few hours.

My head swung to the door as Paul entered. Like Nathaniel, he wore black jeans and a T-shirt. The change in his demeanor struck me. He still looked like himself, of course, just more intense.

He walked to where Christine kneeled.

"It's good to have you back in my playroom, girl," he said.

She moved her hands to the floor and slid toward his feet. "I await your pleasure, Master."

"Show me," he said, and she slid closer and kissed each of his toes, then the tops of his feet. When she finished, she moved to her knees and slid her hands up his legs. "Not yet," he said, and backed away.

She immediately stopped and dropped back to her original position.

That was interesting. Nathaniel had never asked me to kiss his feet. I wondered why, wondered if I would act as quickly as Christine if he asked me to do it.

But I didn't have time to dwell on that thought. From behind his back, Paul brought a black leather collar. "I've longed to put this back on you," he told Christine.

She had told me she no longer wore a collar except when they were in the playroom. Pregnancy and childbirth had changed the dynamics of their relationship, and now they were only dominant and submissive in this room, unlike Nathaniel and me, who were dominant and submissive all weekend.

Her eyes stayed focused on the floor. "I have longed for it as well, Master."

As he put his collar on her, the significance of the ritual hit me. The staking of his claim on her—showing her with both word and deed that she was his. Likewise, by accepting his collar and his claim, she agreed to his temporary control. She gave herself to him. I understood that part from Nathaniel's collaring of me, but what caught me off guard was the look in Paul's eyes as he fastened the collar on her. The intensity of his expression—the pride, the carnal longing—was completely unexpected.

Did Nathaniel look that way when he collared me? Did his expression mirror Paul's?

With the collar fastened, Paul stepped back, eyes still smoldering. "I want you on your hands and knees on the table."

Without moving her eyes from the floor, she crawled to the table and climbed on top.

I wondered why she crawled. Was that something Paul expected? Would Nathaniel ever want me to do that? To crawl instead of walk?

Paul walked to stand in front of Christine, slipped a ball gag in her mouth and buckled it around her head.

"I'm going to work you a bit harder than I have lately," he said, his hands softly stroking her shoulders. "And I want to make sure you don't scare our guests." He leaned down to whisper in her ear, although we could still hear. "Plus I love the sounds you make through the gag."

He slipped something into her hand.

I felt Nathaniel's breath on my ear. "It's a bell," he whispered so low, I knew the couple before us couldn't hear. "It allows her to use her safe word while she's gagged. If something happens and she needs to stop or slow the scene down, she'll drop the bell."

I moved forward slightly. Nathaniel had never used a gag on me before, and I was quite curious. I remembered Christine's recommendation to tell Nathaniel to push me harder when I wanted and to bring up things I'd like to do.

While Paul went about collecting things from around the room, I kept my eyes on Christine. I would have thought she'd look vulnerable, and she did, but it wasn't her vulnerability that drew me. It was the beauty of her trust, the grace of her submission. There was an elegance of sorts in her position I had not anticipated being there.

Paul came up behind her and ran a hand down her backside and again, the look in his eyes captured my attention. "You want this badly. I can tell." He slid a vibrator into her, her moan muffled by the gag. "So needy already."

My mind spun as it tried to take in what was happening before me. I tried to work my mind around the fact that the man who had made breakfast for me this morning was using a vibrator on his wife. In front of me. I couldn't look away.

He started spanking her. The sound was light at first, but slowly grew in intensity. I wondered, briefly, how it would feel to be spanked while filled that way.

After a bit, my mind concentrated, not so much on what Paul was doing, but how the two of them looked. The way he completely focused his attention on her. The utter concentration of his expression. There was nothing in the world that existed in that moment for him except her, and I wondered again if Nathaniel looked the same when I gave myself to him.

His statement from earlier in the week came back to me. About how, for the wedding, he didn't want to be in the mind frame required when I wore his collar, and I suddenly knew exactly what he meant. How intently he must have to work the entire weekend: to keep his focus *and* to plan all the necessary details. To make sure, above all, that I was okay and cared for at all times.

I shifted my attention to the couple before me, and while what they did was interesting—Paul had switched to a wooden paddle—it was the way they moved that captivated me. They looked to be dancing an intricate dance: his movement echoed and received by her. Her moans, in return, spurred him to further action. What played out before me was a give-and-take I had not expected, and the entire scene portrayed a delicate beauty I had not believed possible.

I was so engrossed in watching that give-and-take, I barely noticed when Paul picked up a flogger. I wanted to be Christine. Wanted it to be Nathániel working hard to bring me the pleasure only he could. I wanted to play again, now that the image of how beautiful my submission must be was firmly embedded in my head.

Eventually Paul stopped, granted Christine permission to relax, and she dropped her head to the table. He removed both vibrator and gag, kissed her cheek, and whispered something to her we couldn't hear. When she looked up at him, the love and trust in her eyes so touched me, I tightened my grasp on Nathaniel's knee.

I thought back to our first weekend back in the playroom, when he'd cupped my chin and commanded me to look at him. Had I looked at him the same way Christine looked at Paul? Conversely, could I remember Nathaniel's expression being as fierce and feral as Paul's? It bothered me that I couldn't recall it, and I made a promise to pay closer attention next time.

Paul told her to move to the the center of the room, and she slipped off the table to comply with his wishes. The middle of the room held what looked like a complex pulley-and-rope system. I leaned forward again, recognizing from Internet research the equipment needed for suspension scenes. Nathaniel didn't have any of this in his playroom.

Paul took his time and slowly buckled Christine into what looked like boots, securing her to the ropes and pulleys hanging from the ceiling. It was obvious in watching them that they were a couple who had been together for years. There was no awkwardness, no hesitation, just control fully given and control fully assumed.

Once Christine was in position on the floor, Paul walked to a switch on a nearby wall. Within seconds, the pulley lifted her legs in the air and she rolled up—a smooth, practiced move she must have done many times. When her head hung a few feet off the ground, the pulley stopped. He walked to her, nodded, and she unbuckled his jeans.

I wanted to look away, but I was unable to do so. Then, right as I was trying to decide if I should close my eyes, just before Paul's zipper opened, a soft scarf covered my eyes. Nathaniel whispered to me, "Sight isn't the most important part of this scene."

No, I wanted to yell as soon as I realized I'd be blindfolded for the foreseeable future. *I want to see.*

But I recalled the beauty and trust in Christine's submission and knew I was submitting to my own master by wearing the blindfold. Knew he had his reasons. So I sat a bit straighter and concentrated on my other senses.

At first my sense of touch felt the most noticeable. The softness of the pillow under me. The movement of air around my bared belly. The hard bones and strong muscles of Nathaniel's knee under my fingers. Even the silkiness of the blindfold.

Then came the sounds. The ragged intake of Paul's breath as Christine did whatever it was she was doing. The whispery words of encouragement, too low to make out, but spoken in a tone I completely understood. From above me, the steady sound of Nathaniel's breathing. Even my own heart. The once quiet room became a cacophony of noise.

I could no longer measure the passage of time with anything save my breaths and heartbeat. I tried to find something else and settled on the rhythmic sounds coming from the couple in front of me.

Christine let out a low whimper of pleasure, and I wondered what was happening. Then I recalled Nathaniel's whisper and knew what was happening wasn't what he wanted me to get from the experience.

You are brave and strong and fierce, he'd said in bed the night before.

I'd thought them to be romantic words, meant to soothe, to ease me into sleep. But hearing and experiencing the scene before me, they became so much more.

I saw Christine's braveness in her supine position on the floor as she waited for Paul's command.

I heard her strength in the sounds of Paul's words as he softly encouraged her and eventually gave in to his own desires.

I felt the fierceness from both of them with emotions so fiery they damn near lit the playroom with their heat.

It's you, I had whispered back to him. *You let me be brave and strong and fierce.* I'd meant it when I'd said it the night before, and I still believed the words to be true. Yet there was another facet added to my understanding, and as the couple before me continued, I sat in blinded awe of that knowledge.

Chapter Ten

——ABBY——

Nathaniel took my hand and I jumped at his touch, unprepared for the jolt of desire that accompanied his hand wrapping around mine. He placed my hand in my lap.

"Get in your waiting position," he whispered, his husky voice sending another wave of longing through me.

I slipped off the pillow and moved into the position I took when in his playroom. While kneeling on the floor, I strained my ears, trying to hear what was happening. I hadn't been in Paul's playroom long enough to know what furniture Nathaniel was near, much less guess what he might be doing or getting.

And were Paul and Christine still in the room? Were they watching me? Nathaniel said he wouldn't push my exhibitionism limits this weekend, but would this be considered exhibitionism? I mean, I was just kneeling.

I tried again to hear, to pick up on any voices, any whisper. Then it hit me—it didn't matter. Didn't matter what Nathaniel had planned. He was in control. I gave him that power, and to worry would be second-guessing him.

If Paul and Christine were in the room, I wanted my submission to be a mirror of what I had just seen play out before me. I realized then that I didn't even care if Paul and Christine were in the room. I wanted them to see. Wanted to show them how proud I was to serve my master.

Bare feet padded to me.

"Stand up, Abigail," Nathaniel said.

I scrambled as gracefully as possible to my feet, but the change in position, combined with the blindfold, disoriented me, and I swayed a bit.

He caught me, slipped his arms around my shoulders. "Steady, my lovely." He didn't move his hands, but kept his hold on me. "I need you to trust me."

Yes. Anything.

"Paul and Christine have left. Only the two of us are in here."

My heart pounded. We were alone. Alone. Oh, the things he could do when we were alone.

"You are to answer any question I ask immediately and honestly," he said. "Understand?"

"Yes, Master."

Master.

The word meant so much more now that I'd watched Paul and Christine.

Master.

I shivered in the new appreciation of its meaning. Every time I spoke it, I renewed my commitment to him. Reminded him I was with him by choice. Had given control to him. Confirmed I wanted him.

Had a six-letter word ever carried so much meaning?

He took my hand. "Come with me."

We walked. I wasn't sure where we were going. We weren't leaving, were we? I didn't want to leave. I wanted to stay in the playroom. I wanted Nathaniel to take me, to use me, to . . .

But it was his choice, and if he wanted us to leave, he'd have good reason.

He pulled us to a stop. I didn't think it was near the door. It was hard to get my bearings, but I thought we were near the wall opposite the door.

"Undress," he said, dropping my hand.

I'd undressed for him numerous times, as both his lover and his submissive, but it seemed different somehow. More intense.

I imagined him watching as I hooked my thumbs into my waistband.

"Top first."

I reached behind my back and unhooked my bra. It fell to the floor and, almost immediately, his hands were on me. Walking me backward until my back hit something wooden.

His thumbs rubbed my nipples, and I bit the inside of my cheek. His mouth ran softly across my neck. "You did so well this morning. I'm so proud of you."

I couldn't tell what made me happier—his hands and mouth on me or his praise.

"I'm so proud. I decided to give you a little reward." His hands took one of my wrists and locked it into a soft cuff above my head. He repeated the action to the other wrist, and his teeth grazed my earlobe. "By fucking you good and hard while you're bound to Paul's cross."

Ah, hell, yes.

While he talked, his hands moved—over my shoulders, across my chest, tweaking a nipple, stroking my belly. I became a quivering mass of need, spurred along by his deep, husky voice.

"I do have one of these in my own playroom," he said, oblivious to my desires, or maybe he knew exactly what he was doing. "Next time we're in there, I'll bind you with your back facing me." His touch grew rougher. "Your ass completely exposed." He grabbed the fabric at my hips and jerked it down, baring me completely. "Would you like that, Abigail?"

I gasped as the cool air hit my aching flesh. His fingers grazed my clit.

"Yes, please, Master," I said in a half whisper, half groan.

Fingertips traced lazy circles across my bare flesh, dipping occasionally into my wetness. "You enjoyed the rabbit fur. I think it's time to move up to suede."

I shivered just thinking about offering my backside to his flogger.

"But for now," he said, spreading my legs, "we have other business to attend to. Wouldn't you say?"

He was deliberately baiting me. Between the promises of what waited for me in his playroom, his hands on my body, and the anticipation of what he was getting ready to do, I could hardly form a coherent thought.

"Whatever you wish, Master."

He chuckled. "I'm so glad you see things my way."

With one movement, he picked my legs up and thrust into me. My backside hit the wood behind me with a force that drove him deeper.

"Don't hold back," he said, and I wrapped my legs around him. "This room's soundproof." He pulled back, rocked into me again, and I let out a loud moan. "I think."

Part of me wanted Paul and Christine to hear. After all, it only seemed fair. I wanted them to know what Nathaniel did to me, how I responded to him, how he commanded my every move, my every thought and, it seemed, sometimes my every breath, during our weekends.

He thrust into me again, and Paul and Christine left my thoughts completely. I concentrated only on the feel of him as he drove me closer and closer to release. He shifted my legs, angled his hips, and hit that sweet spot deep inside me.

I couldn't hold back anything then. I yelled.

He continued his thrusts, stroking inside me again and again, until I was dizzy with pleasure. His breaths came in short gasps, and he moved a hand between our bodies.

I let out another yelp as he rubbed my clit. "Please, Master," I begged.

His voice was tight. "Please, what?"

Oh, God, his fingers. His cock. Being vulnerable and at his mercy. "Please, Master. I can't hold on anymore."

He thrust again. "Come, then."

My climax swept through me with the next pass of his hand.

"Hold on," he said, taking my hips and pushing me against the wall, legs still wrapped around his waist. With quick, deep movements, he entered me over and over, driving himself toward his own release.

I felt another climax building and, as he spilled himself deep inside me, his movements caused me to come again.

For the next few minutes, he rested against me, breathing hard and heavy. When we'd both recovered somewhat, he gently lowered my legs to the floor. He quickly unlocked my wrists and spent several minutes rubbing my arms and shoulders.

Then, finally, his fingers reached behind my head and the blindfold fell away. I met his eyes for the first time since we'd left the hallway to enter the playroom.

It was there.

The intense longing, passion, and love I'd wondered about was there. I sucked in a breath.

"Are you okay?" he asked.

"Yes, Master." I stood and basked in wonder at the emotion in his eyes. "So much more than okay," I whispered.

After, he took me back to the guest room. I sat in his arms while he leaned back against the headboard. As much as I wanted to talk after our morning, I was glad he held me—I still felt more comfortable touching as we talked.

"I want you to be completely honest with me now," he said, and I relaxed further into his embrace. "What do you think so far?"

"I have so many thoughts, so much information to process," I said. "But first, thank you for setting this up. I was worried at first, but it's been so helpful."

"How so?"

"Everything," I said, not sure how else to describe it. "Starting with Christine. She's so confident, so sure of herself."

I heard the worry in his voice. "Have you had doubts about yourself?"

I dropped my head, and my hair fell forward. "Not when I'm with you. It's when I'm at work, or talking with Felicia. Even when I'm around Elaina and Todd. I used to wonder if there was something wrong with us."

"And now?" he asked, voice thick with emotion.

"I don't wonder anymore," I said, wanting to reassure him. "Seeing Paul and Christine, the life they've built. I'm not ready for children and everything, but I see now that when I am . . . I'll be okay."

"*We'll* be okay," he corrected.

My heart leapt at the underlying meaning of his words, and I turned my head to kiss him. "We'll be okay," I repeated.

"Anything else?" he asked, stroking my hair.

"So much." I leaned back into his embrace once more. "Christine helped me understand how important it is to give you feedback. I see now it's not telling you what to do."

"I'm glad someone finally got that point across."

"I never wanted you to think I was telling you what to do."

"There's a world of difference between telling me what to do and telling me what you like or want more of," he said in the firm but gentle voice I loved so much.

"I know. Christine said if it was easier, I could tell you on a weekday what I'd like to do."

"Or you could tell me on a weekend."

I shook my head. "I can't imagine doing that."

He was quiet, and I wondered if he'd change the subject altogether, but then he spoke again. "What if I gave you another safe word?"

"What?"

"We could add 'green.' "

"What would that do?"

He took a deep breath. "If you wanted me to speed up or push you harder."

"Really?" I asked, excited about the prospect.

"Yes. If you feel more comfortable saying 'green' instead of telling me directly," he said. "But I will still ask for you to give me detailed feedback later."

I wondered why he hadn't given me *green* weeks ago when we discussed the safe words, but then decided he probably hadn't thought I'd ever want him to push me or that I'd feel comfortable using it.

"I like it," I said. "Let's use it."

"What else did you and Christine talk about?" he asked, instead of talking further about safe words.

"Listening to her talk about the twenty-four-seven relationship she had with Paul made me curious. I wonder how something like that would be."

He stiffened behind me.

"Just for a week or so," I hastened to add. "Not for an extended period or all the time."

He spoke carefully. "If, at some point in the future, you still want to explore something like that, I would not be opposed to extending our weekend play. But only for a specified period of time and only when you can prove to me you're able and willing to give me feedback."

"Fair enough."

"It's not something I'm particularly interested in. But if you want to try, I'll do it for you."

I was starting to see the benefits of giving feedback. "Thank you."

He kissed the top of my head. "I'm almost afraid to ask, but anything else?"

"The scene with Paul and Christine. I never realized how it looked. How"——I stopped for a second—"*beautiful* it was."

"Beautiful?"

"Mmm," I said, tracing his fingers, intertwined with mine. "The trust. The control. How they played off and balanced each other."

"Almost overwhelming."

"The way he looked at her . . ." I stopped.

"Yes?"

"To think of you watching me. Looking at me like that."

He moved his hands to my shoulders. "Look at me."

I turned in his lap.

Met his eyes.

Gasped when I saw the truth of his next words.

"I do," he said. "Always."

Chapter Eleven

——NATHANIEL——

I stared into her eyes and saw she finally got it. Finally understood. At least in part. She gasped, and I hoped she found
what she was looking for in my eyes.

"Does it make sense now?" I cupped her cheek, stroked her
skin. "Do you understand, just a bit, how I feel when I see what
you give me?"

"Yes," she said, still searching my eyes. "I see it now."

"Good." I drew her close and kissed her, my lips hard and urgent. I wanted to taste her. Feel her under me.

She moaned into my mouth and wrapped her arms around
my shoulders. For just a minute, I let myself go and gave in to
the need I'd held back since seeing her amazement in the playroom. Only when she pulled me toward her, trying to bring me
down on top of her, did I stop.

"No," I said, pushing back from her. "We can't. Paul's ordered lunch." I honestly wanted to tell him we'd eat later and
spend the next few hours alone with her in bed, but we couldn't.

We were guests in Paul's home, and he'd been nice enough to ask me when he should plan to have lunch delivered. I felt I should honor the time frame I gave him.

She sighed. "Yes, sir."

"Later," I whispered to her.

She smiled in response. Her fingers danced along my shirt. "Can I ask you one more question?"

"Anything."

Her fingers didn't stop. "Your other submissives," she said. "Did they . . . and you . . . ?"

I dug my fingers into her hair and pulled them through the softness. I understood why Paul had a rule that hair be up in his playroom, but I didn't feel the same. As soon as we left the playroom, I took hers down.

"Did I look at them the same way I look at you?" I asked.

"I understand if you did. I mean, I see more now." Her fingers traced the neckline of my shirt. "Although I guess I've seen only you and Paul. And Christine and I are . . . well." Her hands dropped. "Ah, hell. I don't know what I'm trying to say."

"I do." I took her face in my hands. "And no, I can't think for a minute I ever looked at anyone the way I look at you. You're my one percent."

Her eyebrows wrinkled. "Your what?"

"Before you came to my office that first day," I explained, "I felt complete and at ease with my life ninety-nine percent of the time. But it was the missing one percent that haunted me. Then I found you—my missing one percent."

Her eyes grew wide. "Oh."

"It's you. It's always been you. When you left me, it was you. When you came back, it was you. It will never be anyone else." I brushed my lips across her cheek. "So when you ask if I ever watched anyone, submissive or otherwise, the way I watch you, the answer is a resounding 'no.' " I pulled back from her once more. "And, as much as I'd like to keep you here in bed for several hours and prove it to you repeatedly, I did promise Paul we'd be down for lunch."

She looked crestfallen.

"Later," I whispered. "I promise."

After lunch, the four of us sat in the living room. I'd explained to Abby earlier that since Christine had given birth less than three months ago and was breastfeeding, Paul took extra time and attention when providing aftercare.

"And inverted suspension is particularly intense," I'd said. "Even without the other circumstances."

Christine looked completely content and relaxed, sitting on the couch with Paul's arms around her. Her mother had dropped Sam back off and, after feeding him, Christine handed him to Abby.

I was unprepared for the feelings that struck me when Abby held Sam. Before she came into my life, I'd never given any thought to getting married or having children. Somehow, having her in my life made anything seem possible.

I thought back to the day I found my parents' wedding bands, how I'd slipped my father's on and how strange it had felt. Maybe it wouldn't feel strange anymore.

I sat back in my chair, enjoying the sight of her interacting with Paul and Christine. She had been so nervous that I'd almost called the weekend off. Only the hope that somehow the weekend would help us kept me from doing so. I felt relieved. Everything had gone much better than I'd thought.

Every so often, she would look my way and smile when our eyes met.

Fuck. I want her.

Paul asked her a question about the library, and she turned her attention to him. I settled back into the chair and continued to observe from the sidelines. Sam fell asleep, and she shifted him so he rested more comfortably.

"What are your plans tomorrow, Nathaniel?" Paul asked.

I tore my gaze away from her. "I thought I'd take Abby over to see the Dartmouth campus after breakfast. Show her part of my past. Would you like that?" I asked her.

"Yes, Master," she said.

Master.

Fuck, what her saying that in front of others did to me.

And from the look in her eyes, she knew.

Before going downstairs the next day, I laid out her clothes. "I want your hair up today. I want you to walk the streets of Dartmouth with your neck completely exposed." I ran a finger across her collar. "No one else will know what this is, but I want you to know. To feel it." I kissed her neck. "Every time the wind blows and caresses your skin, I want you to shiver with the knowledge that you wear the mark of my control."

After breakfast, we bid Paul and Christine good-bye. We promised we'd visit soon and even discussed the three of them coming to New York at some point. Christine and Abby hugged, and Christine whispered something to her. Abby laughed and whispered back. Paul raised an eyebrow to me, and I nodded. Yes, the weekend had been a success.

Once we were in the car, I turned to her. "We're going to taste something a little different today," I said. "We're going to explore my old college haunts and we'll look like any other couple." I placed a hand on her bare knee. "Only you and I will know the difference."

She sat up straighter.

"While we're walking, you're to be one step behind me. When we sit, your hand will rest on my knee. You are not to cross your legs or ankles at any point. I'll not require you to call me *sir* or *master* if others might hear. Do you understand?"

"Yes, Master," she said with a seductive smile.

Minutes later, I pulled into a public parking lot near the campus and parked. I got out of the car and walked to her side to open her door. "You look beautiful, Abigail."

"Thank you, Master."

We walked through the main campus, and I pointed out various buildings where my old classes met. We walked past coeds out enjoying the morning sun, perhaps preparing for classes.

At first, she walked carefully, slowly, always checking to make sure she kept in position. Occasionally, her eyes would dart around, as if expecting someone to recognize what we were doing. But gradually, as we continued, she grew more confident, realizing no one paid us any mind.

I stopped at the steps at Webster Hall, near the library I'd studied at frequently while a student, and sat down. She took a tentative seat beside me and placed a nervous hand on my knee.

I placed my hand on top of hers. "I used to sit here and write letters home." I kept talking, sharing parts of myself with her, remembering parts I'd forgotten. Eventually, she eased into a more comfortable sitting position.

At one point, she shifted her legs, moving as if she would cross them.

I leaned close and whispered, "Don't make me punish you. We're relatively inconspicuous now, but if I have to take you over my knee, we'll definitely draw attention."

"Sorry, Master."

"I won't remind you next time. Move your hand higher."

Her fingers moved up my leg, and I stifled a groan at her touch. My plan to show her we could interact in public on a weekend was a good one, but it tested my control. Had we been at home, or even at Paul and Christine's, I'd already have had her bent over something. I looked down at my watch—we still had a few hours before we needed to head to the airport.

I took a deep breath and we talked again. I spoke of inconsequential things—tiny details no one would care about. Yet they were the things I wanted to know about her, the things I enjoyed hearing about her college days and part of myself I wanted to share. So, for the next hour, I reminisced. She laughed at some of the stories I told and opened up, telling me more about her own college experiences. As our time in New Hampshire drew to a close, I knew she finally understood—she could talk to me on a weekend. Even about silly college stories.

For lunch, I took her to an upscale bistro. She bit her lip as she regarded the seating arrangements. I slid into a booth and she followed, sitting close to me and placing her hand on my knee.

"Excellent, Abigail," I said. "When your food comes, you may use both hands to eat."

This time, I wanted to say.

My body was aware of her every breath, every small movement. Every molecule of my body reacted to her. I laid an arm along the back of the booth, so my fingers brushed her shoulder. "Do you see?" I asked. "How it's possible to interact with others while you wear my collar?"

"Yes, Master," she said, glancing around and seeing the relatively empty dining area. "To be honest, the entire day has been"—her voice dropped—"well, it's been a bit of a turn-on. Being with you like this. It's like we're keeping a secret from everyone else."

I reached up and brushed the back of her neck. "Beyond your collar there's a connection between us that is deeper than what others have."

She turned her head. "I think so, too," she said.

I kissed her softly. "Do you want to continue this afternoon in the same way we've spent the morning?" I asked, after our lunch was delivered.

"Yes, Master. I'm really enjoying it."

"A few weeks ago, I wouldn't have been sure if you were being truthful. But after this weekend, I believe you."

"Thank you."

Later, on our way to the airport, I thought ahead to the coming week. With Jackson and Felicia's wedding on Saturday, Abby would be spending every night at her apartment. Her father would be arriving on Thursday, and we'd planned for him to come to my house for dinner. Saturday night would be the soonest I'd have her in my bed again. It would be the longest we'd slept apart since getting back together.

And Saturday felt so far away.

When we were in the jet, buckled into our seats, and the flight attendant had left to sit with the pilot, I turned to her. "When I say *now*, you have thirty seconds to go into the bedroom, undress, and get into position two, page five. Understand?"

The hand on my knee tightened, the need in her eyes echoing mine. "Yes, Master."

Once we were airborne and our ascent leveled, I spoke one word. "Now."

She unbuckled and shot into the bedroom at the rear of the plane. I started counting. When I reached thirty, I slowly undid my seat belt and stood.

She waited in the bedroom for me, on her back, knees bent and spread. I moved into her line of sight. I untucked my shirt and drew it over my head. My shoes, socks, and pants soon joined the pile of clothes on the floor.

I walked to the bed and moved over her, captured her hands in my own, and placed them above her head. "Keep them here. I don't feel comfortable tying you up in a plane."

I took a deep breath, trying to control myself. If this would be the last time I had her for the next six days, I wanted to take my time.

"Come whenever you want," I said. "As many times as you can. And I want to hear you."

I slid against her, wanting to draw out every ounce of need from both of us. Wanting to heighten her anticipation as much as possible. I nibbled. Felt her. Slipped between her spread thighs and tasted her. Enjoyed the tang and sweetness of her desire.

"Touch me," I said, moving back up her body, needing her hands on me.

I groaned as she explored me, running her hands down my chest and moving lower, teasing my cock.

I retaliated by sucking a nipple into my mouth and circling it with my tongue. I flicked the other nipple with my fingers. She arched her back, offering me more of herself. I took it—drawing her deeper into my mouth and sucking harder, biting gently.

I pushed my thigh between her legs and teased her with my knee, grinding slowly against her. Making sure I hit her clit. She rocked her hips against me and moaned as she came softly.

I moved above her. "Open your eyes. Look at me."

Her deep brown eyes met mine, and I positioned myself at her entrance. "Watch my eyes," I said. "As I claim your body, I want you to understand how you've claimed my soul."

I pushed into her. "You wonder if I ever looked at anyone else the way I look at you." I went deeper. "I haven't. Watch my eyes. See the truth of my words."

Her eyes grew wide as I entered her completely, and though my own eyes damn near rolled to the back of my head, I kept my gaze locked with hers. We moved together slowly and purposefully. Each of us offering ourselves to the other; finding and taking from the other what we needed in return.

I slipped a hand between us, gently brushing her clit, and she came again, stronger. Her eyes fluttered closed as pleasure swept through her body. I increased my pace, thrusting into her and enjoying the feel of her constricting around me.

Too soon, it became too hard to hold back, and I came, spilling myself deep within her. Still, I held her to me, not wanting to leave the comfort of her arms. Not ready to have her leave mine. The week ahead would be busy and crazy. I wasn't even certain we'd get a chance to have lunch together.

I turned us to our sides, her back to my chest, and unclasped her collar. "Thank you for serving me this weekend," I said against the skin of her neck.

Her hand slipped up, stroked my cheek. "Thank you for the honor of serving you."

Chapter Twelve

—NATHANIEL—

Abby was scheduled to work only Monday and Tuesday. She took the rest of the week off to help Felicia. Before she left my house on Sunday, we made plans to eat lunch together on Tuesday.

She called on Tuesday morning. Two librarians had called in sick, three second-grade classes were coming for story time, and the library computer was printing out book return dates for June 2007. She felt horrible, but there was no way she could take an hour away from the library for lunch.

So at eleven thirty, I called her favorite Italian restaurant and delivered a picnic lunch at noon.

"Nathaniel," she said, looking up from the front desk, Martha at her side. "You didn't have to bring lunch."

"And if I hadn't, when and what would you have done for lunch?" I asked.

She stepped out from behind the desk. "I would have had a stale protein bar about two hours from now." She hugged me. "Thank you."

"Anytime," I said, delighting in her arms around me.

"Can you stay and eat with me?" she asked. "I can take thirty minutes, if you don't mind eating in the break room."

"I'd love to. Matter of fact, I'm counting on it. I have enough for two." I reached into the bag. "I brought this for you, Martha. A little 'thank-you.'" I handed the startled librarian a pale yellow rose.

"Why, thank you, Mr. West," she said, taking the rose. "I can't remember the last time a man bought me a flower."

"That was very nice of you," Abby said, as we walked out of the main room of the library, leaving Martha smelling her rose. "She'll be all aflutter the rest of the day."

"It was the least I could do. I told you, I never would have left you the rose in the first place if she hadn't caught me with it. Speaking of which . . ." I reached back into the bag. "I think this one's yours." I took out the pale cream rose, just a hint of pink flush on the petal tips, and handed it to her.

Her mouth formed the most adorable O before settling into a mischievous grin. "Why, thank you, kind sir," she said, taking the flower. "But I do believe you just gave my supervisor the same token of your affection."

"I did no such thing," I said with fake shock. "Hers was yellow. Yours carries considerably more meaning." I patted my pocket, checking to ensure the box was still there. "Besides, I might have a little something else for you."

She raised an eyebrow.

"After lunch," I said.

She pushed open the door to the break room. "We'll have to eat in here. There's a grad student working on his thesis in Rare Books today."

I followed her inside. "I suppose we should let him work."

"I'd kick him out if I could."

"It's a long time until Saturday night. Don't tempt me."

I spread out our antipasti and gave her a fork. "How's Felicia?"

She sat down. "Pissed at me."

I looked up from my plate. "Why?"

"She's upset I spent the weekend in New Hampshire."

"Really?"

She waved her hand in dismissal. "She's like that. I think every bride goes through it. I'm not sure what I could have done for her over the weekend anyway. She was with Jackson the whole time."

I forked an olive. "I'm sorry our weekend away caused trouble between the two of you."

"Don't be. Like I said, she's like that about anything and everything these days."

"What are your plans for the rest of the week?"

"Bridesmaid luncheon tomorrow," she said. "Dad gets in on Thursday. Elaina and I are taking Felicia to a spa on Friday before the rehearsal." Her eyes sparkled as she looked at me. "What about you?"

"Todd and I are taking Jackson away for the day Friday." Payback for what Jackson did to Todd when he married Elaina.

"You aren't taking him to a strip club, are you?"

I waggled my eyebrows. "And if we are?"

She looked down at her plate, all nonchalant. "I might have to respectfully protest."

"Respectfully protest? Not firmly reprimand?"

"If I protest, there won't be a firmly anything." Her hand brushed my upper thigh under the small table and worked its way up.

"You better move your hand. Unless you want me to jerk you up from the table, throw you over my shoulder, and bust into the Rare Books Collection, giving that poor graduate student the shock of his life."

Her hand inched upward, lightly stroking the base of my cock. "You wouldn't."

"Abby," I warned in the tone of voice I reserved for weekends.

She looked up at me for just a minute, perhaps trying to decide if I was teasing or not. I wasn't. I started counting in my head—she had until three.

One.

Two.

She moved her hand. "Stupid grad student," she mumbled under her breath.

We chatted a bit about the wedding, our plans for the weekend, how Todd and Elaina's house was being transformed to accommodate the ceremony and reception. Maybe, I thought, we'd be so busy, the time would pass quickly until we could be together again.

My hand grazed hers across the tiny table, and it felt as though the box in my pocket was on fire. I shifted in my seat.

When we finished and cleared the table, she stood up. "I'd better be heading back to work. Thanks again for lunch."

"Before you go, I have something for you."

"Right," she said, picking up the rose. "Something to make up for giving both me and my boss a flower."

I slipped the pale blue box from my pocket.

Her eyes grew wide. She set the rose on the table. "Nathaniel."

"It's just a little something I found and wanted you to have."

"From Tiffany?"

"Open it," I said, passing her the box.

She took it with tentative fingers.

"The bow got a little squashed in my pocket," I said.

She untied the bow and slowly lifted the lid. I knew exactly what she saw when her breath rushed out. Two diamond earrings. Large, flawless ones. My father had exceptional taste.

Her expression changed from shock to amazement. "These are . . . They're . . ." Her free hand danced around her throat.

"They were my mother's," I said. "I want you to have them."

"Your mother's?"

I nodded, even though she wasn't watching me. Her fingertip traced one of the round stones. I'd remembered the earrings on Sunday night, one of the many pieces of jewelry left to me by my mother. Remembered how they sat in the locked box I had that held my parents' wedding bands. As soon as I remembered the earrings, I knew I wanted her to have them.

Wanted her to have another piece of me. To own part of the past that made me who I was.

"I shouldn't," she started. "It's too much . . . your mother's."

"Please." I captured her hands in mine, enclosing the blue box within our grasp. "For me?"

She looked up at me with tear-filled eyes.

I caught a tear with my thumb. "I thought maybe you could wear them to the wedding. If Felicia hasn't picked out other jewelry for you to wear."

"No," she said, and I feared she was rejecting my gift. "She said she doesn't care."

Silence filled the break room and I held my breath as I waited for her to say something else.

"Thank you," she finally said. "I love them. I feel . . . really honored."

"My mother would want you to have them," I said, certain of the fact. "I wish she could have met you. She would love you."

She smiled at me. The gorgeous smile that brightened my day in ways nothing else could. "I wish I could have met her, too."

I wrapped my arms around her, wordlessly, and her hands came up to my shoulders, the box still in her grip.

"I love you," I whispered, kissing her ear. "I'd give you the world if I could, but I'll settle by offering little slivers of myself."

"I love it when you offer me slivers of yourself," she said. "Besides, I don't want the world. I want you."

I pulled back and kissed her. Long and slow and deep. She tugged me close, running her free hand through my hair, her hips pressed against mine.

Someone at the door cleared their throat, and Abby pulled away, but she kept her arms around me.

"Yes?" she asked the teenaged girl who'd opened the door without either one of us hearing.

"Sorry to interrupt, Miss Abby, but I'm supposed to tell you the computer's no longer printing out 2007 due dates."

"Good news," Abby said. "But why did that require my attention?"

"It's printing out 1807."

Abby sighed. "I'll be right there."

The young girl left. "Sorry again," she called through the closed door.

Abby dropped her head to my chest.

"*Miss Abby?*" I asked.

"Don't ask."

I kissed her forehead. "I better go. Let you deal with the nineteenth century."

She lifted to her toes and kissed me. "Trust me, the nineteenth century wants nothing to do with me."

"Call me tonight, okay?"

"I will," she said, lightly brushing a hair out of my eyes. "I love you."

I smiled when the doorbell rang at six thirty on Thursday night. Leave it to Abby to ring the doorbell of my house when she'd be moving in in a little more than a week. I knew she'd told her dad she planned to move in, but I'd be lying if I said I wasn't nervous about meeting the man.

Apollo rushed to the door, guessing Abby waited for him on the other side.

"Calm down," I said, wondering how quickly it would take for him to get used to having her around permanently.

I opened the door and decided I'd never grow accustomed to having her live with me. Even having her over for dinner seemed too good to be true.

I took her hands and kissed her cheek, noticing she wore the earrings I'd given her. "You didn't have to ring the doorbell. I wouldn't have minded if you'd used your key."

She gave my hand a squeeze and returned the kiss. "Old habit." She stepped back and directed me to the man at her side. "This is my dad."

He was a strong, solid man. I knew from Abby he worked as a contractor and had done so for more than twenty years. I shook his hand. "Mr. King," I said. "Welcome to New York."

"Don't call me Mr. King," he said, a small smile playing on his features. "And thank you."

I held the door open wider. "Please come in. Excuse Apollo. He's a bit shy around strangers."

True to form, Apollo stayed stuck to my side, moving only to nudge Abby's hand when she passed him. I smiled, remembering how he'd reacted to meeting her the first time. His reaction to her father was much more normal. My eyes met Abby's, and I nodded toward him.

See? I said with my eyes. *He really doesn't like strangers.*

She rubbed his head as she walked into the foyer, rolling her eyes at me. "Can I help with anything in the kitchen?"

"I have the beef Wellington and potatoes in the oven," I said. She'd told me her dad was a meat-and-potatoes type of man, and I'd planned dinner around his preferences.

"Beef Wellington?" She arched an eyebrow. "Maybe I should go check it out?"

"Your father and I will be in the living room." Better to get this out of the way sooner rather than later.

We sat down—me on the couch, her dad on the love seat. He looked around the room, appraising. I gathered he was a quiet man, much like his daughter.

I cleared my throat. "Abby says you're going to give Felicia away on Saturday."

"Felicia has been like a second daughter to me. She's had her share of hardships. I'm glad she's finally found someone."

"Jackson's completely in love with her. He's never been happier."

He smiled, and I saw the kindness in his eyes, the warmth, and knew Abby inherited more than her quiet nature from her father. "From what Abby tells me, Felicia and Jackson aren't the only ones," he said.

Okay. The straightforwardness I wasn't expecting. Abby had not inherited that.

My mind spun frantically, and I tried desperately to think of how to respond.

I have nothing but honorable intentions toward your daughter?

Not sure that was the entire truth, considering what I told Abby I'd do to her the next time I had her in my playroom.

Fuck. Abby's father is in my house. Sitting directly below the playroom where I teased and tormented his daughter. How would I explain the closed door if I gave them a tour?

You don't, I told myself. *You just ignore it.*

Did I really think he would look at a closed door and say, "Hey, what's in there?"

No, I didn't.

But still. He *could.*

"I understand she's moving in with you next weekend?" he asked.

I pulled myself up straighter and did my best to ignore the sweat running down my back. This was worse than high school prom. What if he forbade Abby to move in? Would he do that? What would I do if I became the cause of more strife between Abby and her father?

The words rushed out. "I have nothing but honorable intentions toward your daughter, sir." I cringed. *Idiot.*

He waved his hand in dismissal. "I know you're a successful man, Nathaniel, and I know Abby has a good head on her shoulders. I'm not going to say I'm altogether pleased with how quickly this is moving or that I'm happy with this whole living-together arrangement." He gave me a look, and I wondered how much he knew of my past with Abby. "But I remember the joy of sharing my life with someone."

Abby had said he'd been alone for a long time.

"So while I'm not altogether pleased," he said, "I'll overlook it for Abby's sake. If you make her happy, well, all I've ever wanted is for her to find happiness."

"Thank you, sir," I said, strangely relieved. "I, too, want nothing but Abby's happiness."

"Hell," he said. "Don't call me *sir.* It makes me feel ancient. Tell me about your cousin. Anything I need to warn Felicia about?"

I laughed, and the conversation shifted seamlessly to football.

We ate dinner in the dining room. I'd wanted to eat in the kitchen, but Abby thought the dining room more appropriate, and after thinking on it further, I agreed. The dining room, while serving a purpose on weekends, was part of the house and should be used as such.

Besides, I thought, watching her direct her dad to his seat, I rather enjoyed watching her acting as hostess in my house. I'd never entertained much, but I decided Abby and I would have to change that after she moved in.

I offered to help her serve, but she rejected me thoroughly and told me to have a seat and keep her dad company. I sat at my place at the head of the table. Abby's dad sat at my right, leaving Abby a seat at my left. I'd set the table before everyone arrived; all we needed was the food.

Abby walked in and stood beside me. My cock gave a twitch, remembering how she served me in the dining room on weekends. I placed a napkin firmly in my lap. This was not a weekend.

Still, my body remembered . . .

And there was the electricity that hummed between us whenever we were together.

She set the beef Wellington before me and lightly grazed my shoulder with her fingers.

I feel it, too, her touch said. *I know exactly what you're thinking.*

Our eyes met as she sat down, and I grinned at her. *Not everything*, my expression teased. *You just wait——when I get you alone again.*

"Did you cook this?" her father asked, interrupting our silent conversation.

I turned to him, slightly abashed at having improper thoughts about his daughter while he sat at my table.

"I did," I said. I hoped he wasn't the type of man who thought cooking was not a masculine pursuit.

"Abby enjoys cooking, too," he said. "You two must have fun in the kitchen."

"We do," I said, and my mind wandered to a snowy day, a steam-filled kitchen, and a lunch of cold risotto.

"We took sushi lessons a few weeks ago," Abby said, kicking my foot under the table.

The corner of her lip went up, and I shook my head at her. *What?* I asked with my eyes. Maybe I'd lost my poker face abilities the last few weeks.

"Do you enjoy baseball?" I asked her dad.

"Oh, yes," he said. "Baseball. Football."

"I have a box at Yankee Stadium," I said. "Maybe you can come down this summer and go to a few games. Abby and I would love to have you stay a few days." Emphasizing, I hoped, that I viewed this not just as my home, but Abby's as well. That he would always be welcome in our house.

Our house.

I felt my stomach flip in the most amazing way and realized that this, this was what contentment was. What was it he had said? *The joy of sharing your life with someone.*

I looked back at Abby and, yes, she felt it too. I reached for her hand and gave it a gentle squeeze. Not just sharing your life with someone, though. Sharing your life with the One.

Chapter Thirteen

——ABBY——

It was pointless, I decided, throwing back the covers and getting out of bed. I piddled around my room for a few minutes, running my hand over the multitude of boxes—clothes here, books there, everything else in between.

I wondered if Felicia was sleeping. She was spending the night on my couch. We'd had a wonderful day—first meeting Elaina at Felicia's favorite spa and treating the bride-to-be to a day of pampering. Later in the afternoon, Felicia and I had returned to the apartment and giggled like schoolgirls while we got ready for the rehearsal. Even that had gone well. Nathaniel stood proudly beside his cousin, a tiny hint of a smile on his lips as Felicia tried unsuccessfully to pry information on where they had been all day.

My bridesmaid dress hung in the closet, waiting for morning. I trailed a finger down the delicate silk material. Felicia had excellent taste. The dress was floor length, ice blue, and formfitting, with bare shoulders except for the chiffon that came up from the waist to drape over one shoulder.

Turning from the dress, I threw a few remaining books into a half-empty box, but finally accepted that sleep wouldn't be visiting me anytime soon.

I stepped quietly into the living room, not wanting to disturb Felicia, only to find her sitting on the couch, drinking a cup of tea.

"I'm sorry," she said. "Did I wake you?"

"No." I walked over to the couch and sat beside her. "I couldn't sleep either. Nervous?"

She tucked her knees under her chin, wrapping her arms around her legs. "Not really nervous, I don't think. Just excited. Maybe a little worried?"

"Worried about marrying Jackson?" I asked, concerned. This was normal, right? Didn't every bride go through this?

"No, not Jackson," she said, and I felt a little better. "Well, not Jackson, the man. More worried about marrying Jackson, quarterback for the New York Giants. The paparazzi and all. Being in the spotlight."

I vaguely remembered her frustration when the engagement was announced. Photographers had followed her for a few days, showed up outside her classroom, even called her apartment a few times. The excitement had died down rather quickly and, truth be told, I hadn't been that much of a help to her, having recently left Nathaniel and living in the fog of depression I'd been in.

"It won't be too bad, I don't think," I said. "He's a famous athlete, sure, but he's not an actor or anything."

"You try setting up security for your wedding and then tell me it's not that bad," she said. "You plan your honeymoon trying to decide where you can be alone most of the time. And you have your wedding gown flashed on television for the world to see."

"Okay. Okay," I said, trying to calm her down, not wanting to see her in full-out bridal rage. "I see your point. The wedding gown thing was tacky."

"Hmph. I'll say."

"But listen," I said. "Jackson loves you. I've seen it. You don't have anything to worry about. If the paparazzi show up, you and Jackson will deal with it together. Plus, you'll have the whole Clark clan to back you up. And you know you'll always have me."

She smiled at that. "Thanks, Abby."

I shrugged. "No biggie. And since you and Jackson will be off touring Europe, I'm sure the wedding hype will have moved on when you do come back to the States. Some other celebrity news will have taken your place."

Jackson had planned a two-week honeymoon for them in Europe. They would visit the UK, France, Italy, and Switzerland. While I'd always wanted to visit Europe, it didn't sound like my idea of the perfect honeymoon. When I got married, I wanted to spend my honeymoon alone, with Nathaniel, not country-hopping.

A shiver ran down my spine.

Honeymoon alone, with Nathaniel.

Gah.

"You're right," Felicia said, oblivious to the inner workings of my brain. "It's just strange, you know?"

"Yeah, strange." And Felicia dealing with the paparazzi wasn't the only thing.

"Everything's strange tonight, isn't it?" she asked. "You and me. We've been neighbors forever, and after tomorrow, everything changes. It's a bit sad."

"You'll still have me. I'm not going anywhere."

"You're moving in with Nathaniel. Talk about strange."

I wanted to ask what was so strange about it, but then decided not to. I really didn't want to discuss my weekends with Nathaniel. While Felicia seemed more supportive, I wasn't sure she could listen at this point and not be judgmental.

"I mean, sure, Jackson's a famous football player, but Nathaniel constantly makes top-twenty lists for wealthiest Americans," she continued. "How does that feel?"

I knew what she was doing—trying to make herself feel better by shifting the focus to someone else. By asking how I handled something she needed to handle as well. I decided to tell her the truth.

"It doesn't feel like anything," I said. "When I'm with Nathaniel, I'm not thinking about his wealth or what he's worth. It's just him. Nathaniel."

"But still," she pushed. "How's it going to work with you living with him? Will you pay him rent? Pay part of his mortgage?"

She'd just called him one of America's wealthiest citizens and she thought he had a mortgage?

"He doesn't have a mortgage," I said. "He owns his house outright. And no, I'm not paying him rent."

"But expenses?"

"Sure, I'll help with expenses." But it was all a guess for me. Nathaniel and I had talked a little about how expenses would work once I moved in, but nothing very detailed. We'd just work it all out once I moved in. "How about you and Jackson? Are you worried about money?"

"No," she said. "Jackson's already made plans to set up a joint account for us. It'll just be odd, having all that money. Come on, Abby. Admit it. You have to have thought about the material benefits of living with Nathaniel."

"Maybe once or twice."

"Once or twice. Sure."

"I know he has a housekeeper," I said. "I guess that will be weird—having someone clean everything for me. But really, I don't think about it. I focus more on Nathaniel."

"I'll be so happy when Jackson retires and we can be a bit more normal."

She was all over the place. Again, maybe this was common for brides. I just decided to go where she led me. "He's playing one more season?" I asked.

"Yes," she confirmed. "This is his last year. He'll probably take some time off and then look into getting a coaching position."

I placed my hand on her knee. "Do this for me, Felicia— enjoy this year. It's going to be so unlike anything you've ever done or experienced." I smiled. "You're going to be fine. Everyone will love you. Jackson most of all."

Her eyes teared up, and she pulled me into a hug. "Thank you."

Our last night as neighbors.

The thought resounded over and over in my head. It seemed so surreal. How was it possible that our lives would be changing so much in such a short amount of time?

I pulled back and smoothed her hair down. "Now, you really need to get some sleep. We can't have tired eyes for pictures tomorrow."

I meant it to be funny, wanting to lighten the mood a bit, but Felicia didn't smile. Her expression was serious as she looked in my eyes.

"I told you I didn't want to know the details of how you and Nathaniel work," she said. "And I still don't. You're so happy lately." She took a deep breath. "But I still need to know . . ."

"Need to know?" I questioned, a hint of dread working its way into my voice.

"That day you left him, you said he finally kissed you." She got that much out and then stopped, biting her lip as if afraid to finish.

"Yes?" I asked, still not entirely comfortable with where this was going, but sensing it was important to her.

"Does he now?" she asked, nearly pleading. "Does he kiss you

on the weekdays and on the weekends? It's stupid, I know, and
I'm not sure why it matters, but if he does, I'll feel so much better. Does he?"

I couldn't stop the smile from spreading across my face. The
answer must have been obvious, because I saw her own smile
before I answered the question.

"Yes, Felicia," I said. "Yes. He kisses me on weekdays and on
weekends, and yes. I'm very, very happy."

Saturday was a blur. Felicia and I were in constant motion from
the moment we woke up, so I didn't have much time to think
about how different the day was from my normal Saturday.

I laughed.

Normal Saturday.

Since when had my Saturdays ever been *normal*?

"Are you laughing, Abby?" Felicia asked. "Fill me in on the
joke. I could use a laugh."

We were in one of Elaina and Todd's guest rooms, and a styl-
ist was fixing Felicia's hair in an elegant upsweep. My hair was
complete, I was dressed, and—looking at the clock by the
bed—showtime would commence at six o'clock. A little more
than two hours.

I glanced back at Felicia. "It was nothing. Just talking with
myself."

"Well, then, run downstairs and grab me a few grapes, would
you?" she asked. "I think I could eat grapes without making
a . . . Ow!" She looked up at the woman combing out her hair.
"Watch it—I'd like to have some hair left when you finish."

Yes, grabbing a few grapes for Felicia sounded like a great
idea. I loved her and everything, but she was driving me, and
everyone else, just the tiniest bit crazy.

"I'll be right back," I said, dodging past her gown hanging from the dress form and heading for the door.

"I suppose I'll still be here."

I hurried down the stairs, holding my dress up so I wouldn't step on it. I didn't want to put my shoes on until absolutely necessary. Once I made it downstairs, I looked around for Nathaniel. I knew he was in the house somewhere—I'd spied his car from the upstairs window—but I hadn't seen him yet.

Oh, well. In two hours, he'd be in the backyard, standing by his cousin's side. If nothing else, I'd see him then. I stepped into the kitchen, careful of the caterer and her crew, and made it to the center island, where a casual buffet of finger foods was prepared for the wedding party and family.

I scanned the table. Grapes, grapes, grapes. Surely, there were grapes. Felicia wouldn't have asked for them otherwise, right?

A large hand cupped my bare left shoulder seconds before a pair of warm lips placed an openmouthed kiss at the nape of my neck.

"My God," Nathaniel said against my skin. "Look at you."

Every nerve I had tensed, and a wave of unfulfilled longing shot through my body.

"Mmm," I said, leaning back in to him while his arms came around me and his lips continued their exploration of my back.

"I've been trying to make it upstairs to you all day," he said, his breath tickling my ear, his hands meandering around my waist, drawing me close. Elaina had kept the men sequestered in the downstairs part of the house, while the women stayed upstairs. "Between Jackson, Todd, and Linda, I haven't had the opportunity to slip away."

I nearly moaned as his lips found the spot right where my neck met my spine.

"How fortunate I took the matter into my own hands and came downstairs when I did," I said.

He turned me around and looked at me with dark eyes. "How fortunate indeed," he said, and bent to give me a soft kiss. But I'd been without him most of the week and wanted nothing to do with soft.

"That all you got?" I teased.

He leaned close and whispered in my ear, "When I get you home, I'll show you *exactly* what I've got. The question is, do you want me to show you hard and fast or soft and slow?"

"Both," I said, stepping closer to him. "I'll take hard and fast first, followed by soft and slow next." I ran a hand under his jacket, teasing his chest. "Or maybe, if you're up to it—"

"Fuck, Abby. I'm always up for it."

His lips crushed mine, and I whimpered as his tongue made its way into my mouth. *His taste.* Damn, I'd missed his taste. I grabbed his lapels and pulled him closer, feeling his erection as he pressed against me. I moaned.

Someone beside us discreetly coughed.

Fuckity, fuck, fuck.

Nathaniel pulled back, and I dropped my head to his chest, hands still clutching the material of his jacket, trying to get my breathing back to normal.

His voice was dry and emotionless when he spoke again. "Melanie."

My head shot up, and I looked directly at the lovely woman standing next to the table.

"You seem to have the most *peculiar* habit of showing up at just the—" Nathaniel started.

I jumped in between the two of them, releasing Nathaniel's jacket. "It's good to see you again."

I said it because it was the sort of thing you said when faced with a person to whom you had nothing else to say. I watched her for a few seconds as she regarded us. She was really quite lovely, with her hair just right and her cocktail dress displaying her elegant frame to her advantage.

It hit me then how very strange it was to be standing next to Nathaniel while we addressed his ex-girlfriend. He had kissed those perfectly made-up lips, had held her and made love to her, long before he'd ever kissed or held me. Even though he'd ended up leaving her, I felt just a little jealous.

You're being stupid, I told myself. What was it he'd said to me last weekend? *It's you. It's always been you.*

I looked at Melanie and knew, deep within the recesses of my soul, that it had never been her, and that made me feel better.

"Abby," she said, holding out her hand. "It's good to see you as well."

I looked up at Nathaniel and saw that he was watching her. I wondered what he was thinking. Melanie's gaze dropped to my neck as we shook hands, and I saw a flicker of surprise cross her expression before she managed to cover it up.

Well, well, well. While Melanie had not been shocked at finding Nathaniel and me together, she was surprised by my bare neck. However, if I wasn't going to spill the details of us to *my* best friend, I sure as hell wasn't going to share them with *his* ex-girlfriend.

"Can we help you with something?" Nathaniel asked.

His voice was still dry and somewhat emotionless, and I wondered if he always talked that way to her. Had he used that tone of voice for the entirety of their relationship? Or had it come later, when he placed upon himself all the needless guilt of not measuring up to her expectations?

In that moment, I couldn't decide if I should love Melanie for not being what he needed—forcing him, if you will, to find a new submissive, namely *me*—or hate her for all the pain and shame he had felt for needing to find a new submissive.

Bygones, I decided. *Let them be.*

"Mom and I went upstairs to see Linda," Melanie said. "Felicia mentioned something about grapes. She said Abby was going to get them but had been gone forever."

"I've been gone for five minutes, tops." I rolled my eyes. "Brides," I added under my breath.

Nathaniel laughed. "And here Felicia and I were getting along so well. She'll never forgive me for holding up her grapes." He turned to me. "Take the grapes on up to Felicia, Abby. I need to get back to Jackson anyway." He cupped my face gently. "You look stunning." He leaned close and whispered so Melanie couldn't hear, "And later tonight, I'll be up for everything your heart, or body, desires."

He kissed me once, quickly on the lips, gave a short nod and a crisp, "Melanie," and was gone.

Melanie looked the littlest bit ashamed. "I'm really sorry," she said. "But I couldn't get to the grapes and I felt bad interrupting, but . . ." She shook her head.

"It's not a big deal," I assured her, taking a napkin and looking once more for the grapes. "I did tell Felicia I'd get the grapes for her."

"Let's look here," she said, lifting the cover off a bowl, exposing the contained fruit inside.

I smiled at the woman whose relationship with Nathaniel had haunted me for so long. All the days I'd spent upset that he had kissed her. The shock and dismay I'd felt when Elaina told me she had never been his submissive. Even the anger I'd felt as Nathaniel relegated his so-called failure with her. I placed the grapes into my waiting napkin and realized all I felt for her now was a faint sort of kindness.

Two hours later, I made my way down the makeshift aisle in Elaina and Todd's backyard. I hated being the center of attention in any way, and for the first few minutes, all I thought about was all the people watching me.

That ended as soon as I looked up to the front and noticed Nathaniel. I'd not had a chance to fully appreciate him earlier. When he pulled me to him, he'd been too close for me to get a good look at just how impressive he appeared. Walking down the aisle, I took it all in—the way his tuxedo hung just so on his shoulders, how the black in his jacket contrasted the deep green of his eyes, the way his pants brushed the tops of his shoes, and his hair, as always, in the disarray I loved so much.

It was as if his gaze and his gaze alone drew me forward. I almost felt the heat coming from his expression and wondered, in some offhanded way, if anyone else noticed. At that moment, it didn't seem so crazy to think he'd one day be waiting for me at a different altar, at a different time, for an oh so very similar reason. The thought made me smile.

You are breathtaking, he mouthed once I reached the altar.

You're one to talk, I mouthed back.

He shook his head in disbelief and, somewhere in the background, the soft strands of a harp began to play.

I noticed Felicia had made it to the front only when she blocked my view of Nathaniel. I mentally scolded myself for not paying closer attention. How embarrassing if anyone realized my focus rested on the best man, not the bride, and I resolved to do better.

But as the minister welcomed everyone and Felicia and Jackson exchanged the vows that would bind them together forever, my mind wandered back to Nathaniel. Our gazes met, and I smiled again.

Anything seemed possible.

Chapter Fourteen

—NATHANIEL—

After the ceremony, the wedding guests stood around, drinking cocktails and eating hors d'oeuvres while Todd and Elaina's backyard was changed into a reception hall. In no time, I took Abby in my arms for our dance together as best man and maid of honor.

"Happy sigh?" she asked, pulling back slightly as a familiar piano melody started to play.

"Happy sigh," I said. "Jackson and Felicia are married. I met your dad and got along with him—"

"Was there any doubt?"

"I always factor in doubt. It's part of my business mentality."

"This isn't business."

I tightened my arms. "I know. But it's a part of who I am. Besides, you didn't let me finish."

"Finish what?" she asked, settling back into my embrace.

I traced a hand across her shoulders and down her back. "Explaining my happy sigh."

"Of course. Continue."

"Where was I?" I said. "Oh, yes, I remember. My cousin has just married. I have a new cousin-in-law. The most amazing woman in the world is dancing with me, and the best news is, she's going home with me tonight."

"That's the best news?"

I swirled us around and caught sight of Melanie talking with Linda. I had almost been rude to her earlier. Thankfully, Abby had been around to temper my attitude. And, truth be told, having Melanie catch me in a passionate embrace with Abby hadn't been that bad. If there had been any doubt I was off-limits, the point had been made now.

"Yes," I said, answering her question. "It's been far too long since I've had you in my bed."

"Nathaniel."

"Admit it. You feel it, too."

Her hand dipped down so it rested below my waist. Low enough to prove her point, but not quite low enough to be considered inappropriate. "Of course I feel it," she said.

"I'm looking forward to having you in my arms as I sleep tonight," I said, tightening my arms around her.

"Sleep? Is that all?"

"No, but if I talk about it too much, I may drag you up to a spare bedroom or haul you into a closet."

"And that would be bad because . . . ?" she teased, pushing her hips against me.

I bent my head and gave her earlobe a sharp bite, right where she liked it. "Because I'm going to take my time once I get you home."

Her breathing was short and ragged. "I thought you agreed to hard and fast first?"

I ground my hips against hers, hoping the movement was inconspicuous to any onlooking wedding guests. "I've changed my mind."

"Changed your mind?" she asked, and I realized we weren't dancing so much anymore, just swaying side to side as the music played.

I moved us forward into more of a dancing motion. "I've changed my mind. I'm going to thoroughly enjoy taking my time with you."

"Hmph," she said, but didn't argue.

I hid my smile in her hair. She was so fucking cute when she was flustered.

The ride home was a torture of sorts. I kept my hand in Abby's, and she passed time by drawing tiny figure eights on it. We spoke of the wedding details, laughing over a few slips, discussing various wedding guests and agreeing how nice it was the paparazzi were nowhere in sight for the entire event. It was an altogether simple conversation, especially considering how tightly strung we both were. How each sweep of her finger on my hand seemed to reach directly to my groin.

"I have to take Apollo out," I said when I pulled into the drive. I loved Apollo, really, but at times, I wished he were potty-trained.

"I'll wait upstairs," she said.

"Foyer, please."

One of her eyebrows rode in the pale silvery light of the house. "Okay."

I kissed her cheek as I helped her out of the car. "Thank you."

After I took Apollo outside and we made it back into the house, I locked the door behind me. She waited for me, rocking slightly on her heels.

"Is there a reason you wanted me to wait for you here?" she asked, eyes full of mischief.

I shrugged out of my jacket and dropped it on the floor. "Do you remember the time I had you spend the entire weekend naked?"

"Vaguely," she teased.

I nodded to the stairs. "And I took you there, on the third step?"

"You remember the step?"

I made it to her and I placed a hand on each of her shoulders. "I remember everything. I remember looking at you, here in the foyer as you waited for me, and realizing even then that you belonged here. With me."

"That weekend?" Her breath swept warm against my neck.

"Yes. I knew without a doubt, that weekend."

"I never knew."

"I know."

I tipped her head so our eyes met.

> " 'There is a Lady sweet and kind,
> Was never a face so pleased my mind;
> I did but see her passing by.' "

I gently undid her hair and dropped the pins to the floor. They echoed as they hit the marble.

> " 'And yet I love her till I die.' "

She gave a short intake of breath at my recitation of one of her favorite poems, and I smiled at her response. Traced the outline of her lips.

" '*Her gesture, motion, and her smiles,*
Her wit, her voice my heart beguiles,
Beguiles my heart, I know not why,
And yet I love her till I die.' "

"Nathaniel," she murmured softly.

I reached behind her and tugged the zipper of her dress down as far as I could. Then I pushed the soft material from her one shoulder.

" '*Cupid is wingèd and doth range,*
Her country so my love doth change.' "

Her eyes closed and her lips parted. I trailed a line of kisses down her neck.

" '*But change she earth, or change she sky,*
Yet will I love her till I die.' "

I slipped the dress down her body, allowing my hands the freedom to run over her form. Everything felt free now. I was free. Free to love her the way she deserved. Free to accept the love she gave me. Everything felt so . . . possible.

"I love you, Nathaniel," she whispered.

I stilled at her words. It was the first time she'd ever told me she loved me first. How was it possible that four short words made my heart constrict the way they did?

Blood surged through my body in response to her whisper, and I played them over and over in my head.

"God, Abby, I love you," I whispered back. As urgent as our need had felt hours earlier, the urgency had left, leaving in its wake the desire to reconnect.

Her fingers undid the buttons on my shirt. Slowly. She took her time as well, slipping her hands under the fabric, ghosting her thumbs along my nipples. I leaned down and kissed her again. And for a time we stood there, touching and teasing as we undressed each other. Our simple whispers echoed softly in the moonlit room.

"Mmm."

"Yes."

"There?"

"Again."

"More."

"Now."

"Please."

Until, finally, we agreed together.

"Upstairs."

We slept in the next day, woke wrapped up in each other, slowly becoming conscious of our bodies as we stirred. Our touches became more and more urgent, moving quickly from caresses to teasing strokes until we both panted with need.

She rolled me to my back, taking my head in her hands and kissing me deeply.

I moaned into her mouth.

She climbed on top, placing a knee on either side of my hips. She'd never brushed her hair the night before, and it fell in wild, sleep-tousled tangles to her shoulders. Without a word, she rose up and then lowered herself onto me. I lifted up to her, forcing myself deeper inside.

She rolled her hips, and I brought my hands to rest right below the dip of her waist. Not to guide, not to control, simply to feel her muscles work under my hands. To enjoy the way she pleasured herself on my body. To enjoy her.

Her head fell back as she rode me, and her breasts thrust outward. I ran my hands up her torso and cupped each breast, pinching her nipples. She increased her rhythm in response.

She was beautiful in her pleasure—from the faint pink hue covering her body to the soft lustful groans she made as she approached her orgasm. Watching her, my own lust grew, and I slipped my hands down, grasped her hips hard, met her thrusts and matched them with my own. Over and over our bodies came together until her jaw dropped and she climaxed with a short shout.

I held her still and drove myself into her faster and harder, feeling my own release approach. She whimpered, and I rubbed my thumb over her clit. Seconds later, I was rewarded by the feel of her contracting around me a second time. With a grunt and a thrust, my own climax shot through me and I released into her.

She collapsed on top of me.

Several minutes passed before we could speak.

"Good morning," she said finally, not lifting her head from where it rested on my chest.

"I'll say," I said. "What was that about?"

She laughed. "Payback for the Thomas Ford you quoted last night."

"I thought you paid me back for that once we made it up the stairs," I said, remembering the hours we'd spent the night before.

"Oh no. The Thomas Ford quoting definitely required additional payback."

"In that case," I said, running a free hand down her back and feeling her shiver under my touch. "I certainly hope I have a volume of his work in the library."

Later in the afternoon, I returned to the house after taking Apollo out for a quick break. When I left, Abby had been in the living room. It caught me off guard to find her waiting for me in the foyer.

"Everything okay?" I asked as Apollo rushed past her to collapse on his pillow in the living room.

She didn't say anything. Instead she walked and stood before me.

"Abby?"

She dropped to her knees. Her hands came up to the buttons on my blue jeans and she started to undo them.

Ah, yes. The insatiable vixen didn't have enough of me last night or this morning. I felt the exact same way. However, I didn't want her on her knees.

I stilled her hands. "Let's continue this upstairs. Or in the kitchen. Maybe with me on the countertop this time?" My cock hardened at the path the conversation seemed headed.

"No."

No?

Come again?

No, she didn't want to go upstairs? Or no, she didn't want me in the kitchen?

"What?" I asked.

"No."

She was trying to tell me something. I just couldn't decide what.

"Abby," I said, squeezing her hands slightly. "I don't understand."

"No," she said, and then she added softly, "Master."

My jaw dropped, and I hastily closed it.

She sighed and dropped to the floor, sitting in a heap at my feet. "Seeing Paul and Christine last weekend was such an eye-opening experience, and I want so badly to go back into the playroom with you. Then it occurred to me, with the wedding and everything." She looked up. "I don't want you to think I haven't enjoyed the downtime. I have. It's just"—she shrugged—"another week?"

I thought about what she said. Yes, the weekend off had been necessary with our responsibilities the day before, and yes, sleeping in had been pleasant, but there was still that need. Shoved aside and ignored, but still there. Tugging at me. Obviously tugging at her as well.

"And you thought this was the best way to go about getting in there again?" I asked.

Her lips curved upward. "It seemed to be the most direct approach."

"I would imagine it did, but you could have asked."

"This felt more natural."

"You do remember what I told you I would do once I had you back in my playroom?" Besides telling her I would bind her to my cross, I had discussed with her various other elements Paul and Christine used in their play. While Abby had told me she wasn't sure about some of them, I planned to have her experience them. They weren't hard limits, after all.

"Yes, sir."

"Very well, then." I walked to the table in the foyer where I kept her collar. "If you want to play today, who am I to deny you?"

"Thank you, sir."

"You may want to hold off thanking me, *Abigail*." I took her collar and held it out. "Now come here so we can finish what you started."

Chapter Fifteen

——ABBY——

It took just a second for his words to make their way into my subconscious.

Yes, he wanted this, too.

I stood up and made my way to him. His eyes shone with a roguish gleam, and my heart pounded both in dread and wanton longing. What had I unleashed? Did I want to know what rested behind that look?

Yes, damn it. I did.

When I stood before him, I dropped to my knees and waited. Watching.

"I offer you my collar as a symbol of the control I have over you," he said. "When you wear this, you are to obey any command I give without hesitation and to the best of your abilities. When you disobey, my correction will be fitting and swift. I will honor and respect your submission and will keep your mental and physical well-being at the forefront of my mind, while at the same time shaping you into the best submissive possible." He lifted the collar. "Do you accept my collar?"

I loved how he asked me each time before he put it on. How it reaffirmed us and our relationship.

"Yes, sir," I said, and my body shook with anticipation. "I accept your collar and place myself completely in your hands. My body is yours to do with as you see fit."

The cold metal encircled my neck, and his touch calmed me as he fastened the collar. Afterward, his hands rested on my hair in silent command.

"May I serve you orally, Master?" I asked.

His hands tightened their grasp. "You may."

Damn, I loved it when he pulled my hair. I reached again to unbutton his pants and thought I heard a faint sigh when I pulled them down.

He quickly stepped out of both pants and boxers, wasting no time as he brought my head to his cock. His grip on my hair tightened further as he pushed himself into my mouth. I closed my eyes and focused on the feeling of him. I had taken him orally the night before, but there was an undercurrent in his touch that was different as I knelt in the foyer.

"Do you like that, Abigail? Like me fucking your mouth?"

I couldn't answer, of course. Not with his cock in my mouth. So instead, I hummed a response.

"Use more suction," he commanded, and I closed my mouth around him, creating a vacuum and pulling him deeper.

"Yes," he said. He slipped his hands from my hair to rest on either side of my face, and his thumbs pushed against my cheeks. "Harder," he said. "I want to feel my cock as I fuck you."

His hands were rough and demanding as they dug into my skin. He turned his hips to a new angle, causing his cock to strike my cheek as he thrust. During the week, I could bring him to climax within a matter of minutes. That changed on weekends, when he held out longer. I knew part of his reasoning was to allow us both time to slip further into our roles, but I wondered if it also had to do with mastering control of his own body.

I used the time to focus my attention on him and his needs. Serving him. Doing what he wished. As I did, I felt the stresses of the last week and the bustle of the wedding slip away until only Nathaniel remained.

When I felt him shudder, I worked even harder, noting his hands went back into my hair. He held my head still while thrusting in and out of my mouth. The feel of him, rough and feral, captivated me.

This. This was what I had wanted. What I had missed.

He pushed deeply into me and I feared—for just a second— that I'd gag, but I took a deep breath and remained calm as he released. I swallowed greedily, delighting in how I pleased him.

He took a step back, pulling out of my mouth. I redid his pants, then knelt back before him, eyes downcast.

His hand stroked my cheek. "Playroom in ten minutes."

The playroom was empty when I stepped into it, naked, six minutes later. I knew he'd been by, simply because the door was unlocked. I assumed he was in the bedroom. Our bedroom? I wondered.

Focus.

I looked quickly around the room, just to see if I could determine what he had planned, but nothing looked particularly out of place. His cross was in its usual place at the back of the room, but I doubted he'd moved it. I knew we'd go there eventually, but couldn't imagine what else we'd do.

Do you really want to know?

Is it your place to know?

Not really, I answered myself. I just wondered, especially considering the discussions we'd had after seeing Paul and Christine.

I hurried to my waiting spot in the middle of the room. There was no pillow today, so I knelt on the floor, moving into my standard waiting position.

He entered a minute later, and I wondered if he'd been watching me from the door.

His footsteps padded lightly toward me. He was barefoot.

"Your desire for this pleases me," he said. "For today, you may vocalize as needed, but you will not climax until I give permission. I'll be pushing differently, so I need you to feel comfortable with your safe words. What are they?"

"Green, yellow, and red, Master."

He stopped directly in front of me. "Perfect. And if I ask if you're okay?"

I kept my eyes focused on the hardwood. "I'm to answer immediately and honestly, Master."

"Yes. Now, to start our time together today, I want you to lean down and kiss the tops of my feet."

What?

We'd discussed this element of Paul and Christine's play. I told him while I enjoyed kissing his ankles during our lovemaking on weekdays, I wasn't sure how I'd like kissing his feet during playtime. I feared it would feel . . . off or degrading or something.

But how will you know for sure unless you try?

"And when you finish, you are to undress me," he said. "Remember that each item of clothing is an extension of me, and therefore, you will treat them as you would me. After that, you will kiss my cock once."

He wasn't that far from me. I wouldn't have to do anything except lean down to reach his feet. Had he done that on purpose? To ensure I wouldn't have to crawl? But surely if he was having me kiss his feet, he'd have me crawl at some point in time.

Not wanting him to have any reason to think I hesitated, I leaned down, bringing myself closer to his feet, my hands on either side. In order to help, I pictured what I must look like to him—the way I obeyed, my willingness to submit. I remembered Christine and thought not on how I was kissing Nathaniel's feet, but giving myself to him.

My lips grazed his left foot.

It wasn't degrading. It was showing honor and respect to him.

I kissed his right foot, parting my lips as they touched his skin.

It wasn't off; it was freeing. And I wanted more.

I went back to his left foot and kissed it again, paying more attention to it than I had before. This was more than Nathaniel; it was my master. I went back to his right foot, wanting to be symmetrical and all.

"That's enough," he said, after I kissed his right foot for the second time.

I slowly rose to my knees, dragging my hands along his legs, peppering kisses as I went. I got to his waist and took my time undoing his pants, slowly taking them down. He stepped out of them, and I took them and folded them neatly. He was already shirtless, so I didn't have to undress him above the waist. I stroked his hips and kissed his erect cock once, just like he'd told me, before settling back into my waiting position.

I tried to settle my mind and focused on my breathing, trying to get into the place I needed to be to serve him. Then his hands were on me, moving my hands so they rested on my knees. He gently pushed my knees apart so they were roughly the width of my shoulders. Finally, he tipped my head back so my breasts pushed forward.

He stepped back. "This is your inspection position. I'll use it for various reasons, one of which is to ensure you are following my commands on personal grooming."

I felt horribly exposed in this position, and a faint twinge of worry started to work itself into my head.

"I must say, Abigail," he said, and his tone did nothing to alleviate the worry. "I'm rather disappointed." He bent down and stroked me. "I thought I made myself clear on your responsibility to wax."

I didn't move. "I have an appointment with my waxer on Tuesday, Master."

"Tuesday is no good when it's Sunday and you haven't prepared yourself for me."

"It's a weekend off," I said, suddenly worried. I'd known I needed to be waxed, but I'd thought I was perfectly within bounds to wait until after the wedding. "And I didn't have time—"

"Are you arguing with me?"

The inspection position was starting to feel a bit uncomfortable. "No, Master," I said. "I'm simply explaining—"

"You're talking back. In my playroom."

If he'd just let me explain.

"I'm not talking back," I said. "I'm trying to explain—"

"I don't want explanations, Abigail," he said, cutting me off again. "I want obedience."

Oh, hell.

"Go back to your waiting position," he said. When I'd done so, he continued. "I told you, and you agreed, that you would be waxed as often as possible. You should have waxed last week, simply because you are to be prepared for me at any time. You

asked to play today. I would have thought you to be fully prepared."

Okay, he actually had a point.

"And," he said, "if you can ask to play, I can ask to play, and if
I ask on a Wednesday, I expect you to be ready. Now, being a
Wednesday, you can turn me down, but I wouldn't think you
would do so often. After all, I didn't turn you down today,
did I?"

"No, Master."

"Second," he continued. "You are never to talk back, argue,
or be belligerent in my playroom. Do you understand?"

"Yes, Master," I said. "But I——"

"Fucking hell. Are you doing it again?"

I held completely still and didn't say anything. Fucking hell,
indeed. What had I done?

He walked around me, and I knew he was thinking. Thinking about how to punish me.

"You wanted to play today," he said. "You asked for this and
you are not prepared. Not in body, or it seems, in mind. Therefore, you will not be allowed to climax at all today."

That didn't seem too bad. After all, in an hour or so, the collar would come off. Surely I could hold out until then, and if
need be, finish myself a bit later.

"Matter of fact," he said. "You are not to climax again until I
grant you explicit permission."

I didn't like the sound of that. At all.

"Stand up," he said, and I scrambled to my feet. "To whom
does this body belong?" he asked, gripping my shoulder.

"To you, Master."

His hands ran down to cup me. "And these breasts?" He
stroked between my legs. "And this pussy?" He gave my backside
a firm slap. "This ass?"

"All yours, Master."

"Who controls your orgasms?" he asked. "Decides if you deserve one?"

"You, Master," I said, my voice soft.

"Speak louder."

"You, Master," I said, with more force.

"No climax until I permit one," he repeated. "If you're lucky, I won't make you wait until Friday night."

Friday night? Was he serious? Five fucking days?

"Do you understand, Abigail?" he asked.

"Yes, Master," I said.

In that second, I wished he'd just told me to move to the whipping bench. At least a spanking would be over and done with. This punishment of no release . . . well, that was punishment of a different sort.

"Look at me," he said.

I lifted my eyes and met his. His gaze was still intense and took my breath away. His disappointment didn't hide that.

"Now that we have taken care of that," he said, "I believe we still have the matter of what I said would happen when I had you in here next."

Finally.

"Move to the cross, Abigail. Face it and do it quickly. I expect no more slipups today."

Neither did I. If he had to spank me on top of not allowing me to climax . . .

I walked over to the cross and stood before it. It was nothing more than a big X with cuffs at either end for wrists and ankles.

He walked up behind me and took my left wrist, cuffing it to the cross. Then he took my other hand and attached it to the other side, leaving me in a half spread-eagle, my arms pulled high and wide.

My heart pounded as he took my hips and moved me a step away from the cross so I was slightly bent.

He nudged my feet apart. "Stay like this and I won't bind your ankles. Move an inch and I'll use the lower cuffs."

I was damn sure not going to do anything else to provoke him.

"Lift your ass to me," he said.

When I was properly positioned, he stroked my backside a few times, then smacked it with hard and fast slaps.

Fuck, it was going to be a long afternoon.

Scratch that. It was going to be a long five days.

"Focus, Abigail."

I turned my attention to him, to what he was doing and how it felt. As always, his spankings left me needy and wanting. I resisted the urge to lift my butt to him. Instead I focused on the sensation coursing through my body, how the slight pain radiated throughout and combined right between my legs.

Something else trailed around my backside: the rabbit fur flogger. He worked it fast, unlike before, when he'd used soft, slow strokes. Nothing painful, just light brushing strokes interspersed with an occasional smack from his hand. I tried to determine a rhythm, but couldn't do it. There was no reasoning to what struck me or when, so I eventually stopped trying to find a pattern and just felt.

I jumped slightly when something different hit. It was a bit harder, landing on my left ass cheek with a hard thump.

"Suede," he said. The flogger hit again. "Are you okay?"

It felt good, different from the fur, but not as hard as the leather strap.

"Yes, Master."

He alternated for a time, switching from my backside to my thighs. Again, I tried to find a rhythm, but quickly gave up. The heat from below my waist grew exponentially stronger, and it took all my focus not to bring my legs together for friction.

A long finger slipped between my legs. "How wet you are," he said. "Imagine how good it would feel to have me inside you now. How full."

I know, I wanted to shout. *I know. Please.*

Then something was inside me, and I let out a squeak when I realized it was one of his vibrators.

"Just a taste," he said. "Not too much. Bratty submissives don't get to release."

He slid the vibrator in and out of me a few times, and it took all my strength not to give in to the need to orgasm.

"Please, Master?" I finally begged when it became too much.

"No," he said, sliding it from my body. I knew then why he'd bound my wrists: I was so overwhelmed by sensation, I'd probably collapse if he hadn't.

But he wasn't finished.

He started back with the suede flogger, and my skin was even more sensitive for this second round. It felt as though all my nerve endings were in overdrive, standing at attention, waiting for the thud to hit again. I moaned when it did.

"Are you still okay?" he asked.

"Yes, Master," I said. The flogger hit right where my legs met. "Oh, yes." I groaned as the pain struck and subsided into pleasure over and over.

I wasn't sure how much time passed. I turned my reflection inward, wanting only him, focusing only on him and what he was doing to me. Only he knew how to do this to me. Only he could play me the way he did. Could create such a dichotomy of feelings in me.

"You're being punished," I heard from what seemed far away. The blows landed slower, softer.

I breathed in and out.

Slower.

Softer.

"But I haven't done anything wrong," he said. "So I get my release."

The flogger stopped and a new sound replaced it. Friction. Somewhere.

"Where do you want it?" he asked.

I knew what I wanted. It was dirty and primal, but I wanted it. "On me, Master," I said. "I want you to come on me."

"Fuck."

"Please."

"Hold still," he said, but I wasn't sure where I'd be going. "Fuck," he said again.

A warm wetness landed on my back. I swore as he came, feeling his release hit and then drip off.

"Yes," one of us said. I wasn't sure who.

Then he was closer to me and breathing heavily in my ear. "You did well, my lovely." He undid one wrist and then the other. "I am so very pleased."

I nearly fell into his arms. He helped me gently to the floor, where he held me. His lips were on my face, my hair, my lips, and he whispered words of praise, telling me again and again how much I'd pleased him.

Afterward, when he'd cleaned us both up and removed my collar, he carried me outdoors to his hot tub. We sat for a time, relaxing. The coming down after play always left me feeling soft, pliable, and tired. But today, there was something more, and it bothered me.

He must have picked up on my mood. "Abby?" he asked. "Is something wrong?"

It was the *Abby* that did it. I almost shook my head, but my eyes filled and I knew I couldn't lie to him.

"Your disappointment," I said, watching the water bubble around me. "I feel as if it's a weight I carry."

"Come here," he said. I moved into his lap, and his arms came around me. "Is this because I won't let you climax?"

It sounded silly to my ears. How could such a thing even make me sad? But it did, so I had to tell him. "I think it's because it's still lingering between us. When you spank me, it's over and done with and we move on, but this is still there. I remember it every time I look at you, and it reminds me of how I messed up."

"Look at me," he said, and I looked up to see his eyes. There was a sadness there, but a firm resolve as well. "It's supposed to be there. That's why it's a punishment. How effective would it have been if I allowed you to release tonight?" He didn't give me a chance to answer, but slipped a hand between us and one of his fingers slipped, just for a second, into me. "Don't you know there's a part of me that wants nothing more than to take you here and now? A part that longs to drive into you over and over and feel you climax around me?"

"Don't tell me you're going to pull that 'This is harder for me than it is for you' crap," I said.

He smiled. "No. I'm very much aware that it's harder for you than it is for me. If it had just been one offense, I might have allowed you to come sometime today. But when you added the petulance on top of—"

"I was *not* petulant."

"When you wear my collar, my word is law," he said. "We agreed you would be punished if *I* decided you neglected your waxing, not that we'd call a conference in the middle of the playroom to discuss it. I decided you should have waxed before the wedding and that's it. Bottom line. You continually tried to argue with me."

"I didn't see it as arguing," I said. "I saw it as explaining."

"If I ever want an explanation, I'll ask for one. Understood?"

"Yes," I said, still a little pissed.

"Yes, what?"

"Yes, *Nathaniel*," I said, emphasizing his name. The collar was off and it was a Sunday afternoon. "Now look who's being petulant."

"FYI," he said, working his hand back between us. "A bit of petulance on weekends every now and again can be fun." He pinched my ass. "I like you feisty."

Chapter Sixteen

——ABBY——

Sunday night we went to bed relatively early and spent time talking. My back rested against his chest and his arms wrapped around me. I still felt just the slightest bit peeved he wouldn't let me bring myself to orgasm, but my more rational mind understood his reasoning.

"I know you had concerns about feet kissing," he said. "How do you feel about it now?"

I thought back to our time in the playroom. "It surprised me how much I enjoyed doing it. I thought I wouldn't, but I did. It felt so . . ." I searched for the right word. "Humbling? Not sure that's right, but I felt even more under your control when I did it." Although, I supposed, not so much under his control that I'd been able to hold my tongue about the waxing.

"How about you?" I asked. "What did you think of it?"

"I didn't like it as much. But I wouldn't have known beforehand."

That surprised me. "You didn't know if you'd like it and you still had me do it?"

"Yes. How else would I find out what *I* liked?"

"I don't know. I just assumed you'd had enough experience that you'd know what you liked and wanted."

"But I've never had anyone nibble on my ankles while she made love to me," he said, stroking my arm. "Only you've ever done that, remember? The weekend I asked you to move in? I wasn't sure how I'd feel asking you to do something like that in the playroom."

I kept forgetting the dynamics of our relationship were new to him. "Since you didn't like it and I did, will you be asking me to do it again?" I asked.

He laughed. "You expect me to tell you all my plans?"

I pushed my butt against his groin. "Yes."

"Well, it won't happen," he said, then whispered in my ear, "Wait and see."

I shivered at his words. Mmm. He was right—waiting and seeing was so much better than knowing in advance.

"I have a concern," he said, voice growing serious. "You seemed to have trouble focusing today."

"You picked up on that?"

"Yes, and I'm wondering if it would help if you started yoga again."

I hadn't kept the yoga up after he recollared me. I worked out three times a week of my own prerogative and planned to use his gym during the weekends as time allowed, but I had not re-started yoga. Though, now that he mentioned it . . .

"I think it would help with your focus, and as we progress, would aid in your breathing as well," he said.

"I'll think about it. See when and how to fit it into my sched-ule."

"Maybe it's something we can do together."

"Really?" It would be a lot more fun if he joined me.

"I need to keep my mind sharp, too, you know."

I told him I'd definitely think about it, and the conversation switched to the upcoming week. The movers would be at my apartment on Wednesday to get my boxes, and I'd requested only that day off of work. I didn't think it would take much to get me settled into Nathaniel's house.

As we talked, I began to notice him shifting slightly behind me. Pushing away, so he wasn't as close to me anymore.

"You okay?" I asked. It wasn't like him to withdraw from me. Especially before falling asleep.

"Fine."

"Then why are you . . ." I scooted back in to him, bumping his erection as I did. "Oh."

He moved away again and sighed. "It's just, holding you like this? I can now say, with great certainty, that your punishment is literally *harder* for me than it is for you."

I groaned. "Tell me you didn't just make a dirty joke."

"I did."

I snuggled against him. "Sorry about your little problem there, but you'll excuse me if I'm not inclined to help out at the moment." Let him experience a bit of his own medicine.

"I wasn't going to ask you to help," he said. "But if you don't mind, would you stop wiggling your ass against me?"

"You mean like this?" I asked, treating him to another ass wiggle.

He groaned. "Yes, damn it."

"I'll try to stop, but you know I have a tendency to move while I sleep."

"Good night, Abby," he said in a tight voice, kissing the back of my neck.

I wiggled again. "Good night, Nathaniel."

I'd called my old yoga instructor Tuesday and reenrolled us both for yoga. Nathaniel had been right. It would help both my concentration and breathing. I was glad he'd left the final decision up to me, though. I was even gladder he would attend with me.

With him not allowing me to orgasm, we hadn't had sex of any kind since he came on me in the playroom Sunday. I wondered just how long he planned on dragging this out. In all honestly, I thought maybe he'd have initiated something Tuesday. Especially since I'd been waxed earlier in the day.

So, Friday night at six found me in the foyer once again with Nathaniel repeating the words that would make me his for the weekend. He vowed to push me while respecting and guarding my limits, all the while keeping me the focus of his attention. In return, I gave myself completely to him.

After I was collared and he'd released in my mouth, he put a finger under my chin and tipped my head up. "Dinner in the dining room in one hour."

His kitchen was familiar to me, and I'd moved most of my belongings in on Wednesday. It still didn't feel completely like home, but I felt more comfortable than I had before. I was glad he wanted to eat in the dining room, as it would help keep me in the proper role.

I stood at his side while he ate the salmon I'd grilled for him. My own dinner waited for me in the kitchen, and I assumed he'd have me eat when he finished.

My mind wandered as he ate. I watched his arms and how his fingers wrapped around his glass. My eyes moved to his mouth as he ate a bite of the meal I'd prepared for him. There was no feeling in the world that compared to serving him. My trust in him grew stronger with every minute we were together, and my desire for him increased each time I looked at him.

Knowing how intently he focused on me turned me on further. There was no doubt in my mind that he was thinking of me while he ate. Maybe he was deciding how he would work me. Or maybe he was planning how many orgasms he'd let me have.

Fuck. He will let me orgasm, won't he?

My need for him hadn't vanished during the week. Instead, it had bloomed. He would probably need only to touch me and I'd be putty in his hands.

I knew my punishment had not been easy on him either. After the craziness of the week before the wedding, I knew we had both looked forward to a more restful week.

Although, come to think of it, we'd *rested* a lot.

Deep in my thoughts, it took me a few seconds to realize he'd spoken and commanded me to kneel at his side. When I'd done so, he placed a hand under my chin and tipped my head up. "For the rest of the weekend, you are to keep your head below mine," he said.

What?

"Anytime you enter a room I'm in, your head is to be lower than mine." He stopped briefly and then continued. "I'll leave it to you to decide how to comply with my request."

I looked into his eyes and saw a hint of playfulness.

I like you feisty, he'd said last weekend.

Mmm . . . Maybe this would be fun.

As he finished eating, my mind raced. If I left the dining room before he did, how would I clear the table? Would I have to crawl to the kitchen? How would I carry his plate? Maybe I'd have to walk on my knees.

Ugh. That wouldn't be fun at all.

Fortunately, after eating, he placed his hand on my head one more time, instructed me to eat in the kitchen and to meet him in the playroom afterward. Then he stood and left, letting me clear the table.

Finally.

Half an hour later, he waited for me when I stepped naked into the playroom. Unprepared to find him waiting, I hurried to stand in front of him and knelt down at his feet.

Am I late?

No, I decided. He hadn't given me a time to meet him.

"Move to your inspection position, Abigail. Let me see if you're better prepared today."

I moved into the position he'd shown me the weekend before, and he knelt between my knees.

"Excellent," he said, stroking my bare flesh. "This is what I expected." He stood up and instructed me back into my waiting position.

When I had, he spoke again. "You've borne your punishment well. Remind me again why you were punished and look into my eyes as you do so."

I met his gaze. "I was unprepared for you, Master, even though I asked to play. Then I was insolent and argumentative while I wore your collar."

"And should I allow you to come tonight?"

Yes! Damn it, yes!

But I knew that wasn't supposed to be my answer. "If it pleases you, Master, and if you think I deserve it."

"Is that how you really feel?"

The temptation to look down was strong, but I forced my eyes to remain on his. "No, Master," I said honestly. "I want to come badly, and it's hard to push aside my wants for yours."

It shamed me to admit I wasn't yet where I needed to be in my service to him.

"Your honesty pleases me." He stroked my cheek. "Don't feel guilty over your feelings. I know it's still early in your journey. I know you aren't yet able to completely put aside your wants. You'll get there eventually."

He understands. Relief replaced the guilt immediately. "Thank you, Master," I said, smiling.

"I know you, my lovely," he said. "I know your thoughts and your mind. I know every line of your body. And I know the desires you have hidden deep within." He bent slightly, and his voice dropped. "They echo my own."

Gah.

Putty. I knew it.

He hadn't yet told me to drop my eyes, so I watched him as he commanded me again. "Crawl to the padded table, Abigail," he said.

Crawl?

I'd known it was coming. I'd known he'd want me to try it at least once. To be honest, I'd expected to like it once I tried it, much like the feet kissing. Therefore, I was surprised when I made it to the table and found I hated every second I moved on my hands and knees. I didn't hate it so much that I'd safe word over it, but I hated it so much I was certain my displeasure showed when he looked at me.

It's all about him, I told myself. *Trusting him. Letting him decide.*

And I'd liked the feet kissing. I wouldn't have known that unless he made me try.

I really hoped he didn't like the crawling.

I moved carefully onto the table, making sure my head stayed below his. Once on top, I stilled myself and waited.

"On your back," he said.

His footsteps echoed in the room as he made his way to where I was. I noted he had four ropes in his hand.

He held them up. "I'm going to tie you to my table," he said. "Before I bind a limb, I'll press a rope to your lips and you'll kiss it."

His expectations really shouldn't have turned me on the way they did.

A soft rope touched my lips. "This is for your right leg," he said.

I kissed the rope. "Tie my right leg, Master."

He pulled my right leg and tied the rope around it. Another rope touched my mouth. "Left leg," he said.

I pressed my lips against it. "Please bind my left leg, Master."

Like before, he used the rope to bind my leg. He repeated the action two more times—first with my right arm and then with my left. Each time, he put the rope to my lips for me to kiss. Each time, I asked him to tie me.

When he was finished, I lay spread-eagle on the table.

His hands ran from my shoulders, down my breasts, across my belly, and came to rest between my legs.

A long finger slipped inside. He added a second. I forced my hips to remain still.

"Your body recognizes me," he said, feeling the evidence of my need. "It knows its master."

I was nearly panting for him; there was no point in arguing.

Besides, I learned that lesson the hard way.

"Close your eyes, Abigail. We're going to try something again."

I had a good idea of what he was going to do.

"No vocalizing until I say," he said.

I sucked in a breath at the first pass of the Wartenberg wheel. Like before, he used one to start with—running it lightly across my chest, avoiding my nipples entirely. Then he added a second and worked them in unison, running opposite each other. They crossed my body, each a perfect mirror of the other, each coming close to a nipple and then rolling away again. I realized immediately when I'd moaned, and after a week of punishment, I wasn't about to mess up again. My body shook as the wheels rolled over my nipples, but I remained silent.

"Very good, Abigail. Shall I continue?"

I caught myself seconds before I answered. He gave a short laugh. "I do believe one time is all it will ever take for you. Be still."

The wheels rolled down my body lightly. The sensation was odd—when he ran them both in parallel, it almost felt as if I were being unzipped. Then they separated and ran over my pelvic bones, and I caught my breath and held completely still. The spiked wheels came right to my sensitive flesh before rolling away.

I was going to go mad while tied to his table, and I hoped he didn't touch me *there* at all. My senses were so heightened, so on edge, a mere touch would send me into an earth-shattering release.

I panicked for a second. What if he wanted me to climax without permission? What if he decided to test me to see how long I could hold out? I couldn't do it, not after almost six days of denial.

Oh, fuck. I am going to fail. Again.

Should I use my yellow safe word?

He must have sensed my worry because the wheels stopped. "Are you okay?" he asked.

"Yes, Master, I think so."

"You think so? *Think so* isn't good enough. Open your eyes. What's wrong?"

His hands were at my feet and ankles, checking the ropes.

"It's not the ropes," I said. "It's me."

"Are you in pain?" he asked, worry clouding his expression as his hands reached my arms.

"No, Master. I'm just afraid."

He quickly untied the ropes binding me to the table, and I felt silly for causing him undue alarm.

"It's nothing, really," I said.

"Sit up. Tell me."

I sighed and pulled myself up, swung my legs over the edge of the table. "I thought for a moment I was going to orgasm, and while I was working on holding it back, I thought maybe you wanted me to fail. Wanted me to come without permission."

"And you panicked?"

"Yes."

"I didn't want you to fail," he said slowly. "I wanted to show you how much you'd grown from the last time we tried something similar. I know you're on edge. I feel that." He stroked my cheek. "I told you. I know your body."

"I'm sorry, Master."

"Don't ever apologize for being honest."

He stood for a minute, thinking. Both his hands were on either side of my legs as he stared at the wall behind me. What I wouldn't give to live inside his brain for a second.

Finally he looked up, his expression intense. "Your punishment has ended. Come when you wish."

With that, he pulled himself up on the table, took my face in his hands, and kissed me. Pushing me back down, he came up over my body, pressing his weight on me.

Yes. Yes.

Relief swept over me, and I felt almost giddy. Then his hands were on me and the giddiness left as quickly as it came. Longing, desire, and need took over, and it didn't take long for me to get right back to the spot I'd been seconds before. I imagined he felt the same—his erection was hard against my belly.

He pulled back, and I saw my answer in his dark eyes. He

pushed my knees up and out so I was spread before him. Then he lifted my legs and put them around his waist, drawing me closer to him.

Neither of us moved. His cock barely brushed my entrance, and I resisted the urge to raise my hips to him. Instead, I enjoyed the delicious anticipation of almost having him inside me and knowing he soon would be.

Almost.

Almost.

He moved a fraction of an inch, pushing the head of his cock slightly into me.

Ah, yes.

The feel of him taking me was one I never grew tired of—how he stretched me and possessed me.

With one hard thrust, he pushed the rest of the way inside, and just like that, I came undone, climaxing around him.

He smiled wickedly. "All better now?"

"Oh, God," I said, still awash in sensation. "Yes, Master."

It was all he needed. He started a hard rhythm, thrusting into me repeatedly. Driving himself toward his own release. I'd been right—the week had been just as long for him—because it didn't take long before he was twitching inside me, nearing orgasm.

His hand came between our bodies, and he ran a thumb around my clit. "Can you come again?" he asked, breathing heavily. "For me?"

He had been right earlier; my body knew its master. This time was no different. My swollen flesh responded at once, sending a new wave of pleasure through my body.

He groaned and released inside me.

We lay on the table for a few minutes, and I rejoiced once more in how it felt to have his pleasure-spent body on top of me.

How my own release left me weak and rubbery. He trailed kisses up my body, coming to rest fully on me. When he made it to my mouth, he kissed me long and passionately.

"You need to go on to bed," he finally said, and kissed me again briefly.

It was an odd request. I knew it couldn't be after nine. Why did he want me to go to bed so early?

Maybe he planned on waking me in the middle of the night. After five days of no sex at all, it wouldn't surprise me. Or maybe he had plans for a really long and intense day tomorrow.

Maybe both?

However, it wasn't my place to guess, and whatever he had planned, I wanted to be ready.

"Good night, Master," I said, slipping from the table and making my way to the door so I could go to my room.

"Good night, my lovely."

Chapter Seventeen

—ABBY—

He didn't wake me up.

I had thought he would—expected it, even. I lay awake for some time, listening for either the piano or his footfalls outside my door. Even when I finally closed my eyes, I told myself it was just for a brief rest. Surely he would take me at some point during the night.

I certainly hoped he would.

Instead, the alarm clock woke me up at six o'clock. Unless I was told differently, I needed to have breakfast ready and in the dining room at eight every Saturday and Sunday morning. Since I wanted to work out before cooking, I had set my alarm for six.

I dressed in my workout clothes and walked to his gym.

Our gym, I corrected myself. This was my house now, too.

The sound coming from the other side of the door stopped me from entering. Nathaniel was running on the treadmill. My hand hovered above the doorknob. I had to keep my head below his. If I started running and he did sit-ups or something, how would that work? Would I have to stop what I was doing and get into a position lower than his?

I looked outside. It was raining.

Damn. Can't run outside, either.

As much as he said he liked me feisty, it was too early for me to deal with the mechanics of keeping my head below his in the gym. I'd work out later.

Since I had plenty of time, I went back upstairs, took a shower, and dressed. Then I went back downstairs and decided to cook eggs Benedict.

He wasn't in the dining room when I entered with his plate, so I set his breakfast down, the table complete with coffee carafe and pitcher of orange juice, and waited. When he came in and sat down, I knelt at his side.

"Good morning, Abigail," he said. His hair was still damp and he smelled like soap.

"Good morning, Master," I said. If everything went according to plan and I didn't mess up this weekend, maybe we could shower together next week before work. I loved showering with him.

"Eggs Benedict," he said, picking up his utensils. "This looks delicious."

"Thank you, Master."

"Why don't you fix yourself a plate and join me."

He remained in his chair, so I moved on my knees to the doorway and stood up when I made it to the hall. I didn't like the crawling thing at all and would most certainly bring it up when he asked, or whenever we were in the library next.

I carried my breakfast into the dining room, crawling once again, and sat across from him.

"How did you sleep?" he asked.

"Very good, Master. You?" Dining room protocol was still a gray area for me. I knew I wasn't to speak as freely as I could while eating in the kitchen, but certainly I was allowed to ask him how he slept.

"It felt odd having the entire bed to myself," he said. "But other than that, I slept well."

I nodded, understanding what he was saying.

I noted his orange juice was nearly gone, so I lifted the pitcher to pour him more.

"No, thank you," he said. "I don't care for more. I'm almost finished."

We ate for a few more minutes in silence. The only sound in the room was the clicking of our utensils against our plates.

"Would you like to work out this morning, Abigail?" he asked when his plate was empty and he sat drinking the last of his coffee.

"Yes, Master," I said, not even surprised he would know what I wanted. After a time, one got a bit acclimated to it. "I would."

He nodded. "After you finish eating and clean up the table and kitchen, you're free to use the gym."

"Thank you, Master."

"Be in the playroom at ten thirty." He stood up. "And be sure to stretch really well."

My heart pounded just thinking about what that could mean.

I was waiting for him in the playroom, naked, at 10:25. A pillow sat under the chains in the middle of the room, so I knelt on it in my waiting position. He entered the room shortly after I did and walked to me.

"I trust you had a good workout?" he asked.

"Yes, Master," I said.

"And since I told you to do so, can I also assume you stretched like I asked?"

I still felt the post-workout endorphin high running through my body, though now it was paired with the unmistakable tinge of lust and need. "Yes, Master."

"Very good. Stand up for me."

I stood, but kept my head down. He took one arm and then the other, securing me by the wrists so my hands were above my head. Secured, but with enough slack to allow for limited movement.

"Look at me," he said.

When I did, I noticed he wore black jeans with a short-sleeved T-shirt tucked into them. He'd never worn a shirt in the playroom before that I could recall. I wondered what that could possibly mean—maybe he meant to have me undress him later?

"Abigail," he commanded, obviously not unaware of my wandering thoughts.

I focused my eyes on his, instead of the hard muscle under his shirt.

"You will not come until I give you permission," he said. He leaned close and nipped my ear, causing a jolt of need to shoot through me. "You will not fail."

When he said it, I believed him.

"You will not fail *me*," he said. "Repeat it to yourself if you have to. I want you to understand and agree. Say it for me."

"I will not fail," I repeated back.

His hand cupped my chin. "You won't, my lovely. Trust me."

I nodded.

"Say it or I won't tell you what I have planned for you today."

"I trust you."

He dropped my chin and moved behind me, hands skirting down my back. He delivered a playful slap to my backside. "I think this ass needs a sound spanking for neglecting to call me *Master*. What do you think?"

Gah. Yes, please.

"Whatever would please you, Master."

"Mmm," he said, trailing kisses up my back. "It pleases me for you to trust me. It pleases me for your skin to turn a delicious shade of pink under my hand and to hear your moans of delight as I take you to new heights." His hands rubbed my shoulders as he whispered again. "Remember the feeling you experienced last weekend?"

I remembered how he flogged me, the sweetness of surrender when I let go and let myself feel. "Yes, Master," I said in a whisper.

"I'm going to do it again."

I shivered at his words.

"Beautiful," he said. "How your body responds to my voice." His lips traced my shoulder blades, his voice a low murmur against my skin as he spoke in quiet tones I couldn't make out.

I wasn't aware of him having a flogger in his hand, but when he pulled back, the soft tails of rabbit fur brushed my back softly. He slowly worked the flogger up and down. Grazing. Stroking. Caressing. My body ached for his touch and wanted it, either gentle or firm.

My eyes closed as he walked to stand in front of me, still trailing the flogger against my skin. He dragged the tips along my breast, and I stifled a moan.

"No," he said. "I want to hear you. Want to hear every whimper, every moan, every sigh." The fur dipped low and brushed my sex. I lifted my hips, searching for more.

"Not yet," he said, walking behind me to slap my backside again.

I groaned, but the sound was cut off when I felt the soft thud of suede hit my lower thighs.

"Not even close," he said. "I'm going to show you just how

much you've grown since our first weekend." The fur followed the same path of the suede. "And what did I say earlier?"

"I will not fail, Master."

"Exactly." The suede struck my left ass cheek. "You will not fail."

He didn't say anything then, choosing to communicate with the flogger instead. Sometimes he used the fur, and sometimes he used the suede. Often, he'd use them together. I found it easier this time to simply let the feelings he evoked in me take over. My eyes remained closed and I whimpered when the tips of suede struck between my legs from behind. Moaned when it was replaced by fur.

More. I needed more.

I searched my brain, desperate for the feeling to continue and struggling to remember the words.

"Green," I said, almost shouting. "Green. Please."

The next strike of suede landed harder, a sharp bite against my right cheek. "Like that?" he asked.

"Yes." I hissed as the pain subsided into pleasure.

The following blows landed hard and quick, exactly what I wanted. I moaned in response, ready and willing to be carried anywhere he wanted to take me. I didn't feel the rabbit fur anymore, only the suede. Every so often, his hand would smack my backside, his fingers stopping to slip inside me, stroking and teasing my sensitive flesh.

"Beautiful," he whispered when I trembled at his touch.

He pressed against me, the denim of his jeans rough on my sensitive skin. I felt every part of him—his erection pressing my backside, his arms coming around my shoulders, his fingers rubbing and twisting my nipples, his breath hard and panting in my ear. I arched my back, desperate for him to enter me and put an end to my longing.

"Not yet," he said again, once more crashing my hopes of an easy release. "Later. When I decide you're ready." He undid the cuffs binding my wrists and tenderly massaged my upper arms. "Open your eyes," he said, slipping to stand in front of me.

His intense gaze met me. "Are you okay?" he asked, his hands still working magic on my arms.

"Yes, Master."

He didn't respond, but took my hand and led me to the corner of the room, where a blanket had been spread. "We're going to take a little break," he said. "I want you to have a seat and wait for me."

The blanket felt soft and inviting. He must have placed a mat of sorts underneath.

"It's going to be a long day, Abigail," he said. "I hope you were telling the truth when you said you slept well and stretched properly."

Chapter Eighteen

——ABBY——

I felt light-headed imagining what he could have planned that required me to have slept and stretched well. Were we going to spend the entire day in the playroom?

Holy fucking sh—

"Abigail," he commanded.

My head snapped up to meet his eyes. "Yes, Master?"

"Stay here in your waiting position. I'll return soon."

I moved quickly into my standard kneeling position and dropped my head. My knees sank into the soft mat beneath the blanket, and I was thankful he decided to have me wait on the mat instead of the hard floor.

There was no way to measure time in the playroom. Even if I'd been at ease and free to look around the room, there was no clock to indicate if it was past lunch. How long had it been since I first entered at ten? My eyes itched to look for a window, but even those were covered with room-darkening shades, so I kept my head down.

I heard him when he returned and felt the mat give as he stood to my side.

"Relax, my lovely," he said, sitting beside me.

As I slid to sit on my backside, I noticed he held a platter: a large one, filled with numerous, yummy-looking items.

"Tapas," he said. "I'm hungry."

What? So he decided to have a snack in the playroom?

"Here." He placed the platter in my hands. Everything looked delicious: meatballs, bread with aioli, and skewers with veggies.

"Banderillas." He nodded toward the skewers and then opened a large bottle of water at his side. "I'll start with one of those."

I looked back to the wooden sticks lined with cucumbers, olives, and baby onions. He'd start with one of those?

Beside me, he waited.

He wanted me to . . . ?

Oh. Oh!

Oh.

"But first," he began, reaching inside his pocket and pulling out the nipple clamps and chain. "I want to decorate you a bit."

I swallowed and put the platter down. I remembered the pinch of the clamps and the sharp pain when he released them. The way a tug on the chain sent a jolt of need to the ache between my legs.

I moved to my knees and thrust my chest out, both in invitation and acceptance. My nipples hardened at the thought of what he would do.

He worked with a comfortable ease, rubbing first one nipple between his fingers and then the other. He teased me. Taunted me. Whispered to me how beautiful I was.

I still gasped when the first clamp latched onto my nipple. He slipped a finger between my legs and drew lazy circles around my clit, teasing and taunting again before returning to slide a clamp onto my other nipple.

"Beautiful," he said when he was finished. He sat back on his heels. "Now you may serve me."

I picked up a skewer, noticing immediately how the chain swayed when I moved. Everything I did caused the chain to move, to slightly tug at the clamps. It would be a long lunch break. I hid a smile just thinking about it.

"Now, Abigail," he said, pulling the chain and making me moan.

I looked back down at the platter. Should I take the veggies off the skewer and feed him by hand or just put a banderilla up to his mouth?

He hadn't given me any instructions, so I was fairly certain I could do either one. What would he want?

I wasn't sure.

I knew, though, what I'd want if the situation were reversed.

I slipped a cucumber off a wooden skewer and fed it to him. His lips parted. His tongue brushed my fingertips as the cucumber disappeared in his mouth.

Fuck, that was fun.

The bulge in his jeans told me he was just as turned on as I was. I fed him an olive and a baby onion, each time offering him the food from my fingers and feeling the electric shock as his lips brushed my hands. Between that and the still-noticeable ache of my nipples, I was a quivering mess when I lifted a small piece of aioli-covered bread up.

Again, the chain swayed. Again, his lips lightly kissed my fingertips.

It was the same when I fed him the meatballs. Same when I went back to the banderilla. How was it possible feeding him was such a turn-on?

I wasn't sure, but it was.

I realized serving him was just that: offering myself to him in any capacity he wanted. It was the sexual offering of my body. The way I served him breakfast in the dining room. How I prepared myself for him, whether that preparation be yoga, jogging, or waxing. And it was as simple as feeding him an olive.

"Are you hungry, my lovely?" he asked, eyes dark with longing and need.

"Yes, Master," I whispered.

He silently took the plate from me. His eyes watched mine as he slid a cucumber from a skewer and pressed it to my lips. I parted my mouth, accepting his offering.

When I'd chewed and swallowed, he brought his bare fingers to my mouth.

"I have marinade on my fingers," he said. "You need to clean it off."

I took his fingers, one at a time, into my mouth and gently licked off the marinade. When I finished, he took an olive and fed me. Again, he lifted his fingers and again, I cleaned them of every trace of marinade.

Once he bumped a nipple as he dropped his hand to the platter, and I stifled a whimper. Nathaniel feeding me, combined with the ache of my nipples, left me feeling wanton and primal, because it wasn't his finger I wanted in my mouth.

"Patience," he ordered as I shifted in my seat. "I'm going to extract every ounce of pleasure I possibly can from your body, and when you don't think you can bear any more"—he tugged the chain—"I'm going to show you what you have left."

I shivered, believing his every word.

He smiled at my response, picked up a meatball, and finished feeding me lunch.

"You've had the clamps on long enough," he said when we'd finished. "Stand up and put your hands behind your back."

Lunch had turned me on more than I would have imagined. He'd fed me at a leisurely pace. Every so often, he'd hold the water bottle to my lips and instruct me to drink. Only when I'd had my fill of the water would he have some himself.

In between feeding me, he played with the nipple clamps. Sometimes, he would lightly bump one as if by accident, but I knew he never did anything accidental. Other times, he would brazenly tug the chain or flick the skin around a clamp. No matter what he did, though, the end effect remained the same. By the end of lunch, I was a trembling mass of need.

At his command, I waited until he stood before rising to my feet before him. I dropped my head and waited for further instruction.

After removing the clamps, he tied my upper arms behind my back with a soft rope. "Move to the table," he said.

I spent the short walk to the table doing my best not to think ahead. Instead, I tried to focus on doing what he told me to do, not trying to anticipate or guess his next plan. It took a few minutes to work my way onto the table, what with my arms behind my back and all.

When I'd managed to get onto the table, in what had to be one of the most graceless moments of my life ever, he positioned me on my stomach so my lower body rested on a padded wedge and propped my upper body up with pillows.

I heard him walk away only to return seconds later. His hands worked their way around and fastened a blindfold around my head. I felt a fleeting moment of panic, but calmed when he stroked my hair.

"Are you okay?" he asked.

"Yes, Master."

"*Yellow* or *red* if you need me to slow down or stop," he said, still caressing my hair. "I have a few more things to do in preparation. Relax."

His voice was low but held his normal no-nonsense tone. Between that and his hands making their way down my neck, across my shoulders, and tapping lightly along my spine, I felt myself yield.

"Lovely," he said, hands never leaving my body.

I realized after a bit that the preparations he mentioned had to do with me. *I* was what he was preparing.

Gah.

My suspicion was confirmed when he took one of my arms and tied a rope to my wrist. I shifted slightly on the table.

His hand came down across my bottom in a hard slap. "I didn't tell you to move."

I held perfectly still as he tied another rope to my opposite wrist. His hands moved lower and massaged my waist, his strong fingers kneading my lower back. I relaxed further.

My lower body was already exposed to him, but he took my left ankle and tied it to my left wrist; then he repeated the action with my right ankle and right wrist, exposing me even further. I felt helpless.

"Beautiful," he said.

I didn't feel particularly beautiful. I felt helpless and awkward.

The sound of a camera clicking behind me made me jump.

"Just because you might not believe me," he said. I heard his footsteps as he walked around me. Again the camera clicked.

Holy fuck. He was taking pictures of me.

"Just look at this," he said, slipping a finger into me briefly. "I think you rather like the idea of me taking pictorial proof of your beauty."

He moved closer to my head and *tsk*ed. "But look at this. My fingers are all messy again."

Said fingers brushed my lips, so I opened my mouth and cleaned them off. He was right; the thought of him taking pictures did turn me on, especially bound the way I was.

"Look at you. All spread out, waiting for me." His fingers skimmed my entrance. "Just think about all the things I could do to you."

He swirled his fingers around my clit. "The things I could do here." He thrust two fingers deep inside me, and my body shifted. I moaned as my aching nipples rubbed against the pillow in the most agonizingly delicious way.

He chuckled.

"Or here." He moved his fingers and they teased my other entrance. I sucked in a breath.

Oh, yes. Again. I want him to consume me again.

I let out a whimper when he spread the warm lube on me.

"So needy," he said. Some sort of plug slowly circled where he'd prepared me. "Remember?" he asked. "Paul and Christine?"

I searched my mind, trying to decide what he meant.

"How you wondered what it felt like?" He pushed, gradually inserting the plug into me.

I was stretched.

Stretched and open and exposed and waiting.

He delivered a hard smack to my backside.

"Remember now?" he asked.

Oh, yes.

"Answer me."

"Yes, Master."

His hands were gentle again, teasing me, running along my slit. They slowly grew rougher and pinched my outer lips. Then he spanked me again. He alternated, spanking and teasing, until it became hard for me to tell what was pain and what was pleasure. Under his hands, they combined.

Something hard and leather pressed against me. *A leather strap?* He ran it up and down, playfully slapped it against my clit and brought it down hard against the flesh of my backside.

I groaned.

"Like that?" he asked.

"Yes," I half said, half moaned.

The strap came down harder and hit right where the plug was.

Dear, sweet heavens.

"Yes, what?" he asked.

"Oh, God," I panted. "Yes, Master."

He struck me again. "Better."

The leather gently tapped my growing, aching need, and his fingers once more circled my clit. I felt as if I was balanced precariously on something and almost fell completely when he brought the strap down hard. Harder.

I didn't want it to ever end. For a while, it felt as if it wouldn't.

The plug inside me. His fingers teasing me. And the strap, how it somehow brought both of them together in a mixture of pain-touched pleasure.

"I'm going to take you like this," he finally said, his breathing heavy. "Filled as you are. Nice and spread out."

I heard the sound of a zipper and felt a rush of air. He steadied his hands on my hips, and with one hard, deep thrust, he buried himself inside me. I yelped. The sensation was incredible: filled by both him and the plug. Stretched and pulled and bound, I wondered how much my sensitive skin and teased body could stand.

"Come when you want," he panted.

He pulled out again and again and filled me over and over. Slowly and deeply, he took me. His thrusts were controlled, measured. I was balancing again and wanted to hold on to how I felt.

My body shook with impending release, my muscles tight and tense. He moved faster behind me. Moved faster inside me. I clenched my fists as he entered me, as he thrust and hit the plug. Again.

I was . . .

I was . . .

Screaming my release.

I felt weightless.

Or heavy.

Yes, that was it. I was too heavy to move and my body couldn't hold me. A faint tremor shot through me.

Residual effects of my massive orgasm, I decided.

His hands caressed me as he untied me, his voice soft and low. I couldn't make out what he said, but it didn't matter. He was there. My limbs were loose and untangled, but he was gentle.

He removed the blindfold. The playroom was dark.

"Relax," he said. "Rest now."

His lips touched mine once in tender affection before my eyes closed.

Chapter Nineteen

—NATHANIEL—

I held her while she slept.

I'd carried her from the playroom to our bedroom, where I wrapped her in blankets and stroked her hair. Our day had been longer and more intense than ever, and I wasn't sure how she would react. I did, however, expect her to sleep afterward and knew she'd be sore the next day. When she woke, we would spend some time in the hot tub, relaxing and soothing her muscles.

I couldn't help but compare my actions and plans with Abby to what I'd done with my previous submissives. I took care of them, of course, but even after a day like the one I'd just put her through, they would have slept in the submissive bedroom. Never, never in my bed.

I asked myself if it was different because it was *our* bedroom? If Abby had never agreed to move in with me, would I have had her rest down the hall?

No. I knew, even if she'd kept her apartment, she would be resting in my bed.

The shadows in the room were growing long when she finally stirred. I kept my hand on her shoulder, lightly caressing her while she woke. She stretched against me, unknowingly pushing her backside into my groin and releasing a soft moan.

She is sore.

I had water and Motrin waiting for her, but the most important thing in that moment was for her to know I was with her. She'd fallen asleep in the playroom; she might have been disoriented.

I propped myself up on an elbow and whispered to her. "You're in our bedroom," I said. "When you feel like getting up, let me know."

"Mmmm," she mumbled, still half asleep.

"I made chicken Caesar salads for dinner tonight," I said, knowing it was one of her favorite light meals. "I thought maybe we'd go down to the hot tub when you got up."

She became more talkative in the hot tub. Especially when I suggested she sleep in our bed for the night.

She twisted in my lap and faced me. "May I ask a question, Master?"

"Yes," I said, pleased that she felt more comfortable talking with me during a weekend. "Of course. Speak freely."

"If I wasn't me," she said. "If I was one of your other submissives, would you be asking me to share your bed?"

"No. But I fail to see what that has to do with anything."

"If the bedroom down the hall was good enough for them, why isn't it good enough for me?"

A strand of hair had slipped from her ponytail and dangled in front of her eyes. I tucked it behind her ear. "You aren't one of my previous submissives," I said. "You're you."

"I don't want you to treat me differently."

"I appreciate that, but everything about you is different. And," I said, lifting her chin slightly with my hand. "My previous subs were experienced. You are not."

Her nostrils flared. "And *I* fail to see what that has to do with anything," she said, repeating my words to me.

"Are you being petulant again?" I asked, partly teasing, but partly serious.

"No, Master," she replied quickly. "I just want you to explain it to me."

I took a deep breath. "Would you agree that our time in the playroom today was longer than ever?" I asked. "And more intense?"

She nodded.

"There can be certain"—I searched for the word I needed—"*feelings* after such intense and lengthy play," I said. "It can be hard—coming down."

She sat, deep in thought for a few minutes. "Is it the same for you?"

"Yes," I said. "But I've gotten used to it. I know what to expect. How I react. And I have ways to deal with it."

"Would you mind if I don't sleep in our bedroom tonight?" she asked. "It's just, I want you to be the exact same with me as you were with your previous submissives."

"You want to stay in the other bedroom tonight?" I knew I'd never treat her *exactly* like I did my previous submissives, but I did appreciate the context of her request.

"I'd like to," she said, running a tentative hand down my chest. I stifled a groan. Sore as she probably was, I didn't want her to do anything else strenuous.

"Promise me you'll come to me if you need to talk?" I asked. "Or at the very least, call Christine?"

"I promise."

"We'll still talk tomorrow," I said. "Probably Monday as well. I want to make sure you're okay."

"I'm fine," she assured me.

"Are you sore?"

"Just slightly." She shifted in my lap. "Nothing horribly uncomfortable."

"I want you to take more Motrin before you go to sleep tonight. You'll probably really feel sore tomorrow." I'd planned for a very relaxing Sunday, nothing too active or intensely physical. I dropped my lips down to hers and gave her a quick kiss. "You'll let me know if anything feels too uncomfortable?"

She smiled against my lips. "Yes, Master."

On Sunday, after I took off her collar, I pulled her to the couch and started rubbing her feet. It had not escaped me that she felt more comfortable talking while we touched, and I wanted her comfortable while we talked. Plus, it helped soothe me.

"Favorite thing we did this weekend?" I asked by way of leading off.

She dropped her head back against the couch and sighed. "When you took me yesterday. It was so surreal. All of yesterday was. I can't even remember parts of it." She smiled. "Did you carry me to the bedroom? I don't remember walking."

"Yes. You were completely out of it."

"Is that normal?"

"It obviously is for you," I said. "I was expecting you to crash, though, based on your previous reactions."

"I want to feel that way again," she said, with an evil gleam in her eyes.

"Excellent. I want to make you feel that way again."

She reached for one of my legs. "Why don't you swing your legs up here and let me rub your feet?"

"No. Let me do this for you."

"I'd like to return the favor."

"Remember when I told you how I had ways to handle my own feelings when I came down?" I asked.

"Yes."

"This is one of them." I worked on the upper part of her foot. "It helps me." She didn't say anything. "It's not that I did this with my previous submissives, because I didn't. I've just found it helps with you." I cocked an eyebrow. "Humor me?"

She thrust her foot into my hand harder. "Sure, as long as you make it good."

I brought her foot to my lips and kissed the soft underside. "Don't I always?"

She only shivered in response, so I dropped her foot back down and continued rubbing.

"Least favorite thing we did all weekend?" I asked.

"No question," she said. "I hate crawling. Hated it. Hated it. Hated it."

"Really?" I asked. Not that her answer surprised me. I'd noticed her look of displeasure a few times.

"Yes, I don't want to do it a lot."

"That's too bad," I said. "That you didn't like it, I mean."

"You liked it?" She lifted her head up off the arm of the couch. "Tell me you didn't like it."

"I liked it," I said, and she just groaned.

"Why? Why can't you like me kissing your feet? Why do you have to like the crawling?"

"Because when you kiss my feet, it doesn't show off your ass."

"What?"

"I said." I smiled. "When you kiss my feet, it doesn't show off your ass."

"You were watching my *ass* while I crawled?"

"What did you think I was doing?" I asked. I ran a hand up her bare thigh and tickled the edge of her shorts. "You have an incredible ass."

"I'll take your word for it. I've never seen it."

"That's no problem. I have pictures."

Her cheeks flushed. "Oh, hell."

I chuckled. "Want me to get them?"

"No."

"Later then," I said, resuming my work on her feet.

"Hmph," she replied. After a few seconds, she spoke again. "So you're going to make me crawl again?"

"Is it a hard limit?" I asked, instead of answering.

"No."

"The fact is, Abby, that I'm the dominant in this picture and I like it when you crawl. But I am glad you're open and honest about your likes and dislikes. I need that information."

I knew I would ask her to crawl again, just like I knew I'd have her kiss my feet again, even though it wasn't something I particularly liked.

I worked on her foot in silence for a few minutes, using my hands to relieve and relax her.

"What was the head thing about?" she asked. "That came from nowhere."

"It was a mental thing," I explained. "Something to help keep you in the right frame of mind. I thought it would help you focus."

"Oh."

"Did it work?"

"I suppose it did," she said, and I switched to her other foot.

I ran my hand down her foot and cupped her heel. "I want to discuss Friday night."

"I should have said *yellow* when I panicked."

"Yes," I agreed. "But outside of that, I was a bit too aggressive in my plans, and I'm sorry. I should never have pushed you like that following such a lengthy punishment."

"I thought you'd be upset with me for not safe wording," she said.

"That, too, but the safe word wouldn't have been necessary if I'd made better plans."

"I don't want to disappoint you."

"You safe wording could never be a disappointment," I said. "I can only push you if I trust you'll *yellow* or *red* if you need to. And yes, I expect you to *yellow* even if you're panicked and think I'm pushing you toward failure."

"I wasn't sure."

"Promise me you'll use it in the future," I said, refusing to discuss anything further until she'd agreed.

"I promise," she said. "I used *green* this weekend, didn't I?"

I thought back to the day before, when I'd flogged her while she was bound to the cross. I'd had a submissive *green* on me before, and while the use of the word still gave me momentary pause, I'd not reacted the way I feared. Abby saying "green" had evoked feelings of pride and pleasure, for the most part.

"Yes," I said. "You did. I was so pleased you felt comfortable enough to tell me what you needed."

"I felt right on the edge of that feeling. You know the one?"

"Subspace. Not from personal experience, but yes, I know which one you're talking about."

"I just knew if you went faster and harder, I'd get there," she said, her eyes drifting to a far-off bookshelf as she remembered.

"And you did?" I asked, wanting to confirm what I knew, but she didn't answer. "Abby?"

"Huh?" Her eyes came back to mine and she smiled. "Yes, I did." She slipped her foot from my hands and sat up. "Thank you."

"You're welcome, but I wasn't finished with your foot massage."

"I want to say 'thank you' with a kiss," she said, shifting closer to me. "Proper-like."

Her lips were near mine. I couldn't help but look at them. "I would say, 'No thanks are needed,' but I really want that kiss."

"Oh, yeah?" she asked, moving to sit in my lap.

"Mmm," I replied as her lips grazed mine.

She initiated the kiss, and I let her lead, enjoying her tongue as it ran along the outside of my mouth. I parted my lips slightly and tasted her. Her thanks were soft and slow and long. I could have stayed with her in my lap for hours, but I knew she was still sore.

Later, I told myself. *Maybe later tonight.*

When we finally broke apart, she stayed in my lap, my hands stroking her hair as she leaned against my chest.

"The honeymooners return next weekend, right?" I asked.

"Yes, Friday night. Felicia said something about us coming over for lunch on Saturday the last time she called. I told her we'd see. I wasn't sure how else to answer her."

"No need to sequester ourselves. We could go over for an hour or two. We're always going to have to balance our weekend time." I rubbed her back. "If you want to go, that is."

"I've missed her."

"I know you have," I said. "Just because it's a weekend doesn't mean we do nothing but stay in the playroom."

"Though that would be fun," she teased.

"Agreed, but I don't want to push you." I ran a hand down her back. "Still sore?"

"Just a little." She shrugged. "Nothing I can't deal with."

"Let me know——"

"Nathaniel," she interrupted. "I'm a big girl and I know my body. I already said I'd tell you. I'll tell you."

"Sorry. Just making sure."

"You've *already* made sure."

"Let's change the subject," I said. "I've made a grocery list for the housekeeper. It's in the kitchen. I need you to look it over and see if you want her to pick up anything else."

"You don't do your own grocery shopping?"

"No," I said, trying to remember the last time I went grocery shopping.

"Never?"

"Not anymore," I said. "I don't need to. Why?"

"It's just weird. Having someone do all that."

"You'll get used to it," I told her. "Besides, between my company and weekend time with you, I don't have time to run up and down grocery aisles looking for bread and milk."

"You say that like it's beneath you," she said. "You know most people do it and don't think twice about it."

"Are we going to argue about grocery shopping?" I asked. "Really?"

She stilled in my arms, weighing her words or actions, perhaps. "No," she finally said. "I don't want to argue with you."

"Good. I don't want to argue with you, either." I kissed her again. "Want to go for a walk?"

"Yes," she said, getting up and stretching. "Fresh air would be great."

————————

She waited for me that night in our bed, with the sheet pulled up to her neck, a sly smile on her face.

"Hiding?" I asked, crawling in beside her.

"No. Just a little surprise."

Her shoulders were bare, so I decided it probably wasn't new lingerie. I couldn't imagine what else it could be. "For me?" I asked.

She nodded. "You need to unwrap it," she said, thrusting her chest out.

"Oh, really?" I moved close to her and traced the line of her collarbone. "Well, it just so happens, I love unwrapping my surprises." I dropped my lips to brush along the same path as my finger.

"Mmm," she hummed. "Lower."

"I'll get there," I said, swirling my tongue in the hollow of her throat. "Eventually."

I wanted to ask if she was still sore, but knew it would probably make her angry. If she wanted me . . .

Well, I wasn't going to argue.

I delicately lifted the sheet. "Whatever could be hiding under here?" I asked, taking a little peek underneath. "Holy fuck, Abby," I said, momentarily stunned.

"You like them?"

Them were nipple rings, or something very similar, decorating each of her nipples. Unlike a normal ring, these were red and circled her nipple. She hadn't had them on earlier, and she'd been at the house all afternoon and evening.

"Nathaniel?" she asked.

"Oh, yeah," I said, tracing one. "I like them. I like them. A. Lot."

"I thought I'd see how they were."

"What brought this on?" I asked, my eyes still firmly locked on her chest.

"Christine's pierced, or at least she used to be. Did you know that?" She sucked in a breath as I lowered my head to gently tongue her exposed nipple.

"No," I said. She'd had a bra on the last time I'd seen her in the playroom, and the time before that had been years ago.

"She said it was very sexually stimulating, but suggested these first."

"Smart woman, Christine," I said, switching over to her other breast. "I knew introducing you was a good move."

"Plus, I didn't want to do something permanent like piercing if you were totally against the idea."

My cock grew uncomfortably hard. "*Piercing?*"

She nodded. "Just one nipple, maybe? I don't know."

Fuck.

"You were thinking about getting a piercing?" I asked.

"Yes. Do you hate the idea?"

I sighed and brought myself back up so I could look in her eyes. "I think you have a beautiful body, Abby. I'll admit, the idea of piercing is, honestly, quite a turn-on, but I don't want you to rush into anything." I traced a nipple again. "Let's start with these."

The sly smile came back. "I have dangles, too."

"Dangles?" I croaked.

"Mmm." She rolled over so she straddled me. "Maybe I'll surprise you with those tomorrow."

Chapter Twenty

——NATHANIEL——

Something had been off all week. I couldn't put my finger on it, and Abby and I never got into an out-and-out fight, but something was off.

In all honesty, it was a busy week. Then again, they all were. I still attended one counseling session a week, Abby and I had dinner with my family on Tuesdays, and the week prior, she had enrolled us for couples' yoga on Monday and Wednesdays.

Friday morning Sara sent me a reservation reminder for my upcoming business trip to China.

Fuck.

I'd forgotten to mention the trip to Abby. I hoped she wouldn't have any trouble taking off time from the library. Surely a week wouldn't be a problem. We could leave early on a Saturday and return the next Sunday night. Maybe we could both take the following Monday and Tuesday off to relax. I'd pamper her with a spa day. She still talked about the one she'd had with Elaina and Felicia prior to the wedding.

A few hours later, I met Abby for lunch at our favorite Italian deli. She'd arrived first and sat at an outside table. I gave her a quick kiss before taking my seat.

"How's your day?" I asked. I thoroughly enjoyed having lunch with Abby, how it broke up stressful days.

She smiled and took a sip of water. "Good," she said. "Yours?"

"Same."

After we ordered our lunch, we made small talk, mostly concerning Jackson and Felicia's return home and our lunch plans with them the next day.

"I keep meaning to tell you," I said, changing the subject. "I have a trip planned in two weeks and I was hoping you could go with me."

"Two weeks isn't good for me."

"No way I can change your mind?" I wiggled my eyebrows. "I've heard I can be very persuasive when I need to be."

"I have a conference in two weeks," she said, hiding a laugh and acting completely unaffected by my wiggly eyebrows.

"That sounds horrifically boring and uneventful," I said. "Come with me to China. Let me persuade you."

"You're going to China?"

"Ah, my powers of persuasion are working. Yes. China."

"Your powers are doing no such thing," she said. "I have to attend this conference if I hope to be in line for Martha's job when she retires."

"Martha's retiring?"

"In a few years. Besides, I don't have a passport."

"You don't?" I asked. How did she not have a passport? "We'll have to take care of that. We can get you one expedited."

"Because I'm going to be doing so much international travel?" she asked, and at once, the light mood of our lunch was replaced by the underlying tension I'd noticed all week.

"I hope you do a lot of international traveling," I said. "With me."

She shifted uncomfortably in her seat, but before she could say anything, the waiter returned with our lunches.

"That'll be great," she said, once he left. "I can't go to China, but you're right. I need a passport. I'll take care of that."

It didn't sound too great, not by her tone of voice, but she changed the subject and I went along with her. I knew I should say something else, should ask her if something was wrong, at least try to find out what was going on in her head. But the more I thought about it, I decided to wait. After all, why have a heart-to-heart at an outside café? Besides, if something was wrong, wouldn't she tell me?

I was distracted at work that afternoon by the persistent nagging that something was wrong. Or maybe wrong wasn't the right word, but something was off. I felt even more certain. I had several meetings that afternoon, but fortunately those were run by my senior executives, so all I had to do was show up.

It was close to six when I made it home that night. Any other Friday night, I'd have been smiling as I thought through my plans for the weekend. My plans that night, though, consisted of sitting Abby down and having a long talk before we did anything. I wasn't sure what, if anything, was wrong, but I intended to find out before collaring her.

She was waiting for me in the foyer. She sat on the plush bench, Apollo at her feet, and gave me a nervous smile when she saw me walking in.

I dropped my briefcase at the door and sat down next to her. We didn't touch, and the tension between us was palpable.

"Hey," she said.

"Hey," I answered back, confused, uncertain, and a little scared. "What's going on?"

"Nothing urgent," she said. "I just wanted to talk with you."

We still weren't touching, and her words did little to make me feel better.

"I was thinking the same thing," I said. "Matter of fact, I was going to insist on talking. You haven't seemed yourself this week."

She sighed. "The newspaper did a feature on you and your business. Did you see it?"

The newspaper had actually interviewed me weeks ago, and I'd completely forgotten about it. I tried to remember what they'd asked me that would have her acting so strangely.

"No," I said. "I didn't see it."

"Why didn't you tell me you weren't pulling a salary this year?"

"What?"

"Why didn't you tell me you decided not to take a salary?" she repeated.

Oh, right. *That.*

I shrugged. "It was something I decided before you became my submissive the first time. I guess it never occurred to me to bring it up in conversation."

"You just didn't think it was important?"

"No," I said. "Not really. Why?"

"It's just confusing for me," she said. "Who can just decide they don't need a salary?"

"I'm a wealthy man, Abby."

"I know," she said. "I just never realized *how* wealthy you are."

"Is my wealth a problem for you?"

"I just need to get used to it."

"I don't understand."

"Sometimes, I feel . . . I don't know." She stumbled over her words. "It's like I don't recognize my life."

Her words nearly shattered me, and I didn't know how to re-spond.

"That sounds horrible," she said in a rush. "Even to me, because I've never been happier. Really. I've hesitated saying anything because I didn't want to sound ungrateful, or unappre-ciative, or like I didn't want to be with you."

My chest grew tight. "You don't recognize your life?"

She turned to face me. "Damn it. I'm sorry."

"Don't be sorry, Abby," I said, forcing myself to remain calm and not to assume the worst. She had, after all, said she wanted to be with me. "I'd much rather you tell me about it than let it sit and fester." I'd done too much of that in the past. "But I'm still not sure exactly what the problem is."

"It's just, I felt useful before. Now I feel somewhat insignifi-cant."

Insignificant?

"What?" I asked. "How can you feel that way?"

She used her fingers to count. "You don't need me to clean or keep the house up. You're completely capable of cooking for yourself. I don't need to do laundry or grocery shopping. You certainly don't need my salary. Hell, you don't need yours. I'm not contributing anything to expenses financially, and I just feel completely insignificant in the middle of all this," she said with a wave that encompassed the entire foyer.

I thought for a few seconds, unsure what would be the best way to respond and uncertain how to show her the fallacy of her thinking.

Finally, I stood to my feet and held out my hand. "Come with me."

She tentatively placed her hand in mine, and I gave it a gentle squeeze as she stood. I led her up the stairs, past the playroom and our bedroom, down the hall, to a single door. I opened it, showing her another set of stairs. I didn't think she'd ever been in the attic, and she followed me as we made our way up.

The attic was huge and ran the entire length of the house. White sheets covered old furniture, and several trunks lined the walls. A few windows were scattered here and there, allowing light into the dusky space.

It'd been a long time since I'd been in the attic, and a rush of memories came back.

"This was my favorite place to hide when I was little," I said. "I would sit up here for hours: playing pirate, reading, or exploring." I walked over to a white lump and lifted the sheet, showing her the armchair underneath. "When I remodeled, I had them leave the attic untouched. They stored a lot of the original furniture from the house up here."

She ran a hand over the leather chair. "It's your history."

I smiled. "I came up here a lot during high school. Spent hours here. It was a struggle for me, trying to decide what to do." I faced her. "Do you know I had an appointment at the Naval Academy?"

She nodded. "Linda told me once."

"Part of me wanted something different, to go somewhere no one knew me. To start over." I thought back to those long-ago days when I was a teenager, desperately trying to find my place in life. "I'm not sure anyone knows, even now, how hard I struggled with myself. I felt trapped into who I thought the world wanted Nathaniel West to be, and I didn't want to feel trapped." I turned to face her. "I wanted to be significant."

The window nearest us overlooked a large oak tree in the backyard. I pointed to it. "Do you see that tree?"

"The oak?" she asked, moving to stand closer.

"Yes. I want to build a tree house there one day. For our children."

I stood completely still and let my words sink in. I heard her sharp intake of breath.

"It's a huge step for me to think that, Abby," I said. "For me to allow myself to think that one day you and I will marry and have children. But it's you who gave me the freedom to dream." I turned and framed her face with my hands. "The wealth, the housekeeper, the salary I'm not taking this year? They're nothing. They're the insignificant things, Abby. Not you. *You* are the most significant part of my life."

"Nathaniel," she whispered.

"I love you," I said. "And that's all that matters. If you want to go grocery shopping and do the laundry, do it. If it'll make you feel better to help with the utilities, help with them. But please, *please,* don't ever lose sight of what you mean to me."

She closed her eyes. "I'm sorry."

"No." I kissed her eyelid. "Don't apologize. Moving in with me, changing your entire way of life, of course it's been stressful. It's going to take some adjustment."

"I didn't handle it very well."

"We're here now, aren't we?" I slipped my arms to her waist and drew her closer. "Isn't that all that matters?"

She laid her head on my chest and sighed. "Yes."

The weight of the week dissipated, leaving in its place a sense of joy and peace. The air around us was silent, and I allowed the old memories and doubts I had as a teenager to be replaced by the new dreams made possible by the woman I held.

She sighed. "I messed up our weekend."

"What do you mean?" I murmured into her hair. Frankly, the weekend was going better than I imagined it would when I pulled into the driveway earlier.

"It's past the time you normally collar me," she said.

"I can collar you later tonight," I said, shifting my plans for the weekend around in my head.

Her arms tightened around me. "Sounds good to me."

"One more thing," I said. "I need you to know that while I appreciate the fact that you want me to treat you the way I did my previous submissives, it won't ever happen."

I pulled back to catch her gaze and watched her wrinkle her forehead.

"You're not one of my previous submissives," I said. "I told you before that I cared for them, but it's not the same as what I feel for you. Not even close."

"I've never questioned that."

"And yet you still asked me to treat you the same," I reminded her. "Still asked me what I would do with them."

"So tell me," she said. "Would you have postponed your weekend play for them the same way you did tonight?"

I nodded. "If something was wrong between us, yes." At the surprise in her eyes, I continued. "But I would never have thought to bring them up here, or to share with them what I shared with you. I've talked with Paul a lot about this, Abby, and you're not the same as them. It doesn't bother me to treat you differently. Don't let it bother you."

"I'll try," she whispered.

I pulled her to my chest. "Don't compare yourself to them. You are completely different. *We* are completely different."

We spent the next several hours exploring the expanse of the attic together. Every so often, one of us would catch the other looking outside at the oak tree and we'd share a smile.

Chapter Twenty-one

——ABBY——

He had told me to expect some sort of role-play, and on Sunday morning, I waited in the living room, reading. I hadn't seen him since breakfast. He'd left the dining room shortly after eating, instructing me to dress in the outfit he had waiting in my closet.

I'd never worn garters before. The ones he laid out for me were black, and I'll admit, made my legs look sexier than normal. It'd never occurred to me to wear such things, and I decided to plan a shopping trip with Felicia for sometime the next week.

I pulled absentmindedly at the skirt. It was ridiculously short and fell just past my upper thighs. I felt certain a glimpse of garter would peek out from the bottom whenever I walked. The jacket wasn't much better; it was tight and barely covered my chest. There wasn't even a blouse, just a black lace bra that showed when I moved the right way. I had to admit, though, just sitting and thinking about what he could have planned was a turn-on.

How would I know when he was ready? Would he come find me?

He would have to, right?

I thought back to Friday night. How he'd wanted to talk as much as I had and how he'd postponed our play until he made sure everything was right between us. It still put a silly grin on my face every time I thought about his mention of the tree house and how he wanted the same things I did.

We'd spent hours in the attic, looking through old trunks, and each time he uncovered a new piece of furniture, it was as if he uncovered another part of himself. He'd eventually collared me, and for some reason our ritual felt more intense than normal. Later, when it was time to sleep, he invited me to share his bed, and turning him down never crossed my mind.

Lunch with Jackson and Felicia the day before had been wonderful. I'd rarely gone so long without seeing her, and she still had a glow about her. For once, I didn't feel jealous that she shared a connection with Nathaniel that I didn't. After our Friday-night talk, Nathaniel and I both felt more secure in our relationship, with where we were and where we wanted to eventually be.

I stood and walked to the bookshelves so I could put away the book I'd been pretending to read.

"What do you think, Apollo?" I asked. "Should I find something to do or give up?"

Apollo cocked his head to the side, gave a soft grumble, and rolled to his back. I took the hint. Belly rub it was.

My phone beeped with an incoming text.

"Sorry, Apollo," I said, moving to the table beside the couch to get my phone. "It's probably Felicia."

But it wasn't Felicia. It was Nathaniel. My heart pounded when I read the message.

My office. Now.

I stared at the message for entirely too long.

His office?

His office, *where?*

I went to the desk in the library first. Nothing. He wasn't even in the library. He had an office across from the dining room he used when he worked at home.

I ran as quickly as the black, strappy shoes would let me, expecting to find the door shut. Instead, it stood open. I peeked inside, but again, the room was empty.

He didn't mean his *office* office, did he? The one in the city? There was nothing else he could mean, though.

I grabbed my purse and keys to his second car, rubbed Apollo on the head, and went to the garage. A note waited on the seat.

> *Yes, Ms. King,*
>   *I meant my office in the city. The weekend security guard will let you inside the building.*
>
>   *Sincerely,*
>   *Mr. West*
>
>
> *P.S. You're late.*

So much meaning in such a short note, I decided as I drove to his office. For one, I would be allowed to call him "Mr. West," and for another, I was apparently late. The thought thrilled and titillated me.

I pulled into the parking garage across the street from his office and realized I would have to walk in public in the outfit he'd picked out for me. I felt an odd combination of pride and excitement.

I scurried across the street to the tall building that housed his company.

"Yes, ma'am," the weekend guard said when I made it to the front door.

I knew the weekday guard, spoke to him frequently anytime I visited Nathaniel at his office. This guy, though, wasn't the older gentleman I recognized. This guy was young and unfamiliar.

"Ms. King to see Mr. West," I said, tugging at my skirt. I wondered if he saw the garters when I walked inside and then mentally chastised myself. *Does it matter?*

"Yes, ma'am," he said. "Mr. West is expecting you. Said to send you right up." He looked only at my eyes. His gaze didn't drop to my outfit at all. "I need to see your identification."

"What?" I asked. "Oh, right." The weekend guy wouldn't know me like the weekday guy would. I pulled my wallet out and flashed him my driver's license.

"Thank you, ma'am," he said, and then waved me through to the elevators.

Nathaniel's office was on the top floor, and though I'd been inside his office multiple times, this time was different. This wasn't a normal meet-you for lunch or it's-time-for-our-yoga-class meeting.

Sara wasn't at her normal place, of course, with it being a Sunday. The large wooden door of Nathaniel's office was closed, and I stopped for a moment, unsure how to continue.

He would have heard the elevator ping when it arrived on the floor, wouldn't he? Should I knock or text him? Maybe he'd open the door for me?

But he'd had me drive all the way to his office. Surely he wasn't going to open the door for me.

I knocked.

His voice was low and commanding when he answered. "Enter."

I pushed the door open with a hesitant hand. He sat at his desk, thumbing through papers. At my entrance, he looked over the tops of them and scowled at me.

"Come in, Ms. King, and close the door."

The door closed behind me with a loud click.

"You're late," he said.

I'd decided exactly which angle I was going to play on the way over, so I flipped my hair behind my shoulder and tilted my head.

I like you feisty, he'd said two weeks ago.

He liked feisty? I'd be feisty.

"I wasn't sure what time you wanted me, Mr. West," I said.

He raised an eyebrow. "Didn't my summons say *now*?"

"Maybe. I really don't remember."

"That's an ongoing problem of yours, isn't it?" he asked. "Forgetfulness?"

I shrugged.

He set the papers down. "I've heard you are quite forgetful lately. That you've been otherwise occupied when you should be working."

"I have a lot on my mind," I said. "But I get my work done."

He scanned the papers in front of him. "According to this, you make personal phone calls on company time."

"One or two."

"One or two an hour, perhaps," he said. "Are you calling a man?"

I shifted my weight. "I call my boyfriend sometimes."

He looked at me from head to toe and then motioned to my outfit. "Does your boyfriend know you dress this way?"

"Oh, no, Mr. West." I played along, trying to pull the hem of my skirt down. "My boyfriend doesn't see me like this. I wore this at the request of my master."

I thought maybe my admission would trip him up or that he would at least show some sort of acknowledgment. Instead he nodded. "Ah, I see," he said. "You're a kinky girl."

I thought about the previous weekend and smiled. "Very."

"I bet you like dressing this way," he said. "Like showing your body off for your master."

"Yes," I said, running my hands over my hips and jutting my chest out just a tad.

"And I bet you like showing it off to other men as well, don't you, Ms. King?" He pushed his chair back. "Like the security guard downstairs?"

"He was okay." I ran my hands up my body, skirting the swell of my breasts. "But I was really more interested in what you thought, Mr. West."

He stood up and walked to me, his eyes never leaving mine. "Is this the attitude your supervisor has to deal with?" he asked. "This inappropriate flirting?"

I gave him my best smile. "You never answered my question. What do you think of my outfit?"

He moved to stand behind me, and his hands came around my body to cup my breasts. "The jacket is too tight." He pulled at the fabric and the buttons scattered to the floor. His voice was low and deep as his hands slid to my hips. "And the skirt is too short," he whispered in my ear.

"Perhaps you would like them better off?" I asked, pushing back into his groin and smiling at the feel of his erection.

"Ms. King," he said, as if in shock. "You do realize the gravity of your actions? I could fire you for your impertinence." Those were his words, but his hands didn't move from my body.

I spun to face him and batted my eyelashes. "But, Mr. West, I need this position."

"I have no choice," he said, and took a step backward. "I have to let you go. I can't have this disrespectful, outlandish behavior distracting my other employees."

I walked slowly toward him, slipping the tattered remnants of my outfit to the ground, stepping out of it. "Surely there's something I can do."

"I don't know. It's a very serious situation."

"There has to be something."

His gaze traveled up and down the length of my body. "There may be one thing."

"I'll do it," I said. It was odd how the role-play bolstered my confidence, how it affected even the way I walked. My hips swayed as I approached him. I ran a finger down his chest. "Please."

He turned and walked to his desk, slowly removing his belt as he went. When he stood to the side of his desk, he faced me, flexing the leather in his hands. "I don't know if you're up for this."

Holy fuck. Is he going to spank me with his belt?

"I assure you I am, Mr. West."

"Come here."

I walked to his desk.

"Hold out your hands," he said.

He took them and looped the belt around them, binding my wrists together. I didn't struggle as he pushed me forward, and I rested my forearms on the desktop with my ass facing him.

Making sure I saw every move he made, he walked behind his desk and opened a drawer. I sucked in a breath when he withdrew a wooden paddle and placed it on the desk.

He has a paddle in his office?

In the span of a few shaky breaths, he'd moved behind me. His fingers nipped the skin of my thighs as he undid my garters. He roughly rubbed my ass through the scratchy lace of my panties before slipping his fingers under the waistband and slipping them over and down my hips, exposing me to him.

"You've been a very naughty employee, Ms. King," he said. "I'm going to have to punish you."

I wiggled my ass. "Whatever you think best, Mr. West."

His hand came down on my backside with a satisfying smack. "I'm going to make sure you understand the consequences of your actions." While he spoke, he continued spanking me. "You need to understand exactly what I expect from my employees. What is allowable. If you forget, I'll be obligated to remind you again."

He *tsk*ed as he slid a long finger between my legs. "Why do I get the feeling this isn't a deterrent for you?"

My ass felt warm and sensitive from his spanking, and I bucked my hips trying to get his finger deeper. "I don't know, Mr. West. Maybe you should punish me more."

He collected the paddle from the desk. "If you insist, Ms. King."

"I'm afraid it's the only way I'll learn my lesson."

The paddle smacked against the skin of my ass, and I moaned.

"Here are the rules you'll obey if you continue working for me." As he spoke, he brought the paddle down over and over.

"You will dress appropriately."

Smack.

"No more garters and ill-fitting outfits that show off your body."

Smack.

"No more personal phone calls to your boyfriend during office hours."

Smack.

"No more flirting with male employees. Including me."

Smack.

"No more forgetfulness."

Smack.

"And when I tell you to come to my office immediately, you're to come to my office immediately."

Smack.

"Am I understood, Ms. King?"

Smack.

Before I could answer, his hands were on me, teasing and tickling my swollen flesh.

Fuck me. Fuck me. Now.

He landed a slap to my ass, but with his hand instead of the paddle. "I asked you a question, Ms. King."

Right. Right. Right.

"Uh," I pretended to stammer. "What was the question again?"

He spanked me harder. "Do you understand how you are to act when you are in my employ?"

I shifted my legs, desperate for friction. "Yes, Mr. West. I understand."

He sighed. "I should fire you anyway. I've never had to do anything like this before."

The office fell into silence. The only sounds audible were the steady *tick, tick, tick* of a clock on his desk and the faint hum of a mini refrigerator in the corner.

I slowly lifted myself from the table and looked behind me. He'd moved back a few steps, but was smiling.

"You'll probably have me arrested," he said.

I unbound my wrists and dropped the belt to the floor. "I'd never have you arrested."

He shook his head. "Treating you like that."

"I needed it."

"No," he said. "There's no excuse for the way I acted."

"But I'll be good now, Mr. West." I reached behind my back and unclasped my bra. Slipped the straps from my shoulders. Dropped the flimsy garment to the floor. "Let me show you how good I can be."

He adjusted his pants.

Yes.

"I just spanked you for that sort of behavior," he said.

I shook my head. "I'm not flirting. I'm showing you what a good girl I am." I hopped on his desk, biting the inside of my cheek at the slight tinge of discomfort. I scooted forward and brought my feet up to rest on the desk, bending and spreading my knees, making sure he saw exactly what he wanted. "Please, Mr. West."

He moved closer, looking for all the world like a cat stalking its prey. "How good can you be?"

"Come find out. I'll make it worth your while."

He unbuttoned his pants as he walked. He wasn't wearing anything underneath.

"Oh, Mr. West," I said, eyeing his cock. "You're so much bigger than my boyfriend."

A smile played on his lips. "Am I?"

"Yes," I said. "But perhaps a wee bit smaller than my master." I looked up and met his eyes. "He's huge."

He laughed softly and stepped out of his pants. With two short steps, he was before me, standing between my legs.

"Let's get you out of this shirt, shall we?" I asked, my hands making quick work of the first two buttons. I grew impatient at the third, grabbed the material and jerked. "Oops," I said as his buttons bounced off the desk and floor.

"You ripped my shirt, Ms. King," he said. "I'll have to spank you again."

"I look forward to it, Mr. West." I slipped the torn shirt from his shoulders, running my hands across his chest.

"Mmm," he hummed. "You certainly look delicious."

I leaned back, offering my breasts to him. "Why don't you have a taste?"

He answered with action, dropping his head to my neck and running his tongue along the hollow there. His teeth nibbled their way down to one nipple and then the other. He suckled me gently, almost reverently, before trailing kisses back up and whispering in my ear. "Just as I thought. You're delectable."

I captured his head with my hands and did my own whispering, surprised at how easily the words came out. "You should taste my pussy."

He bit my earlobe. "I'm shocked, Ms. King." But he slid a finger between my open legs, dipping momentarily into me, and brought it back out. He licked it with the tip of his tongue. "Though, how very true."

I pulled him to me, drawing pleasure from the feel of his chest against mine, his warmth surrounding me. I ran my nails lightly down his back. "I can't wait to feel you inside me, Mr. West."

He pulled my legs around his waist. "Then far be it for me to make you wait any longer."

With one forceful thrust, he entered me, filling me completely. "Fuck, Ms. King."

We didn't talk anymore, focusing our attention on the movement of our bodies. Enjoying the way they pulled and pushed against the other. He growled low in my ear, and I responded with my own guttural moans.

Each thrust forced my hips to move along the hard wooden desk, and the feel of it, combined with the lingering ache of his spanking, drove me to work faster to my orgasm. He thrust even quicker, even harder, sending currents of pleasure swirling through my body.

"Mr. West," I gasped, tightening my legs around him.

"You were right, Ms. King," he said with a powerful thrust, hitting a spot deep within me. "You are good."

My need to release grew stronger, and I struggled to hold back until he gave permission.

"Can I?" I begged. "I'm going."

He thrust again. "Yes."

His head dropped to my shoulder, and I trembled as his teeth grazed my skin.

"Fuck," I said. "Harder."

His only response was a sharp nip to my shoulder, but that's all it took. My climax shot through me, and I came hard. He continued his rhythm, his pace unrelenting as he drove himself to his own climax. The muscles of his back tightened under my hands, and I felt him release inside me.

With a soft sigh, he relaxed. "You have a job here for as long as you want, Ms. King."

Chapter Twenty-two

——ABBY——

He left for China two weeks later on a Friday night. I drove with him to the airport, wanting to be with him as long as possible. He held my hand the entire way, and the long week apart stretched endlessly before us.

"It'll be the longest we've been apart since March," he said, staring at the road as we approached the airport.

It's only a week. It's only a week.

I wanted to cry just thinking about it.

"I wish I could go with you," I whispered.

He lifted my hand to his lips, brushing my skin softly. "You're doing what's best for you and your career. I have the utmost respect for that."

I blinked back a tear. "I love you."

He kissed my hand again and his lips lingered as he inhaled the smell of me. "Abby," he whispered, his breath as gentle as a caress. "I love you."

The night before, we'd stayed up making love into the early

hours of the morning. He had been slow and reverent in his affection, taking his time and memorizing every detail of me. Even when he finally entered me, he moved unhurriedly, as if we had all the time in the world.

As the sun rose and we woke in each other's arms, we came together again, but with a fierceness and urgency born of the knowledge we'd soon be separated for more than a week. Our hands and voices were hurried, and we pulled and pushed until at last we collapsed together, where we rested before finally forcing ourselves to leave the bed.

At the airport, I stayed with him until his pilot discreetly coughed and nodded toward his watch. Even then I stayed on airport property until the jet disappeared into the sky. Only then did I head to his car for the long, lonely ride back.

Once there, I stepped into the foyer and threw his keys on the table. I'd never stayed at Nathaniel's house—*my house*, I corrected myself—alone before. I walked through rooms, checking the alarms, even though Nathaniel had done so before he left.

When I was satisfied I was safe, I made my way upstairs to our bedroom. It wasn't until I passed the playroom that I remembered Nathaniel's words from earlier that day.

I won't be able to collar you this weekend, he had said at lunch. *But I do have certain tasks for you.*

He said he'd have envelopes waiting in the submissive bedroom. *Although I want you to sleep in our bedroom, if you wish.*

Yes, I knew, I did wish to sleep in our bedroom. Even though he wouldn't be in our bed, I could sleep with his pillow, and perhaps the sheets still carried his smell.

I stopped briefly in the small bedroom. A stack of envelopes waited for me. On top was a package wrapped in brown paper and labeled with his neat script.

Friday night.

I took a peek at the envelope underneath.

Saturday, 8:30 a.m.

Since the package didn't have a time on it, I carried it to our bedroom and placed it on the bed. I returned to it once I'd taken a long, hot shower. I'd decided to sleep in one of Nathaniel's dress shirts, so I clambered up on the bed and tucked my legs under its hem, and then I slowly unwrapped the package.

It was a leather-bound journal.

I turned it to the first page, and my heart leapt when I found his inscription.

> *I know you often have difficulties expressing your feelings with spoken words. I thought, perhaps, you might feel more at ease writing them down.*
>
> *I want you to use this journal as a place to write your fears, your doubts, and your heartaches, as well as your joys, your hopes, and your dreams. I'd like to see you use it as a place primarily to detail your submissive journey, though I understand there will be some crossover from our daily lives as well.*
>
> *To start you off, I will give you several assignments. My only request is that you be completely honest with your writings. Nothing you put in this book will ever be held against you.*
>
> *You've given me so much. I know you will give me this as well.*

I ran a finger over the ink, somehow feeling closer to him with that simple act. I flipped through the empty pages. Christine told me she kept a journal, but I'd never gotten around to picking one up for myself.

Leave it to Nathaniel . . .

I reached for the envelope that had fallen out of the journal and lifted the flap. A single sheet of paper was inside.

> *We discussed earlier this week that once I returned*
> *from China, we would attend a play party together.*
> *Write down a list of your fears, and for each one suggest*
> *a way to counteract it. On another page, make a list of*
> *benefits you hope to obtain by attending.*
> *We'll discuss upon my return.*

Was he serious? It was like an assignment a teacher would give me.

Would he grade it?

If he felt I failed, would he punish me?

I giggled at the thought, but then remembered how scared I'd been the first time he suggested the party and decided writing my fears down might be a good idea. I reached across the bed to my nightstand and dug through the drawer before finally finding a pen trapped underneath a bag of toys.

It was surprising how freely the words came once I started writing. I felt unrestrained and uninhibited. I wrote without stopping, just putting down what came to mind and filling page after page with both my fears and what I hoped to accomplish.

When finished, I looked at the clock, surprised at how quickly time had passed. The flight to Hong Kong took sixteen hours, so I didn't expect to hear from Nathaniel anytime soon.

Yawning, I turned off the light and slipped under the covers. Apollo jumped up to rest beside me. Perhaps it was the lack of sleep the night before, but I drifted off within minutes.

Saturday, 8:30 a.m.

I turned the envelope around in my hand, anxious to see what it held. Would it be another writing assignment? I slipped my finger under the flap and opened it.

> *It's 8:30 on Saturday morning and I'm still in flight. I hope you had a restful night's sleep and that Apollo kept you company. I gave him a stern talking-to before I left.*

I smiled at his words. He'd made a lot of progress in the last few months, and I loved seeing the funny, playful side of him. I rubbed Apollo's head and continued reading.

> *We've been in the playroom countless times in the last few months, but we haven't come close to exploring all the different ways we can play. This morning, I want you to go into the playroom and look around. Find a toy, item, or piece of equipment we haven't used but that you would like to experiment with next time we play. Write it down in your journal so we can discuss later.*
> *I might decide to use it.*
> *P.S. You have only an hour. Felicia will be by at nine thirty to take you shopping and out to lunch.*

I took a quick glance at the next envelope.

Saturday, 3:30 p.m.

Plenty of time to enjoy a few hours with Felicia.

I read the eight thirty letter again. I'd never spent much time exploring the playroom by myself. Nathaniel and I had gone through it together before he'd collared me, months ago, and cleanup was now my responsibility, but I still felt it was his domain.

Since I'd already showered and had breakfast, I went upstairs into the playroom. Once inside, I skipped over the whipping bench, padded table, and cross, making my way to the far wall. Handmade cabinets held a multitude of floggers. A few he had used—the rabbit fur and suede. He had others, of course, leather and some braided leather ones; they looked heavier and I wondered how they would feel.

Mmm. Maybe.

The cabinets stood above a large table, made of the same rich wood and filled with multiple drawers. I opened one and saw his collection of plugs and vibrators. Fun toys, but I didn't see anything that stood out in particular.

Attached to one wall was his collection of canes, and I ran a finger across one. I'd talked to Christine about them a few times since our visit, but I still wasn't ready to try them.

I tried to imagine Nathaniel's expression if I told him I wanted him to use a cane on me.

Would he be shocked? Would he agree?

But again, I didn't feel ready yet, so I kept walking.

I rifled through a collection of masks and gags. We'd never played with any of them. I still wondered what it would be like to be gagged.

I picked up a ball gag and tried to imagine him using it combined with a new flogger. That could be fun. His note, though, said to pick one. *One.* How was that even possible?

Taking my journal and pen, I sat in the middle of the playroom and thought. I ran through different scenarios in my head using several of the items I found in drawers and cabinets. They all seemed fun, but I couldn't decide on one thing.

I tapped my pen against the spine of the journal and glanced down at my watch. *Nine thirteen.*

I gazed around the room one last time, smiled, and bent my head to write. I wrote about the toy I picked and, just for fun, added a few details about the scene.

Felicia and I were almost to our first stop, a lingerie store, when my phone rang.

Nathaniel!

"Hello," I said.

His voice sounded tired. "Abby."

My heart warmed just hearing his voice. "How was the flight?"

"Long," he said. "We just landed."

My mind tried to calculate the time difference. "What time is it?"

"A little after eleven at night," he said. "It's like I skipped an entire day."

"That's okay," I teased. I imagined him running his fingers through his hair the way he did when he was tired or frustrated. "Saturday's a drag. You didn't miss much."

"I take issue with that," Felicia said from the driver's seat. "You're shopping with me, and our first stop is a lingerie store. Saturday is not a drag."

He gave a soft laugh. "I'll be talking with you in a few hours.

I just wanted to hear your voice and let you know I'd landed safely."

"What are you going to do now?" I asked, not ready to hang up.

"Check into the hotel and get a few hours' sleep before I start working again."

"On Sunday?"

"I don't have anything else to do," he said in a teasing tone. "Someone refused to come with me."

"You know why," I said softly.

"I know and I understand."

"You should go out and explore," I said. "It's not like you're in China every day."

"Thank goodness. I'll explore some. Though I doubt the Great Wall has changed much since the last time I saw it."

"You're going to see the Great Wall?"

"No," he said. "It's too far away. Next time I'm here, maybe you'll be able to come and we can go together."

"I miss you already."

"I miss you, too."

"We're here," Felicia said.

I'd been so engaged in talking with Nathaniel I hadn't even noticed Felicia parking the car.

"I'll let you go," he said. "You two have fun. Don't get into too much trouble."

"Mmm," I teased. "Trouble sounds good."

"Later," he said with a hint of smile in his voice, but then he grew quieter. "I love you."

"Love you."

I returned home hours later with bags of new clothes and lingerie, several different garters, and a light heart after having plenty of girl talk with my best friend. Married life agreed with Felicia, and I'd never seen her more content and happy.

I hummed as I put away my purchases. Maybe later in the week I'd put on some new lingerie and take a picture to send to Nathaniel.

At three thirty, I opened the next envelope.

> *I hope you enjoyed your time with Felicia. You and my new cousin-in-law are so very different, and yet I know your friendship means a lot to you both. I never want you to feel as though you have given anything up by your choice to wear my collar.*
>
> *Having said that, I know we've discussed before how being a submissive does not make you weak, naive, or gullible. In fact, quite the opposite is true.*
>
> *For your next assignment, I want you to write a thousand words on the following topic:*
>
> *My Submission: What It Means to Me*
>
> *When you have finished, take a walk, eat some dinner, and then write a thousand words on your next topic:*
>
> *My Submission: What It Means to My Master*
>
> *I look forward to discussing both assignments with you and giving you my thoughts on each.*

Whew.

He wasn't lying when he told me he would have me use the journal. The night before had been eye-opening, though, in terms of what I discovered as I wrote. While I'd been apprehensive about a party when he first brought it up, I was now looking forward to it more. Especially since he'd forced me to think about and write a way to overcome my fear.

I couldn't wait to discover what the new writing assignment taught me.

Saturday, 10:30 p.m.

Tonight you will discover how it's possible to serve me long-distance. You have fifteen minutes to undress and get your cell phone.

You will call me from our bed at 10:45 p.m.

My heart pounded as I read his short letter.

Serve him long-distance?

I couldn't wait to find out what he meant by that. Even more exciting was simply the opportunity to hear his voice. I mentally calculated the time difference. It would be morning in Hong Kong.

An early lunch break for him, perhaps?

Fifteen minutes later I waited on the bed. At 10:45 exactly, I hit the send button to call him.

The phone clicked as he picked up.

"Abigail," he said, and I was no longer talking to the weary, worn traveler I'd spoken with hours earlier. The low, commanding voice sending shivers up my spine belonged to only one person.

"Master."

Chapter Twenty-three

——NATHANIEL——

She spoke that one word, *Master*, and I heard the nervous excitement in her voice.

"Have you followed my instructions?" I asked.

"Yes, Master."

"I want you to turn on the speaker, put the phone on the bed, and get into your inspection position," I said. "Tell me when you're finished."

From the other side of the phone came a slight rustling, and I pictured her doing as I asked.

"I'm ready, Master," she said.

"Thank you, my lovely. Now, tell me what I'd see if I were there."

I listened as she described her body, as she detailed her position and posture.

"Very nice," I said when she had finished. "I can see you in my mind, and that's certainly part of what I wanted to accomplish. However, you just spent a lot of time writing on two very specific assignments. With *that* in mind, tell me what I see."

Silence filled the other end of the line as she thought about my words, and then I heard her soft "Oh" and smiled.

"What do I see?" I asked again. "Start with your head."

"You not only see my head tipped back, but also the meaning behind it," she said, all excited.

"Which is what?"

"My throat is exposed. Vulnerable. And I place it in offering to you."

"Yes," I said. "And your chest?"

"Is thrust forward," she answered. "But it's more than presenting you my breasts. My chest houses my heart, and in this position, my heart is vulnerable, too." She spoke with pride. "My heart's one of my body's most important organs as well as being the symbolic center of my emotions. It's almost as if I'm offering you my life. You could harm me, but I trust you not to. You could injure me, but I know you would not."

Her excitement and delight in answering me struck my own symbolic center. "Do you have any idea what it does to me, what it means to me, to see you before me like that?"

"No, Master," she said. "But I'm getting glimpses."

"Then we're both making progress."

"Yes, Master."

"If I were with you, I would walk behind you and tell you to move into your waiting position. What would you do with your head?"

"I would drop it, Master."

"Do it," I instructed. "Then I brush aside your hair so your neck is bared for me. I lean forward and you feel my breath as it brushes against the delicate skin covering your spine."

She gave a shaky intake of breath.

"My lips follow the path of my breath," I continued. "They softly brush your right shoulder blade. I'm running my hand over your left, tracing your fine bone structure under my fingertips."

She sighed.

"I feel you shudder," I said. "Your response makes me harder." I stroked myself in response, but only lightly. We had further to go. "Be my hands as they come around your body. They gently cup your breasts and I feel your heartbeat. It's racing. I rub my thumbs across your nipples and they harden. You're getting excited, aren't you, Abigail?"

"Yes, Master."

"Do you feel your heart?"

"Yes," she said. "It *is* racing, Master."

"I roll your nipples between my fingertips and start kissing down your neck. My teeth graze your skin and my tongue traces their trail." I licked my lips. "Your taste is unbelievable."

I closed my eyes and pictured her. "Lie on your back," I said, because it would be easier for her and because she'd been kneeling long enough. "We're on our bed now. Keep your knees bent and spread." The bed rustled as she complied. "Do you feel the cool air on your pussy? Are you aching to touch yourself?"

"Yes, Master," she said in an almost groan.

"But are your hands on your breasts where I left them?"

"Yes, Master."

"Excellent," I said. "I move them down your body and across the outline of your rib cage. I feel the rise and fall of your chest and notice how you're breathing heavier. Do you feel it, too?"

"Yes, Master."

"I bring my hands lower and move them across your hips. I move myself to rest in between your legs, but I'm careful not to touch where you want me." I closed my eyes and imagined. "Your lips are soft and you part them under my kiss. You sigh softly, and I dip my hand lower to draw lazy circles around your hip bone."

I opened my eyes and looked at the phone to my side as if I could see her through it. *Webcam next time.* "Are you drawing lazy circles?"

"Yes."

"Yes, what?"

"Yes, Master."

"I pinch your right nipple for that slip," I said, and I heard the gasp as she did so. "I move my hand back to your lower body and brush it against your belly. What are you feeling?"

"I feel you warm against my front," she said softly. "Your cock is hard and pressed to my stomach. I want to feel you lower. I push toward you. Wanting."

"I know exactly what you want, my lovely," I said. "And you know I'll give it to you. I'm just not ready yet."

She whimpered, and I smiled.

"I drop my head and suckle you," I said. "I'm rolling your nipple around my tongue, flicking it. Are you pretending your hands are my teeth?"

"Yes, Master."

"Good. Now pinch them because I'm biting and tugging at them. I love the feel of you in my mouth. The slight pull of your skin."

She gasped.

"And I love the noises you make for me," I said, with a smile and a hint of longing that I wasn't with her in person to hear her noises.

"I love making noises for you, Master," she said. "I often find I can't help myself."

"My favorite noise is the one you make when I enter you," I said, brushing my cock, remembering. "If I told you to move freely, what would you do?"

I swore I could hear her smile through the phone. "I'd move

down your body, tease the tip of your cock with my tongue, and
see if I could elicit a few noises of my own, Master."

I chuckled. She'd been more playful since the day of our role-
playing, and I'd been thrilled to see more of that side of her. Just
because she wore my collar on weekends didn't mean she had to
give up that part of herself.

"I'm sure you'll elicit more than that in a few more minutes,"
I said as I grabbed myself. "My cock is so hard just thinking
about it. Would you keep teasing me or would you finally take
me in your mouth?"

"I keep teasing you, Master," she said. "I love your cock, and
I'd spend as much time as you'd let me, licking and nipping it
gently with my lips. I'm licking you now and dragging a fingertip up your shaft." My hands followed her words, pretending she
was in the room doing it herself. "My tongue swirls around the
tip and I finally take the whole thing in my mouth, but just
briefly."

My hips jerked off the bed. "Tease," I said.

"You asked, Master," she said, with a self-satisfied tone.

"That I did, my lovely. That I did," I said, pleased at how
much she was getting into the call. "Where are your hands?"

"You haven't told me to move them. So they're still at my
nipples."

"Move them down your body. Because now it's my turn to
tease. Are your knees still bent and spread?"

"Yes, Master."

"I'm licking my way down your body, paying attention to
every part. Every part except where you want me the most," I
said. "I move my face to the inside of your left knee and kiss the
tiny freckle you have there."

I closed my eyes and pictured it in my head, a tiny little dot,
just in the crease of her knee. "I kiss my way up your inner

thigh, coming so close to your pussy, but right when you think I'm going to touch you there, I move and start back over with your right thigh. Do you feel me, my lovely? Feel my breath on your skin?"

She hummed in reply.

"Louder, Abigail," I said. "Or else I'll stop."

"Yes, Master."

"Good," I said. "On my next pass, I lightly brush the outside of your pussy. You're wet, aren't you?"

"Yes, Master."

"Touch there. Gently," I said. "Then taste yourself and tell me how you taste."

"Slightly salty. A hint of musk and a note of sweetness."

"You're so sweet." My voice dropped. "If I were there, you wouldn't be able to taste yourself at all. I'd keep it all to myself."

"It's all for you anyway, Master," she said, her voice just as low.

Fuck, yes, it is all for me. Mine and no one else's.

"I think I've teased you enough," I said. "Look under the bed on my side and take out the bag I left there."

I waited while I heard her scramble off the bed, picturing the bag she'd find on the floor under our bed. The bed shifted as she climbed back on.

"I have it, Master," she said.

"Open it," I said, imagining the dildo I'd put in the bag before I left. She moaned when she found it. "Like it?" I asked.

"Oh, God, yes, Master."

I smiled. "Good. Get on your back with your knees bent and spread. Pretend it's my cock and suck on it for a few seconds." I heard her movements from the other side of the phone. "Imagine me fucking your mouth and think about how good you're going to feel when I slip out of your mouth and fuck that pussy."

When I decided she'd had the dildo in her mouth long enough, I spoke again. "I'm moving down your body for the last time. Move the toy and pretend it's me. Put it right at your entrance, because I'm going to tease you with my tip for a few minutes."

I played with the tip of my cock, pretending she was in the room with me and I was teasing her.

"I'm entering you with just the tip," I said. "Just the slightest movements of my hips, and you aren't allowed to move yours at all."

"Please, Master."

"No," I said. "Not yet. I feel you tremble beneath me. You want me so badly. I move my hips the tiniest bit more and slip a bit farther inside." My hand stroked more of my cock, but not much. Not nearly what I needed. Not nearly what she needed. "What do you feel, Abigail?"

"You're breathing into my ear," she said. "I feel your muscles clench under my hands, because I'm holding your hips. Anchoring myself so I don't move. I want you. I want you so badly to thrust into me. Please, Master."

"Bounce the toy in and out of your pussy, fast and shallow," I said. "I'm giving you a little friction, but denying you what you want for now."

She groaned, but I heard her movements and I let her tease herself a bit longer.

"Now," I said, stroking myself faster. "I'm thrusting a bit harder and deeper. Do you feel me?"

"Yes, Master."

"Push my cock all the way inside now," I said, grabbing myself tightly. "Come when you're ready, but push it deep. I'm thrusting as hard and as deeply as I can."

For the next few minutes we didn't talk. I concentrated on

my cock and the little whimpers of pleasure I heard from her side of the phone. Her breathing got faster and faster.

"Let me hear you. I'm not finished yet," I said as my own climax built. "Let it out."

"Oh, fuck, Master," she panted, and I saw her in my mind, saw her working the dildo as hard as she could. "Oh."

I lifted my hips off the bed in time with the thrusts of my hand and arched my back, imagining her under me. Just in time, I reached for the washcloth I had waiting and released into it.

From the sounds of Abby's steady breathing, I could tell she'd had her own climax.

"Are you okay?" I asked.

"Yes, Master," she answered, her voice heavy with pleasure. "Thank you."

"If I were there, I'd pull you to my chest, so I could hear your heart," I said. "I'd pepper your skin with kisses and whisper in your ear how much I love you."

"I love you, Master," she said shyly.

My heart clenched at the knowledge that she wasn't talking to Nathaniel, but her master. It wasn't lost on me that this was the first time she'd said *I love you* that way.

"Abigail," I whispered. "My love."

For a time, we stayed as we were, content to have the phone line connecting us. I knew she'd had a long day, though, and that she was probably tired.

"I should let you sleep," I finally said.

"I wish I could stay on the line with you all night and listen to you breathe."

"Soon," I said. "Soon. I'll be home."

"Not soon enough."

We spoke quietly for a bit longer. When I heard her yawn, we said our good-byes and good nights and disconnected.

I propped myself up against the headboard and took a few deep breaths. I still wished Abby had been able to travel with me, but I understood and admired her for staying in New York to attend the conference. Besides, we'd have the rest of our lives to travel together.

Florida, I reminded myself. I needed to tell her about the Florida trip I had planned.

The phone sex with Abby had been incredible. Phone sex was not new to me, of course. Matter of fact, with my previous submissives, it was something I'd engaged in frequently when the urge struck during the week or if I wanted to reward them for something and I thought they'd enjoy it.

Mostly, though, it was just sex, and it amazed me how it was never just sex with Abby. Did it satisfy a need? Yes. Did it help fulfill *her*? Yes. But it was more than that.

Everything with Abby was always more.

But that didn't frighten me the way it used to.

I glanced at the clock beside my bed. She'd be curled up in bed, trying to sleep now. I had only two more envelopes waiting for her to open the next day. The first one she'd open at nine thirty. It was her last writing assignment. Then at eleven, Elaina would be picking her up for Sunday brunch.

I thought ahead to the rest of the week. On Monday, I would have dinner delivered to the house for her. Sushi. With a little note reminding her how much it meant that she'd agreed to a sushi date so many months ago instead of beating the shit out of me like I deserved.

On Tuesday, she was going out after the conference with Felicia. Abby needed to have her address changed and Felicia needed to have her last name updated. It felt right, somehow, to have her sharing my address. I remembered the house being so full of life when I was a child, and I was delighted to feel that coming back.

I thought about the flower delivery I had set up on Tuesday. After she made it home, two dozen cream roses with just a hint of blush would be delivered along with a letter I'd written and given to the florist. Just a little note telling her how happy I was she shared my home.

＊

Wednesday, right before I left a seemingly never-ending meeting for lunch, my phone buzzed with an incoming text. Abby and I often texted or talked right before lunch, so I excused myself from the conference room and went into the spare office I'd been using during my stay.

I scrolled to the text.

Getting ready for bed, she'd typed.

Wish I could tuck you in, I replied.

Me too, she texted back. **I have a little something for you . . .**

What she sent next took my breath away, and I staggered to my chair to sit down. She sent picture after picture of herself, or parts of herself. Parts of her covered, and parts not so covered, with little scraps of lace. A garter here. A tiny slip of a bra there. One nipple playing peekaboo with a brushing of lace. A thong that left very little of her ass to my imagination.

Holy fuck, I typed when the pictures stopped.

You like? she asked.

Let's just say if I were there, I'd remove every last bit of that lingerie. With my teeth.

Oh yeah? she asked. **Then what would you do?**

I looked at my watch. I had a few minutes before I needed to leave the office.

I'd bend you over the foot of the bed.

Sounds good, she replied.

Smack that ass for being such a tease.

squirms

I grinned and typed fast.

Dip a finger into your pussy.

Mmmm, she texted back.

Someone knocked on the door.

Fuck. Fuck. Fuck.

Damn fucking lunch, I typed.

Damn cock-blocking business trip, she replied.

At least you can have some relief, I sent back. **I'll be stuck in a stuffy lunch.**

Drown your sorrow in jiu.

I will, I texted back. **Sweet dreams.**

Sweet dreams *soon*, she wrote. **I have a little problem to take care of first.**

I groaned, picturing her finding a toy in her bedside table, her legs spread . . .

Tease, I finally sent her.

Learned from the best, she replied.

I felt despondent all day. Only two more days until I could leave China, but I knew those two days would drag. I called Jackson when I made it back to the hotel room that evening. He was an early riser and I knew he'd be up.

"Nathaniel," he said. "How's China?"

"Long and boring," I said. "I didn't wake you, did I?" With the time difference, it was just after five in the morning.

"Nah. Just getting ready for my morning run."

We spoke for a few minutes about nothing in particular and made some plans to get together once I returned. It didn't take long for the conversation to turn to his recent wedding and Felicia. He loved talking about his new wife.

"Question for you," I said after hearing a long tirade on their plans concerning his retirement. "Was there a lot of gossip surrounding your engagement?" I honestly couldn't remember; it had been a difficult time for me with Abby leaving and all.

"There was some talk Felicia might have been pregnant," he said with a laugh. "But that wasn't true, of course."

I knew they both wanted children, but I also knew they wanted to wait a few years.

"Why?" he asked. "Are you and Abby—"

"No," I interrupted. "Nothing like that." *Not yet.* "I just know you hadn't known each other for very long when you proposed. It made me wonder."

"Number one," he said. "I don't give a fuck what people think, and I know you sure as hell don't."

I laughed. He was right, for the most part.

"Number two," he continued. "If I found the woman I knew I wanted to marry and she wanted to marry me, why should what other people think have anything to do with it?"

"I don't want people to gossip about Abby," I said without thinking. "I don't want anyone to think less of her."

"Aha!" he said. "I knew it."

I rolled my eyes even though he couldn't see it over the phone. "I didn't say I hadn't thought about marrying Abby."

"You implied it," he said, and then continued without waiting for my response. "Listen, man, Abby's a strong woman."

"I know that."

"And she's secure enough in who she is to not give a fuck if people gossip about her," he said. "Besides, anyone who would think less of her for agreeing to marry you is either an ass or jealous."

I laughed. "Thanks, Jackson. Sometimes I just need to talk things out."

"No problem."

"You'll keep this conversation just between us, right?" I asked. "You won't tell—"

"My wife that her best friend's boyfriend is thinking about popping the question?" he asked. I knew he was smiling.

"Right."

"Your secret's safe with me."

I thought about my conversation with Jackson for much of the remainder of the evening. Before I went to bed that night, I sent Abby a text with three simple lines.

Want you.
Miss you.
Love you.

I called her Friday night, China time, with bad news.

"There've been some problems," I told her, while watching my pilot talk on his headset. He was waving his hands in the air. "We're not going to be able to leave on time."

"How long will you be delayed?"

"We think a few more hours," I said. "I should make it to New York around three in the morning. I'll just get a taxi home."

"I can come pick you up. It won't be a problem."

"I know, but I'd rather you sleep. I'll be there when you wake up."

I didn't stay on the phone long; I was more than a bit pissed I wouldn't be leaving on time, and I didn't want her to think I was angry at her.

Nearly twenty hours later, I tiptoed into our bedroom. She slept, arms wrapped around my pillow, with Apollo curled up by her side. He lifted his head at my entrance, and I pointed to the floor.

After he hopped down with a heavy sigh, I slowly undressed, dropping my clothes in a pile on the floor. I pulled the sheet back slightly, and my heart nearly stopped when I saw that she wore one of my white dress shirts.

Making sure not to wake her, I climbed into bed and gently gathered her in my arms. She snuggled against me with a soft sigh of contentment. I closed my eyes.

Home.

Finally.

Chapter Twenty-four

——ABBY——

There was something important I needed to remember. In my dream, I struggled to remember what it was. Something was going to happen. Something I knew I shouldn't forget. Something. Something. Something.

As I drifted awake, I became aware of warm arms surrounding me, warm arms and the feeling of someone watching me. I slowly opened one eye.

Nathaniel!

"Hey," he said, smiling the heart-stopping grin that always and without fail melted me. There was nothing better than waking up in Nathaniel's arms. Nothing. Nothing. Nothing.

"Hey," I said, returning his smile with one of my own. "When did you get home?"

"Around four." He peeked over my shoulder to the clock on my nightstand. "About three hours ago."

"You're not sleeping?"

"No," he said. "I slept on the plane. I've been lying here, holding you. Watching you sleep." His finger traced my ear. "Did you know you have a little freckle right here, too?"

I felt my face heat. "No."

He squinted and looked at it. "I've never noticed it before." Then his lips closed in and he gently kissed the spot just behind my earlobe. "I wanted to do that, but I didn't want to wake you up."

"Like I'd have complained," I said, stretching my body against his. *Well, well, well.* "You're naked."

He laughed, but then his eyes grew serious. "Yes, and you're not."

"Hope you don't mind," I said. "I borrowed your shirt."

"Oh, no, I don't mind a bit. Looks better on you anyway. I was just thinking how it's really not fair, me naked and you not naked."

"No need to fret. Your housekeeper brought your shirts back from the dry cleaner's a few days ago." I ran a hand down his chest. "You could go get one and be not naked yourself."

"Mmmm," he hummed. "No, thank you."

I reached for him, drew him close, and inhaled his smell. "I missed you."

"Missed you," he said into my hair.

"Next time, I'm going with you," I said.

"Next time, I'll drag you with me," he said, pulling back to catch my eyes.

I drank in the sight of him. Finally home. In bed. With me. The sun shone brightly from the window behind him. "I don't want to get out of this bed all day," I said, then asked, "You don't have any plans today, do you?"

"Oh, yes," he said, rubbing his nose back and forth across my cheekbone. "I have lots and lots *and lots* of plans."

"Which would be?" I asked, hoping his plans matched up with my plans.

"For starters," he said, his breath tickling my ear and one hand tickling my stomach. "I'm going to bring us some breakfast and I'm going to use you as my table——"

"Do I get to use you as my table?"

"Absolutely," he said. "Then I plan to spend hours making love to you in every position known to man, and when we've finished"——he slowly unbuttoned the dress shirt I wore and his voice dropped lower——"we'll make up a few new positions."

I shivered as his fingers lightly stroked the tops of my breasts. I was far from cold, however. Just the opposite, in fact.

"We'll probably miss lunch, making up all those new positions," I said as matter-of-factly as possible with his hands undoing my shirt.

"Then, if it's okay with you," he said. "I want nothing more than a huge pizza covered in meat and vegetables. We could have it delivered and eat outside."

"I don't know. I was thinking lo mein. There's a new Chinese place that delivers."

He pulled back. "Really? You want Chinese?"

I laughed at his perplexed expression. "No. I was just teasing."

"Don't tease me, woman," he said, going back to work on the shirt and finally unbuttoning the last button. "I'm a desperate man."

I slipped beneath him and ran my hands over his bare ass. "You're not the only one."

Funny, I thought the next day as I knelt in my waiting position. *Somehow this wasn't what I had in mind when I answered his question yesterday.*

He'd asked the question sometime on Saturday, after pizza.

We were outside on the patio. I sat in his lap and our feet dangled in the hot tub. It was too hot, really, to be inside the water.

"We should install a pool," he said, head back as he enjoyed the sun. "But do you think it should be inside or outside?"

Outside had several advantages, but we lived in New York, so perhaps inside made more sense. I told him as much.

"The basement is relatively unfinished," he said. "Too bad we can't put it there."

"We could put it outside and enclose it."

"That might work." He thought on that for a few seconds. "We'll call a contractor next week. Have them look over the yard."

I liked how he used the word "we" so often, how it just fell naturally from his lips. I tilted my head up to kiss said lips.

"Why do you have an unfinished basement?" I asked.

He gave me another kiss. Longer. "When I first started the renovations, I couldn't decide if I wanted the playroom down there or not."

"Huh," I said. "A downstairs playroom."

"More like a dungeon."

"That sounds . . ." I thought as I spoke. "Scary."

His hands worked their way to my hair. "Dungeon. Playroom. Same thing, really."

"I like the way 'playroom' sounds," I said. "Dungeons should have chains and ropes and . . ."

He raised an eyebrow.

"Okay," I said with a laugh. "Same thing, really."

He smiled. "Speaking of playrooms, do you want to wear your collar at all this weekend? I thought maybe a few hours tomorrow?"

I ran a finger over his lips, and he captured them in a kiss. I'd missed him so much, I realized. All of him: the sweet, considerate lover of my weekdays and the stern, unyielding master of my weekends. I loved them both, needed them both.

"I'd like to wear it a few hours tomorrow," I said.

Little did I know I'd be wearing my collar as he flipped through my journal, checking to make sure I'd completed all his assignments. My head was down, of course, so I couldn't see what he was reading. I felt certain the "Interesting. Very interesting" comment came when he read the toy I picked and the scenario I detailed.

He sat in a plush chair and I was at his feet. My knees rested on the matted floor of the playroom, not on a pillow.

"Look at me, Abigail," he finally said.

I looked up and met his eyes. Would he be pleased with what I wrote? I couldn't tell by looking at him.

"You have a talent for writing," he said.

Really? I thought most of it was just random stream-of-consciousness musings.

"It seems it is an easier way for you to communicate," he continued. "And the scene you detailed is very creative."

"Thank you, Master," I said. "You inspire me."

I hoped he knew I wasn't giving gratuitous flattery, but speaking the truth. Being his submissive had released and set free a side of me I'd never known existed. The Abby of the year before would never have dreamed of thinking such things as I'd detailed in the journal, much less written them down and let someone read them.

Hell, before him, I'd had such an unfulfilled sex life, I'd almost given up on sex altogether. But now . . .

Well, I *was* kneeling, naked, at his feet.

And we'd had the most amazing sex all day the day before.

"I'm very pleased with what you have discovered, my lovely," he said. "And I want to discuss much of it with you, but for now—" He stood and walked to his cabinets. His bare feet padded as he went. "Your scene has inspired me, and I think you deserve a reward for that."

He turned to face me, and I noticed he had the ball gag and a bell in his hands.

"Go to the table," he said. "Just sit on it for now."

I rose to my feet—he hadn't told me to crawl—and walked to the table. Would he use all of my ideas or just some? I'd picked the gag over another toy, because I thought he'd use something else in addition. Though I'd also written about a new-to-me flogger, I knew he'd use it only if he wanted.

His footsteps sounded again as he walked toward me, but I kept my focus on his face. From the corner of my eye, I noted his shirtless chest and the items he still had in his hands.

"Open," he said. Then he placed the gag in my mouth. He buckled it around my head, and I felt my heart pounding. The hard *thump, thump, thump* shook my body.

"Relax," he said, stroking my hair. "You're fine. Breathe through your nose."

He let me sit for a few seconds, to acclimate myself to the feel of something in my mouth and getting used to breathing.

"Look at me," he finally said, and then continued when I met his eyes. "You can't speak your safe word now, so you need this." He placed the bell in my hand. "If you need to *yellow* or *red*, drop this. Nod if you understand."

I nodded.

"Good," he said. "Now I want you to try it. Drop the bell."

The bell fell from my hand and dropped to the floor with a ring and a thump. He bent down, picked it up, and placed it in my hand.

"Again," he said, and again I dropped the bell.

The next time, he grabbed my wrists and held them behind my back. "Again," he said. He was so close, I felt his chest against mine and his body between my legs. I dropped the bell again. He immediately let my wrists go.

Once the bell was in my hand again, he lifted my chin. "Do you feel comfortable with the bell? Nod for *yes*, shake your head for *no*."

I nodded.

He leaned in close. "It turns me on so much to see you gagged for my pleasure," he whispered, my chin still in his hand. "Excellent idea you had, Abigail." His teeth grazed my earlobe. "Let's try your next idea, why don't we?"

Yes, I thought as he pulled me from the table and bent me over it. *This is more like what I had in mind.*

I looked down at my watch. Almost time to meet Nathaniel in the foyer.

It was the next Saturday and we were heading to a meeting of Nathaniel's BDSM community friends. He said any new members had to attend a meeting prior to being allowed to the party. Since the party was later that night, we were attending the pre-party meeting that afternoon.

My brain was running in all sorts of crazy circles, and my fingers itched to write in my journal, just to make sense of the thoughts floating around my head.

It wouldn't do for me to be late meeting Nathaniel. All I needed was to give him a reason to punish me before we left. Although I'm sure everyone would know immediately what happened if I was unable to sit down.

I took one last look in the mirror. Nathaniel had picked out jeans and a T-shirt for me to wear. The tee had a V-neck, which showed off my collar, and my hair was pulled back into a low ponytail. I didn't think I looked particularly like a submissive. Was that the point?

How did a submissive look anyway?

Would I be able to pick them out at the meeting? I was fairly certain they'd be more obvious at the party.

My party outfit remained in the closet in a zipped garment bag, and more than once I'd had to resist the urge to look at it. Nathaniel had told me there was to be no peeking until I was getting ready.

On the upside, I decided that at least meant I was wearing an outfit. My crazier imagined scenarios had me going to the party naked.

I heard Nathaniel return from taking Apollo out, and I ran downstairs to meet him.

I looked at him with a more critical eye. Would everyone know he was a dominant?

Crazy, I told myself. *He knows all these people. They'll all know who and what he is.*

Which means

"Abigail," he said, a slight smirk lifting the corner of his mouth. "Is there a reason you look like the cat who ate the canary?"

I was certain his question only made my smile grow bigger. "Yes, Master. I just realized that everyone will know."

He walked toward me. How was it possible he could look so damn good just *walking*? "Everyone will know what, my lovely?"

"What you do to me," I said. "Sometimes it feels like we're hiding from everyone. Even though Elaina, Todd, and Felicia know, it's not the same. They're different because they don't participate."

"And by being around those who do?" he questioned, coming to a stop in front of me.

"I can serve you freely," I said. "I can show everyone how much I enjoy being yours." I grinned. "I can't wait."

"You can't wait," he repeated. His hands came up to rest on

my shoulders. "Not exactly the same mind frame of the submissive who had pages of fears last week."

"Yes, Master," I said, pressing my cheek against his hand as his fingers stroked my face. "Writing has helped. Thank you."

"I just gave you the tools," he said. "You had to discover everything else on your own." He moved his other hand so that he cupped my face entirely. "I'm so proud of you."

His lips were soft and light as they brushed against mine, and a shadow of yearning worked its way to my stomach. He must have felt it as well, because it wasn't long before he deepened the kiss. While his every touch claimed me, there was something about a kiss from my master that stirred a longing deep in my soul.

He finally pulled back and gave me one last light kiss. "And I can't wait to show everyone how much I enjoy being yours."

Chapter Twenty-five

——ABBY——

The preparty meeting was being held at a community resource center in the city. Nathaniel had said not everyone attending the party would be at the meeting. The meeting would consist of a lecture of sorts on a predetermined topic, and I'd sign some paperwork afterward.

"We have to protect ourselves," he said, explaining the paperwork. "Can't have just anyone attending the party."

I thought about Samantha and how she had been the one to tell me about Nathaniel. What a huge breach of protocol that must have been.

"It's just as well Samantha isn't in New York anymore," he said, as if reading my mind. "I would have hated to have been the one to talk to her. Especially since it was her faux pas that brought you to me." His tone and words told me how serious he was and how important he considered confidentiality.

We arrived at the center a little before three. Nathaniel led me into the building, his hand lightly resting at the small of my back. As always, his touch calmed me. Even though I was excited, I was still a bit nervous. Certainly, he felt the pulse of excitement running through me.

A middle-aged man waited in a doorway at the end of a short hall. He greeted Nathaniel warmly and nodded at me with a smile.

Normal, everyday people, I reminded myself. If I'd met that man in the grocery store, I wouldn't have looked at him twice. Hell, I didn't look twice at him *now*.

The room held a long conference table, with maybe fifteen people in attendance. My eyes did a quick sweep. There seemed to be an even number of men and women, though not everyone appeared to be paired up.

Of course, I told myself, not everyone would be in a couple. A group of three women stood in one corner, chatting. I noticed how one of them, a blonde, looked Nathaniel up and down. He seemed oblivious to her, but he nodded and smiled at several people. Almost everyone appeared to know him, but no one spoke directly to us.

He pulled out a chair and motioned for me to sit down. It wasn't until he was settled beside me that I looked around the room a bit more closely.

Sitting near the head of the table was the security guard from Nathaniel's office—the one who had been there the weekend of our role-play. He caught my eye, winked, and gave a little smile.

I must have made some sort of noise because Nathaniel gently squeezed my knee under the table. I looked up and he shook his head. *Not now*, he mouthed.

I bit the inside of my cheek to keep from saying anything, but returned the smile and looked at the guy again.

He had longish black hair and sharp, angular cheekbones. He leaned back in his chair, fingers thumping on his knee, head nodding as if in rhythm to a beat only he heard. No one sat near him, and I noticed he didn't wear a collar.

Dominant, I decided. *Definitely dominant.*

Knowing what he was and knowing what I needed in a relationship, I looked closer at him, trying to see if I felt any interest in him. He was nice enough to look at: he had a lean, muscular body, and a dark tattoo encircled his right arm. Outside of the appreciation I might have felt looking at a fine piece of art, I felt nothing. There was no spark, no longing, and no pull toward the man sitting at the head of the table.

I looked back at Nathaniel, however, and my whole body reacted. My pulse beat faster. My gaze dropped from his eyes to his mouth, and I shivered remembering it on me earlier. He alone called to both my body and soul. No one else even came close.

I wondered, though, as I looked once more at the man at the head of the table, if his name had been one of the ones Nathaniel contemplated giving me when I left him earlier in the year. He'd said he couldn't decide on anyone, and I wondered for the first time why. Was the dark-haired man cruel? Was there some defect in his character that made him undesirable as a dominant?

A rustle from the back of the room caught my attention, and I, along with everyone else, turned to watch the woman entering. She completely commanded the room. Even the security guard (I wished I'd at least looked at his name tag a few weeks ago so I knew what to call him) sat up straighter and gave her his full attention.

There was nothing noticeably remarkable about her. She was a large woman with nondescript hair, but her eyes were vivid and she moved with a dramatic grace. Her presence and command were undeniable.

Her name was Eve, she said, and she spoke with calm author-
ity, welcoming everyone and giving a brief rundown of the day's
topic: rope types and usage.

It didn't take long for my attention to wander away from her
discussion on the pros and cons of natural fiber ropes versus syn-
thetic fiber ropes. It wasn't anything I'd ever have to make a call
on, after all. I even noticed the blonde who had ogled Nathaniel
stifle a yawn. She glanced toward us; I gave her a small smile and
shifted closer to Nathaniel. His hand dropped down to my knee,
and I thought back to the previous weekend, when he'd played
out my written scenario.

*The ball gag. The leather flogger that felt sharper against my skin
than the suede. Nathaniel taking me, hard and fast, from behind. His
command to kneel and kiss his feet in thanks afterward.*

Gah.

I shifted uncomfortably in my seat.

Focus, I told myself, and I forced my brain to concentrate on
the many various elements that went into selecting a rope to tie
someone up. Because, really, if you thought about it, who knew
there was so much to think about?

When the talk was over and Eve had answered everyone's
questions, she dismissed us. Nathaniel stood up and pulled my
chair out.

"Ready to fill out paperwork?" he asked.

When I confirmed I was, he led me over to the dark-haired
dominant and requested the necessary papers. Then he left me
alone to read and fill them out. He did so, I knew, to show that
it was my choice. Had I not felt comfortable, we would leave, no
questions asked.

I knew what information I'd be giving since Nathaniel had
gone over what to expect and we'd discussed several aspects.
Ground rules were laid out, and if I agreed, I was to sign the last

page. The last page also collected details on the name I wanted to be called and other required information.

After I read and completed everything, I handed the dark-haired guy my paperwork.

He looked down at it, reading, before he addressed me. "Welcome, Abby," he said, his eyes lit with amusement at something. "I'm Jonah."

I shook his hand. "Hi, Jonah. Good to see you again."

"Likewise," he said, still smiling.

My face felt hot, and I blurted out the first thing coming to my head. "I thought you were a security guard."

"I am a security guard," he said. "But when Mr. West called Mistress Eve, I couldn't refuse."

That didn't make a bit of sense to me. "Just doing a favor for another dominant?" I asked.

His head shook with a confident air. "I didn't ask Mistress *why*. I don't typically question her." He laughed. "Unless, of course, I'm feeling particularly cheeky or want her to punish me."

My mouth fell open. "You're a submissive?"

"I prefer the term *bottom*," he said with a smile. "But, yes. I am."

"Oh," I said, feeling slightly stupid. "I didn't see." I pointed to my collar. "I couldn't tell."

He held up his right hand, and I noticed for the first time the leather cuff he wore on his wrist. "Not all collars go around your neck. Though I have a few of those, too."

"I only have this one," I said. Of course I knew most submissives didn't wear diamond collars. I just thought they'd be more obvious. *Idiot. That's what you get for making assumptions.*

He shrugged, his lanky shoulders rolling under his tight T-shirt. "Mr. West always does things his own way."

It occurred to me belatedly that Jonah would know a lot more about Nathaniel than just how he was as an employer. I wondered how long he'd known him, so I asked.

"I've known him for about three years," he said. "Been working for him for one. He's a good boss. Has a good head on his shoulders. Not many CEOs know their weekend security supervisor." He smiled his lazy grin. "He's a good top, too. I've seen him in action before."

"You have?" I asked, hoping my eyes weren't bugging out too much.

"Sure," he said. "He and his previous submissive, what's her name?"

"Beth," I said, and wondered if she'd be at the party.

"Right. They used to do some demonstrations on occasion."

Nathaniel had been a dom for more than ten years. He'd told me a lot about his past submissives and what they had done. I knew he'd been active in the community as both a mentor and a participant. I didn't feel jealous at the thought of his being with other women before me. I rested comfortably in the knowledge I was the one he wanted. For now and forever. None of his other submissives shared his bed, his heart, or his mind the way I did. They didn't play a part in his tree house dreams.

"You know," Jonah said, interrupting my thoughts. "I'm part of a submissives group that gets together once a month. Would you like to come to our next meeting?"

My last writing assignment while Nathaniel was in China had been to detail where I wanted to be, as a submissive, in five years. I'd written that I wanted to be active in mentoring novice submissives, much like Nathaniel had mentored dominants. I wanted to help others the way Christine had helped me, the way this group might help me.

"That would be great," I said. "What do you do?" It was hard to imagine a group of submissives sitting around talking about, well, being submissive.

He leaned against the table and crossed his arms. "Depends," he said. "Last meeting, one of our members shared her recipe for homemade pasta and we all tried to make some."

My laugh drew the attention of several other people. Even Nathaniel lifted his eyebrow at me. He was talking with the blonde.

"Sorry," I said to Jonah. "Whatever I was expecting you to do, homemade pasta wasn't it."

"That's okay. I suppose it does sound odd at first, and we do have discussions about the lifestyle. Here," he said, taking a piece of paper from the table and writing something down. "Here's my number. Call me and I'll give you the time and directions."

I took the paper. "Thanks."

"I have to go," he said, looking over my shoulder to where Eve must have been motioning for him. "See you tonight."

"Definitely," I said. "It'll be so nice to know one other person."

"Well," he said, eyes dancing with amusement. "I probably won't be much good for you; I'll be tied up." He leaned close. "Mistress and I are doing the Japanese bondage demo."

As he walked away, my face heated thinking about just how much of him I'd probably be seeing later.

"Are you ready to go, Abigail?" Nathaniel asked, coming up behind me and placing his hand on my shoulder.

"Yes, Master," I said, surprised at how easily the word *master* came out. How it didn't seem odd with my current company.

"I saw you talking with Jonah. He's a bright, intelligent man. He leads my weekend security crew."

We started walking out. "It was a surprise seeing him," I said.

"Very handy that Eve was willing to let me use him the way she did."

I remembered how Jonah had acted the weekend of our role-play. How he kept his eyes on my face, never letting them wander to the rest of me. Even when Nathaniel and I had left wearing different clothes, he'd just said a pleasant "Have a nice day."

"Very handy, Master," I agreed.

"I'm quite sure Eve rewarded him handsomely. I told her he was a testament to her training."

His words struck me. "I hope I'm a testament to your training, Master."

"You are, my lovely," he said. "And for coming through your first meeting with flying colors, I'm going to reward you nicely when we get home."

"Whatever you think best, Master," I said with a smile.

My reward consisted of being bound to his table, spread-eagle with my knees bent, ass at the edge of the table, while his lips trailed downward. He nibbled and licked, lower, lower, lower, until, *hell, yes, right there*—

He lifted his head.

What the fuck?

"You can come whenever you want and as many times as you want," he said, his breath warm against my sensitive flesh. "But you can't move or vocalize at all."

Evil. The man was completely and utterly evil.

And I loved it.

I forced my body to be still as he worked me with his lips, his fingers, and his tongue. Slowly and methodically, he pushed me, knowing exactly what to do and how my body would react.

My first orgasm slowly built and softly rippled through me. I held my body still without any difficulties. However, even as soft and quiet as it was, it had not gone unnoticed by Nathaniel.

"Yes," he whispered. "Beautiful."

His hands grew bolder, working my body with long sweeps across my nipples and breasts, long brushes across my belly, until finally he concentrated his full attention between my legs. This time he was more forceful, his nose rubbing my clit—*dear sweet heavens, right there*—while his tongue dipped lower.

It was harder to hold still as my second orgasm approached. My knees wanted to wobble, and I had to struggle to keep my hips still when what I really wanted to do was push them against his mouth. I did it, however, and remained still the second time.

"Excellent," he said, rubbing his nose up and down against my upper thigh as my body settled. "I want so badly to fuck you right now."

He wasn't the only one.

"But I'm going to wait," he said. "You're not allowed my cock until after the party. And even then, only if you deserve it."

Completely and utterly evil. Just as I thought.

It was a modest house, much like Paul and Christine's. Nothing ostentatious and nothing on the outside that gave any indication of what was happening on the inside. Of course, that was part of the reason I had to wear an overcoat. Nathaniel said it wouldn't be respectful of our hosts to show up at their house wearing (or not wearing) any old thing.

Under the overcoat was the outfit Nathaniel had picked out for me: a beautiful black lace corset. The cups were padded so no nipple showed, though peeks of my torso could be seen through the lace. My delicate panties and garters were covered by a skirt so short I'd never wear it in public but was excited to wear tonight. He had hinted he might have me remove the skirt at some point, but even then, I knew a bathing suit would reveal just as much, if not more, of me.

Nathaniel kept his hand on my back as we approached and gave our names to the man at the front door. Once he let us inside, we were met by a woman I assumed to be our hostess.

"Nathaniel," she said, and as was becoming the rule, she looked absolutely normal. "So good to see you again." Her attention turned to me. "This must be Abby."

I exchanged pleasantries with her, but was anxious to see the rest of the house. I was almost desperate to see what happened at a play party. Finally, Nathaniel pulled us away and I could observe more. My eyes wanted to skip around and take everything in at once, but I forced myself to look at one thing at a time.

The first thing I noticed was all the open doors.

"No playing in closed rooms allowed," Nathaniel had said. "If a door is closed, the room is off-limits, and if you're in a room, the door has to be open."

Made sense if you asked me. It seemed safer that way.

I heard soft moans coming from the room closest to us, but Nathaniel wasn't taking us there yet. We stayed in the living room, and though a few people talked to us, the main reason, I knew, was for me to grow used to being there.

I saw one or two people who were completely naked and a handful of others who were close. Most people, like Nathaniel, wore jeans and a T-shirt, though there were several women wearing outfits similar to mine. One woman wore a leash held by a man. She knelt at his feet, looking down at the floor while he talked with someone else.

Minus the now louder moans and the state of dress of several attendees, it could be any party held anywhere.

"Contrary to what others think," Nathaniel had said, "parties aren't huge orgies. Though there are groups and clubs that cater to that sort of thing. It just isn't what I happen to enjoy."

No penetration of any kind was allowed among Nathaniel's group at parties.

"Not even between couples such as us," he said. "Anyone who wants to take play further will have to do so afterward, on their own time and in their own space."

I felt somewhat relieved knowing I wouldn't be seeing people having sex. And standing and people-watching was nice, but it really wasn't why we were there.

I looked up at Nathaniel and lightly brushed his hand, our predetermined signal that I was ready to explore the house more. He raised his eyebrow at me and I nodded.

Together, we moved to the nearest room, the one with the woman moaning. When we made our way through a small press of people, I saw her.

She was bent over a padded table, similar to the one Nathaniel had in his playroom, while being flogged. With a start, I realized she was the blonde who had spoken to Nathaniel after the meeting. I'd meant to ask him what she wanted but hadn't found the time. I couldn't very well ask him in the middle of the party either.

Later, I told myself.

"Notice the way she arches," Nathaniel whispered so only I heard. He stood behind me and, as he spoke, his hands came around my waist. "How she silently pleads for the next stroke of the flogger. How her body craves it."

Watching her body move as the man flogged her, I saw what Nathaniel was talking about. How she moved, how she lifted herself. I watched the man walking around her, toy in hand as he teased, tormented, and played her. I was surprised to find myself moving with her against Nathaniel's body.

Another thing that surprised me was how it was as if we weren't even there. She didn't pay us any mind, and neither she, nor the person flogging, seemed to care or be apprehensive about playing in front of others. Her freedom excited me.

Nathaniel's hands moved up, brushing the side of my breasts. "In your journal, you said you wanted to be a mentor in five years," he said. "Is that still the case?"

The man we were watching brought the flogger down across the woman's ass with a loud snap. I swore I could feel the heat on my own skin, and I pressed back against Nathaniel.

"Yes, Master," I said.

"Would you like to, one day, be a more active participant at one of these parties? To have everyone watch as I flog you and bring you what you crave?" he asked. "To serve me more publicly?"

"Yes, Master," I said, pressing harder against him. I couldn't feel his erection through his jeans, but I was certain he had one.

"Exhibitionist fantasy?"

The football stadium. Paul and Christine's. The library.

Naughty delights made more exciting by the risk of apprehension.

"Yes, Master."

His voice was low and deep. "Take off your skirt."

Chapter Twenty-six

—NATHANIEL—

It had been more than six months since I'd attended my last party and, I had to admit, it felt good being back among my peers. It felt even better with Abby at my side. I enjoyed watching the experience from her novice point of view, but even more so, I enjoyed watching her nervousness dissolve into titillation.

I couldn't focus on the scene playing out before me; my body and mind were drawn to Abby. She moved against me, brushing me each time the flogger tails landed on the blonde's ass. *Mary*, I corrected myself. *The blonde's name is Mary.*

She had sent her application to Godwin, the gentleman who screened my submissives, around the same time Abby suggested submitting her own application the second time. I thought telling Godwin I wasn't interested would be enough. Of course, it escaped my attention that Mary would probably be in attendance at the meeting and the party.

She had approached me after the meeting, while Abby filled out paperwork.

Yes, I confirmed. I did remember Godwin mentioning her.

No, I was not looking for a new submissive.

No, I did not anticipate *ever* looking for a new submissive.

Yes, I would be at the party.

No, I would not be interested in participating in anything with her.

Ever, I had finally added, in hopes of dissuading further conversation.

She took everything well, even though I feared I'd been rather short with her. Another time and in another place, I might have been interested. She was easy to look at and she had a carefree attitude many doms would like, but she was nothing I was interested in. Not when I already had everything I'd ever wanted.

Abby.

At my command to take her skirt off, she kept her eyes on the scene in front of us, but moved her hands behind her. She slowly unzipped her skirt, but not before pushing closer and brushing my cock with her hand.

"Naughty," I whispered, loving her playfulness. "You'll pay for that one, Abigail."

The second stroke of her hand told me she was more than looking forward to it.

She slid the skirt over her hips and pushed it to the floor, stepping out of it one leg at a time. Her eyes were still focused on the scene in front of her when she handed the skirt back to me.

"Fold it and put it in your purse," I said.

I had no plans for her to participate at all that night, nothing beyond a few simple commands. I loved her and I respected her, but I would also push her. Attending the party, taking her skirt off and walking around in a corset, garters, and panties, was enough of a push for one night. I didn't want to scare her, after all.

However, since her long-term goals lined up with mine, perhaps in a few months we would host our own party at our house. Push her a bit more. Maybe do a simple demo scene. On our way home from the meeting, she'd told me about her conversation with Jonah. I was glad he'd asked her to join the submissives group. She would find mentors there, and the companionship and support would help her grow and flourish.

Listen to yourself, West, I scolded myself. *You're thinking long-term goals, growth, and flourishing at a play party. Hell, man, loosen up.*

The scene before us was winding down. I glanced at my watch. Almost time for Eve and Jonah's demo.

"Abigail," I said, pulling her attention away from the couple. "Come with me."

I'd instructed her to walk slightly behind me and to always be within touching distance, knowing that forcing her to concentrate on something besides her nervousness would help calm her. Of course, she hadn't seemed too nervous watching the flogging scene.

I led her through the living area, which was joined to a spacious kitchen. The living room and kitchen were considered neutral areas, I'd told her earlier. No play could be carried out in them, though I knew I could have her serve me in small ways, such as feeding me.

I noticed a small love seat and end table positioned near the kitchen.

Mmm. Later, perhaps.

The bondage demo was being held upstairs in a spare bedroom. Since this was something new to her, I thought it would be a good idea for Abby to see it played out before we tried it.

After we took our places, I looked around the room. There were several people I knew and recognized, but many were new or unknown. I thought Carter and Jen, a couple I'd played with in the past, would be in attendance, but so far I hadn't seen them. I was a bit relieved. Abby knew of them, but I feared it would be somewhat awkward. Besides, there was another couple in attendance that might be more awkward, but so far, so good.

Eve and Jonah were preparing for the demo. Eve stood behind him, whispering something to him no one else could hear. Every so often, he would speak, his lips forming a quiet, "Yes, Mistress."

I had known Jonah for a good number of years and was happy he now worked for me. He'd thrived in the leadership position at work, but in his private life, he craved and needed the domination Eve gave him.

She was certainly dressed for the occasion, with high, spiked heels and a tight black leather skirt and bustier. Jonah, of course, was naked.

While viewing scenes, I'd told Abby she was to be in front of me. I wanted her view unencumbered, and I wanted to whisper in her ear. As she took in the couple before her, I put a hand on each of her shoulders and pulled her to me.

"Jonah thoroughly enjoys this sort of thing," I whispered in explanation, because she might have a hard time reconciling the spirited man she'd met earlier with the one before her. "He loves demos. Exhibitionism," I said. "Almost as much as he enjoys mentoring. He is a complex sort of a guy, so many layers to his personality." I kissed the back of her neck. "Similar to you. I'm pleased he's shown an interest in taking you under his wing."

Jonah would be a good friend for her. A reputable confidant and one I could trust implicitly.

The demo started and Eve spoke, walking a fine line between instructing the attendees and keeping part of her attention focused on her submissive.

She picked up two ropes and briefly discussed their differences.

"I use ropes for two purposes," I whispered in Abby's ear as she watched. I dropped my hands from her shoulders to capture her wrists behind her back. "The first is to immobilize, to keep you in place for my pleasure. Remember the weekend I took the pictures?"

She would recall that weekend, I knew. The way I'd kept her bound while I took her from behind.

"The second," I said, "is to tease and torment you. All based upon rope and knot placement."

I paused for a second so she could pay attention to what Eve was doing. The domme took a piece of rope and bound it around Jonah's upper thigh while explaining the knot she used.

"Done correctly," I said as Eve continued tying the rope around Jonah's hips, "you could wear the ropes under your clothes." I cupped her breasts. "Imagine walking around with ropes binding you here. The pressure. The pulling. The friction." My hands skirted down to her hips. "Or here. How I could put them between your legs with just enough pressure to torment you. I could keep them there for hours, making you go about your day as if nothing's different at all. Not let you find your release."

We watched for a few minutes more.

"She's using black rope tonight," I whispered while Eve talked about several rope safety concerns. "And while that's a nice choice, I think I'll use red on you." Abby's body shuddered as I ran my hands down her back. "Such a nice contrast to your pale skin."

Eve was doing something to Jonah. I could hear his moans. My focus, however, was on Abby.

"The type of bondage I'm wanting to try can be very intense," I said, as in the background Eve commanded Jonah's silence. "We'd need a long weekend. What do you think, Abigail? Does the idea excite you?"

"Yes, Master," she whispered.

"What do you think of the timing?" I asked. The closest holiday was Labor Day.

"I have a long weekend coming up in August."

She'd told me Martha was giving her some time off. "Are you sure?" I asked.

"Mmmm," she hummed, as I stroked her hips. "Yes, Master."

"I'll mark it on the calendar."

When Eve finished tying Jonah up, she spoke silently to him for a few minutes and then slowly started untying him.

"As erotic as it can be to tie someone up," I whispered to Abby, "it can also be erotic to untie them." I swept my hands along her upper arms. "Imagine my hands slowly releasing the pressure of the ropes. My lips softly tracing their path. Can you feel it?"

"I want to, Master."

The first rope fell from around Jonah's arm.

"Do you see the marks?" I asked her. "They're faint, but they're there."

The ropes hadn't been on him long enough to leave a deep impression, but they were there if you looked hard enough. As we watched, Eve started untying his legs.

"When I take the ropes off you, the lines will be obvious," I said. "I'll trace them with my fingers. The sensation will be like nothing you've experienced."

A few minutes later, the demo was over and people started leaving.

"There's a love seat downstairs, near an end table," I told Abby. "Go fix a plate of snacks and grab a bottle of water." I didn't particularly feel like drinking soda, and alcohol was prohibited. "I'll be down in ten minutes for you to serve me. If the love seat is occupied, stand nearby and wait for it."

Feeding me would be a small type of public service, but it would turn her on. Of that, I was certain. Abby had a streak of exhibitionism in her, and this would be a very subtle and nearly inconspicuous way to explore that side.

After she left, I turned and chatted a few minutes with Eve, glancing at my watch to check the time.

"She's very lovely," Eve said when it became obvious my mind was not on our chat.

"Thanks," I said. "She was a bit nervous about coming tonight, but I think she's done extremely well. I'm glad Jonah talked with her today."

She glanced at him; he was bent over, tidying up the ropes and packing them away. At first sight, they didn't appear to go together, but I knew they shared a deep bond.

"He said he invited her to the next meeting," she said.

"I'm happy about that," I said. "It'll be good for her to be around others. Be sure to pass my thanks on to him."

She smiled a sly grin. "Oh, I will," she said. "Most definitely."

I matched her grin and was still smiling as I descended the stairs a few minutes later. I glanced once more at my watch. Abby would be waiting for me. I'd let her feed me for a few minutes and then I'd let her take her own refreshment. By then I would probably have had enough of the press of people. We would leave and I'd take her home, play a bit in the playroom . . .

My smile froze as I reached the bottom stair.

She stood waiting, as per my instruction, at the love seat

with a plate of snacks and a bottle of water. Standing, because the love seat was occupied.

Occupied by the one couple I wasn't eager to introduce her to: Nicolas and Gwen.

My eyes barely registered Gwen. I saw that she was naked, kneeling beside Nicolas, and he held her leash. She didn't see me, and I didn't make a move to catch her attention or to see if I felt anything at seeing her; my focus was on Abby.

Abby shook her head, responding negatively to something Nicolas said. He lifted his arm, perhaps to touch her. Perhaps not, but the possibility existed.

I made it across the room in less than two seconds.

"Don't even fucking *think* about touching her," I said in a low whisper, so as not to draw the attention of other party guests.

His hand froze and he turned to me, a smile of absolute evil joy plastered on his face. "West," he said, dropping his hand back to his lap. "What a pleasant surprise. I haven't seen you in months."

I looked over to Abby. Her eyes were wide.

"Did he touch you?" I asked. "Say anything inappropriate?"

Nicolas was not a bad dom, and I was treading on thin ice to even suggest anything of the sort.

I just didn't care.

"No, Master," she said.

"Master?" Nicolas repeated. "Oh, is she yours, West?" Without waiting for a response, he continued. "Hard to tell with that ridiculous excuse of a collar." He waved to the woman at his feet who wore a thick, black leather collar. "You really should mark your property more appropriately."

I spoke through clenched teeth. "I don't believe I need pointers from you."

"Is that so?" he asked. "I'd have to disagree with you on that.

I'm sure my girl here would do the same, but she's not allowed to talk tonight. Else you could ask her yourself."

Abby was watching us, her head moving from me to Nicolas to Gwen as if watching a tennis match.

Fucking hell.

Gwen kept her head down through our entire exchange. Knowing what I knew of her, I expected no less.

Nicolas was under no such restrictions, however, and he looked Abby up and down.

"I heard you had a new submissive," he said. "And that you were—what's the word? In *love?*"

"Shut the fuck up," I warned, clenching my fists. It wouldn't be wise to start something now. Not in public. Not at a house party.

"She's something else," he said. "Maybe one day I'll have the opportunity to enjoy her."

That crossed the line. I'd have to think on what to do about it when I was in a calmer frame of mind.

I moved, took the plate and water bottle from Abby. *I'm sorry,* I mouthed, before moving to stand in between her and Nicolas.

"Abigail," I said. "Put your skirt on."

A dungeon monitor clapped his hand on my shoulder, immediately defusing the situation. "Is there a problem here, folks?"

"No," Nicolas and I both said in unison.

"I'll have to escort you all outside if you can't be civil," he said.

It would probably look bad for Abby and me to leave. At that moment, I just didn't care. Seeing Nicolas look at Abby. Looking at Abby with Gwen at his feet, imagining . . .

"We were just leaving," I said, putting the food and water down and taking Abby's hand.

But that, of course, wasn't enough for Nicolas.

"When you can't be what she needs, either," he called out as we wove our way through the living room to gather Abby's coat, "be sure to give her my number. I might not mind the sloppy seconds in her case."

His laugh echoed behind us.

The ride home was quiet. Looking back, I knew Abby was probably afraid to talk. That she wasn't sure of what to say. At the time, however, I just assumed she wasn't talking because she had her collar on and didn't want to speak first, or out of turn.

I don't remember much of the drive home. It seemed to take no time at all before I pulled into our driveway and up to the house.

I slammed the car door and walked over to open hers. I didn't say anything as she got out of the car and walked behind me up the front stairs.

"Playroom in ten minutes," I said, because it was what she expected and what I assumed she wanted.

I took Apollo out, but it was all very mechanical. One foot in front of the other type stuff. Nothing requiring me to pull my mind away from Nicolas and Gwen and the myriad emotions they'd caused in me.

Abby knelt in the playroom when I made it up the stairs. I registered the fact that she still wore her party outfit.

You didn't tell her to take it off.

I told her to disrobe and move to the padded table, though to be honest, I really didn't have a solid plan as to what I was going to do. She stood, undressed quickly, and walked to the table.

As she did so, I went to the cabinets, hoping to be inspired by what I found there. I picked up a heavy flogger, remembering the last time I used it. It had been with Gwen. I ran my fingers through the tails.

Nicolas's voice echoed in my head. *When you can't be what she needs, either.*

I was exactly what she needed, I told myself. I turned. She was positioned, bent over the table, waiting.

Why didn't it occur to me that Nicolas and Gwen would be at the party?

Why didn't I think to warn her about him?

I took slow, careful steps to where she waited.

I should have told her when I first saw them.

She waited.

I brought my free hand back and spanked her a few times. She held completely still as the color slowly rose to her skin.

I'll always be what she needs.

I lifted the flogger and struck her on her upper thighs. She gave a short intake of breath. I took it as a sign to move forward and struck her higher. On her ass the next time.

I was still hearing Nicolas's laugh when I brought the flogger down the third time.

She shifted before me. "Yellow."

Time stopped.

"Yellow," she whispered again. "Please."

I blinked.

I stared at the flogger I held in horror. *What am I doing?* "Stop," I whispered as the flogger fell to the ground. Then I spoke louder. "Red. Oh, hell. Red."

She looked up and over her shoulder. "Master?"

"I'm sorry." I shook my head. "I can't."

She looked truly worried for the first time. "Nathaniel?"

I turned and went into the bathroom adjoining the playroom and took a bathrobe hanging from a hook. When I made it back, I draped it around her, then unhooked her collar and slipped it into my pocket.

I was shaking when I took her hand. "Come to the bedroom with me?"

"Nathaniel?" she asked as we walked down the hall. "Are you okay?"

I didn't answer her. I didn't know how.

Once we made it to the bedroom, I climbed onto the bed and pulled her into my lap, smelled her hair. I needed her to ground me after the intensity of the night. I needed to feel her in my arms, to know she was with me.

"I'm sorry," I finally said. "I should have never asked you to go into the playroom tonight. Not after what happened at the party. Thank you for using your safe word."

"What happened?"

"I wasn't in the right frame of mind," I said. "Not after seeing them. I thought I could do it, though. Thought it was what you wanted and that you'd be disappointed if we didn't."

"This is about that couple, isn't it?"

"I'm sorry," I said. "I should have realized they'd be there and mentioned them to you. When I saw them the first time, I should have said something."

"Who are they?" She reached up and smoothed her hands over my hair. I hadn't realized I'd been pulling at it.

"After Melanie and I split," I said. "Well, after I broke it off with her, I dove back into the scene hard-core. I hadn't played in more than six months. I was anxious to get back."

She nodded. "I can understand that."

"Gwen and I met at a party. Gwen's the woman with Nicolas," I said. "I never collared her. We never made it past the test weekend."

"Why?"

"She needed more than I could give."

She tilted her head. "Like Melanie?"

"No," I said, then whispered, "More pain."

I felt guilty remembering how Jackson asked me if I knew of any available women my first weekend with Abby and how I'd joked with myself about giving him her name.

"Oh," she replied in her own whisper.

"Everything with her was always *green*. She always wanted more," I said. "And I couldn't do it. It's like the breath play—I know my own limits. I know how much pain I'm willing to inflict and what I can't."

She nodded. "And Nicolas?"

"Obviously gives her what she wants," I said. "Which is fine. He's an asshole, but he's not abusive. His remark about playing with you was inappropriate, however. I'll think about how to handle that later."

She snorted. "I'd agree with you on the asshole part."

"I'd like for us to talk later about when play borders on or becomes abuse," I said. "I think it's an important topic." I thought for a second. "Maybe have an open-forum-type discussion at the next meeting."

"You mean when someone asks for something that's dangerous?" she asked. "Is that what Gwen did to you?"

"She didn't ask for anything dangerous," I said. "Just more than I was comfortable doing. Which is why it's important to know your limits, both as a dom and as a submissive. I knew how far I was willing to go. I don't so much see it as failing with her. We were just incompatible. I should have known it wouldn't work out. I gave more stringent guidelines to Godwin after Gwen."

"But seeing me standing next to Nicolas?"

I closed my eyes briefly and nodded. "Yes. I think it was what he said: 'When you can't be what she needs either.'"

"Oh, Nathaniel."

"I think it just played upon my old fears," I said. "Made me upset, and I couldn't get into the frame of mind I need to be in to play."

"You didn't actually think I'd leave you for Nicolas?"

"Hell, no. That never once occurred to me." I smiled for the first time in hours. "Progress, yes?"

"I'll say," she said. She smiled so big I couldn't help but lean down and kiss her. "Mmm," she said. "What was that for?"

"For loving me," I said. "For putting up with me. For trusting me." I pulled back, feeling a little better since we'd talked about everything. "I should never have told you to go into the playroom."

"You stopped though," she said. "You didn't let it progress."

"I let it progress enough, and for that I'm sorry."

"You gave me safe words for a reason. Now I see why."

"Why did you *yellow*?"

"Everything felt off," she said. "Not quite right after the party. Then, when I recognized it was a different flogger and it felt harder, I just needed to slow everything down. Get to where I needed to be."

I stroked her back, reached down to cup her bottom. "Did I hurt you? Are you sore?"

"I'm fine," she said. "Promise."

"I love you," I said, just needing to say the words.

"And I love you," she replied, probably knowing how much I needed to hear the words.

"So, Gwen?"

"What about her?"

"You two played?"

I shrugged. "Not for long, but yes. Does it make you uncomfortable seeing submissives I've played with?"

She wrinkled her brow in concentration. "It's weird, but not uncomfortable. I know you had submissives before me."

"That's different from seeing them."

"Yes, but it's still the same. I know your past. I love your past, actually. It's what made you, you." She took my face between her hands and looked deeply into my eyes. "And you, all of you, past, present, everything, are the man I love."

I held her gaze. "You may not have been my first submissive," I said. "But I swear by all I hold holy, you'll be my last."

She leaned close, preparing to kiss me. "I'd better be."

Her lips were soft and gentle on mine.

Exactly what I needed.

Chapter Twenty-seven

——ABBY——

As he worked the rope around my upper left leg, I thought back over the last few weeks and what had happened since the night we both safe worded.

He'd refused to recollar me that night. Instead, we went to bed and slept wrapped in each other's arms. I still recalled the way I drifted off to sleep with his leg draped almost protectively across my thigh. The next morning, we talked more about Gwen and Nicolas and even Mary. By midmorning, we both felt calmer and more relaxed, so we agreed together that I would wear his collar for the rest of the day.

I felt more connected with him after that night. I'd known, of course, that he would slow down or stop if I safe worded, but somehow experiencing it reconfirmed just how much I could trust him. He said the situation did the same for him, that he felt better knowing I would safe word if I needed.

I went to the submissives group meeting, and Jonah was quick to introduce me around. In addition to the lifestyle knowledge I gained, I was surprised by the different feelings I had toward some members of the group.

Jonah was like my older brother, laughing and cutting up at times, protective and supportive at others. As one of the more experienced members, he was looked up to by everyone. I quickly learned that he and his mistress were both highly regarded in the community.

Nicolas's actions had not gone unnoticed the night of the party, and according to Jonah, he had been asked to leave shortly after Nathaniel and I left and was told not to come back. Gwen was still welcome, though, and I was more than a little shocked to see her at my first group meeting.

She seemed an independent, self-assured type of a woman. I barely recognized her as the naked submissive who knelt at Nicolas's feet. Even more shocking was the almost complete lack of anything I felt toward her, especially considering she'd played with Nathaniel.

The woman I felt the most jealous toward was Jen. When I thought about it, I knew it made no sense. Jen was in a committed relationship with Carter, had played with Nathaniel only a few times and only with Carter in attendance. Still, I suppose that's how jealousy worked. It didn't have to make sense. Especially when I knew Nathaniel felt nothing for Jen. For the most part I ignored it.

Toward Mary, I'll admit, I felt a bit superior. I had what she wanted. Nathaniel was *my* master. Nathaniel was *my* lover. It was his collar I wore and his hands that guided and owned my body on weekends. She could send in her application to Godwin all she wanted. There was no way and no how he would ever be hers.

"Is there a reason for the vindictive-looking grin, Abigail?" Nathaniel asked, bringing me back to the business at hand.

"No, Master," I said. I thought about sharing what I'd been thinking, maybe add in a bit of snarky attitude, but decided not to. There was a time and place for feisty, after all.

He raised an eyebrow. "Do we need to move to the whipping bench in order to settle your mind?"

Uh-oh. Definitely not the time for feisty. It didn't escape my attention the way he used *we*. It would be my choice.

"No, Master," I said, hopefully removing from my face any lingering traces of the smile.

He shot me a stern look before resuming his knot tying. We had spent time over the last few weekends (and one really enjoyable Wednesday night) working up to this point. One day he'd bound my chest with multiple ropes and knots; another day he'd bound my legs. The weekend would be a combination of them all.

Since he hadn't told me not to, I closed my eyes and concentrated on his hands while he wound the rope around me. He worked methodically and slowly, taking the rope and winding it around the upper part of one leg before moving to the opposite one.

His lips trailed up my belly and he spoke in soft tones. "I bind you for my pleasure," he said. "You'll spend all day and night in the ropes." He brushed a hand between my legs. "I'm going to place some knots here to tease you and you're not allowed release until I give permission."

Fuuuuck.

He kept right on talking. "I have a dress for you upstairs. You'll wear it to Linda's. No one will know or be able to tell what you have on underneath." He chuckled low in his throat. "Or what you don't have on."

Something told me there weren't panties laid out with the dress.

"I'll put some quick-release hooks here," he said, brushing right below my navel. "When you need to use the bathroom, you'll have to ask me, and I'll remove the rope between your legs."

The picnic at his aunt's house would be in a few hours. Everyone would be there. Due to our demanding schedules, the entire family hadn't been together for nearly a month. I was looking forward to it.

Nathaniel placed a thin rope between my legs, making sure it rubbed me just so.

Looking forward to it for more than one reason.

"This is just the beginning," he whispered.

"You look beautiful," he said as we drove to Linda's house.

"Thank you, Master."

True to his word, the ropes were discreetly covered by the dress he'd picked out. Underneath, I had ropes around my upper thighs, my waist, and between my legs. He'd refused to let me wear a bra. Instead, red ropes were wound around my upper body, both above and below my breasts, with more rope in between. Though the dress was short-sleeved, a high turtleneck covered the rope that looped behind my neck in a halter-top fashion.

When I moved my arms just the right way, the tension of the ropes and the pull of the dress fabric against my exposed nipples caused my body to shiver.

"I think I'd like to listen to some jazz," he said.

Yes, when I move just like that.

"Thank you, Abigail," he said with a grin that told me he knew exactly what I was feeling when I changed the satellite radio station.

"No, Master," I said as soft jazz filled the car's interior. "Thank *you*."

An hour later, I stood in the backyard talking with Linda and Elaina while Todd, Jackson, Nathaniel, and Felicia played an unevenly matched game of basketball. I'd gracefully declined joining in, especially since I had a dress on. Sports were not my favorite pastime, though playing with the ropes around my body would have made things interesting.

"Nathaniel told us you're going to Florida next month?" Linda asked.

"Orlando, yes," I said. "I'm looking forward to it. I haven't had a real vacation in years."

"Neither has Nathaniel," Elaina said.

"I'm afraid this won't be much of one," I said. "It's a finance conference, and he's the keynote speaker." We would check in on a Saturday and stay until the following Friday. I was looking forward to the trip as it would offer new ways to play.

"Just promise me you'll get him out of his suit for a few hours," Linda said. "He could do with a little rest and relaxation."

Elaina leaned in and whispered, "I'm sure you'll get him out of his suit for more than a few hours."

I laughed. "I'm sure I will." We'd be in Florida for weekday time as well as weekend time, and if I had my way, he wouldn't be wearing his suit outside of the conference. He wouldn't be wearing much of *anything*.

Linda shot her what was supposed to be a stern look, but she succeeding only in making us laugh louder. I loved the closeness of everyone. Loved how they'd welcomed both Felicia and me with open arms.

True to Nathaniel's word, no one had been able to tell what I had on under my dress. I liked to think Linda didn't know of our lifestyle. She'd never given either of us any indication she did, after all. Regardless, the two of us had grown close over the last few months, and I very much considered her a second mother.

Elaina was the sister I never had. Though she knew about my and Nathaniel's relationship on a high level, she never spoke of it with me and, truthfully, that was the way I wanted it.

Jackson, I didn't know about. Nathaniel told me he didn't think he knew, so for the time being, I'd pretend he didn't know. Felicia may have told him, but even if she had, he never treated me any differently than before.

I didn't know the basketball game was over until I was surrounded by two very strong, very warm arms.

"Ugh," Elaina said from beside me, pushing Todd away. He'd captured her in the same type of hug Nathaniel had me in. "You're sweating."

Mmm. Nathaniel.

"Are you okay?" he whispered.

"Yes," I said, not adding the *Master*. We were too close to his family and they might overhear.

His arms pressed tighter around me, hitting the ropes just right. "Are you sure?"

I closed my eyes and leaned against him as a wave of desire swept through me. "Very."

"You'll let me know if anything becomes uncomfortable?" he asked.

I nodded. "Yes."

"You're doing great," he whispered. He pulled away before I could respond. "Can I help you do something for lunch?" he asked his aunt.

"No," she said. "Everything's ready."

Jackson walked up beside us and took the drink Felicia handed him. "Missed you playing with us today, Elaina."

Elaina brushed imaginary lint from Todd's shirt. "Apparently, they didn't teach Todd in medical school that pregnant women could exercise."

It took about four seconds for what she said to sink in, and then everyone spoke at once.

"You're pregnant?"

"Why didn't you say something sooner?"

"How long?"

Through it all, Elaina and Todd stood there, looking around at their family and smiling.

"I'm ten weeks," Elaina said, once we all shut up long enough for her to get a word in. "We heard the heartbeat yesterday."

Before Nathaniel and I could join the rest of the family in congratulating the parents-to-be with hugs, he slipped an arm around my waist.

"The tree house will be a lot more fun with nieces and nephews joining in, won't it?" he whispered to me.

I turned my head to him, and our lips met in a soft kiss.

When we made it back to our house (it was still something of a shock to view the imposing mansion as *ours*), he told me to go upstairs and prepare his shower. It was a new type of command, but not an altogether unexpected one. He was still sweaty, after all, and in need of a shower.

By the time he took Apollo outside and made it up the stairs, I'd started his shower and set towels on the warmer bar. Because it just seemed like the right thing to do, I also stripped out of the dress. I couldn't decide whether to kneel or stand, so when he walked in, I was still standing.

He glanced at the dress on the floor. "Everything okay, Abigail?"

"Yes, Master," I said. He still had his clothes on. He looked delicious.

"Do you need to use the bathroom?"

Well, yes. Now that he mentioned it, I did.

"Please, Master."

He walked across the floor and quickly undid the rope between my legs. Not before taking the time to play with my exposed nipples, of course.

I moaned at the press of his thumb.

He laughed and gave me a swift smack on the ass. "Hurry up and make your way back here. I need your help."

His bathroom was huge. During the weekend, I thought of it as his bathroom, even though evidence of my cohabitation was scattered around one of the vanities. On weekends, I usually used the bathroom connected to the submissive bedroom.

When I made it back to the main portion of the bathroom, he had undressed. I tried not to think about how he looked even more delicious undressed but failed miserably. He smiled as if he knew exactly what I was thinking.

Damn.

"Later, Abigail."

Right. He'd said no release until he permitted.

Double damn.

He trailed his hands down my body, teasing and tickling as he worked the rope back between my legs. Standing so close to him, both of us naked, was a challenge in remaining still, but I managed to pull it off.

He hooked the rope back, gave my clit one last, soft caress, and whispered, "You're doing such a great job."

I shifted my legs, accustomed now to the pull against my

body and the constant low-level tormenting tease of the ropes. "Thank you, Master."

He smiled. "I'm ready for my shower."

Oh, right. Shower.

I opened the door to the huge shower, checked the water to make sure it was the right temperature, and stepped back to let him enter. He breezed past me, and I wondered for a second if I should follow. I wasn't sure. Surely I could get the ropes wet? It wouldn't hurt anything, would it?

"Abigail?" he asked, standing just to the side of one of his overhead showerheads.

"Yes, Master?"

"I require your assistance," he said. His voice was low and held just a hint of gruffness. The tease of the ropes increased a notch or two, but when I stepped into the shower, I forced myself to focus on him instead of my body.

It wasn't that hard to do. He stood under a showerhead while I adjusted the side nozzles, and then he sat down on one of the tile benches.

During the week, we often showered or bathed together. Showering together was one of our favorite ways to wake up. On evenings, we sometimes shared a bottle of wine while relaxing in his huge bathtub.

But, I reminded myself, this wasn't Nathaniel. This was my Master.

I took his shampoo and squeezed some into my palm. I worked my fingers into his hair, gently scratching his scalp the way I knew he liked.

"Mmm," he said after a few minutes. "Feels good, Abigail."

My chest *accidently* brushed his shoulder. "Thank you, Master."

After finishing his hair, I started on the rest of his body, working my way from the top down. I savored bathing him, from the way my hands slid over his chest and back as I soaped him up, to the way he closed his eyes in pleasure as I angled one of the shower nozzles over him when I rinsed him off. All the while the numerous side and overhead nozzles kept us both warm and filled the shower with steam.

I worked my way lower, and he stood to accommodate me. I skipped over his erection on purpose and soaped up his upper thighs, my fingers massaging down first one leg and then the other.

When I made it to his feet, I knelt on the shower floor, picked up his right foot, placed it on my knee, leaned down, and kissed it.

His hands made their way to my head. "Again," he said.

I placed openmouthed kisses on top of his foot and all along the side before switching to the other foot to do the same. Finally, I placed his left foot down and looked up. He was staring at me, his eyes dark, and I felt warm, but not just from the steam surrounding us.

"You missed a spot," he said, hips moving forward just a bit.

I ran my hands up his legs. "Oh, no, Master. I didn't forget anything. I was saving the best for last."

"Is that so?"

"Yes, Master," I said, taking more body wash and soaping my hands up again.

I washed him gently, carefully cupping his sac in my hands and cleaning him the best I could. I lingered over his length, gripping him hard and making sure I didn't miss an inch of him. Didn't miss a centimeter.

His eyes had been closed, but he opened them when I removed my hands from his body.

"Finished?" he asked.

"I'm finished bathing you, Master," I said. "But if you don't mind, there's something else I'd like to do."

"Tell me."

"Can I show you?"

"No," he said. "I want you to use the words."

He wanted me to use words? I'd use the words.

"I want your cock, Master," I said, not even feeling the tell-tale heat of my skin that generally accompanied any sort of dirty talk on my part. "In my mouth."

He was silent. I listened to the water beating down on us, fearing he'd tell me *no*. It was his prerogative after all. He could tell me *no* just as easily as he could tell me *yes*.

I steeled my spine. Promised myself I wouldn't take it personally if he said *no*.

"I would like that very much," he finally said.

My heart sped up, but I waited. He still hadn't said *yes*.

"Go on, Abigail."

"Thank you, Master," I said, because I knew that just because I wanted him, it wasn't a given he'd let me have him. Not on a weekend.

He tasted of soap and I licked him, swirling my tongue around his cock before sucking him in all the way. He was thick and long and hard, and as always, it took me just a minute to adjust to having him in my mouth.

His hands found purchase in my hair, and he rocked his hips slightly, but for the most part he allowed me to take my time. Slowly, I worked up a rhythm until I found my pace.

It had been my request to serve him, and he allowed me to do it my way. He kept his hands in my hair, but he didn't move other than to slightly rock his hips in time with my mouth. The movement of my body pulled in delightful ways against the ropes, and I wondered, not for the first time, when he'd permit my release.

"Fuck," he said, so low I barely heard him above the water pounding us both.

I took his word for the encouragement it was and moved faster. My hands slipped along his skin. It was difficult for me to hold him since his body was so wet, but I doubled my efforts and managed. My hands played with his backside, and I ran a tentative finger along the crack of his ass.

He bucked against me in obvious pleasure.

Well, well, well. That would be something interesting to explore.

"Fuck," he said again, thrusting deeper into my mouth. I dug my fingers into the backs of his thighs and relaxed my throat moments later, as he filled me with his release.

He looked completely sated when he helped me to my feet. "Thank you," he said.

"My pleasure, Master."

The gleam in his eyes told me he would more than reward me for my service, and I couldn't wait to see what he had in store for me.

On Sunday, he took me into the playroom, where he restrained me with more ropes and used several different floggers. He started with the rabbit fur and worked up to leather, drawing out in me the feeling I'd started to crave. The one the other submissives I'd spoken to craved as well.

By the time he finished, I was quivering with need and felt certain I'd come in one never-ending wave if he so much as looked at me. I thought he'd take me in the playroom, but instead, when I was somewhat recovered and able to stand, he took my hand and led me to our bedroom.

I stepped inside behind him, noting how the room was dark

thanks to the light-limiting shades. Candles flickered from the dresser and nightstands, and soft piano music filled the room.

"On your back, in the middle of the bed," he said.

The push and pull of the ropes felt familiar now, though my excitement grew as I tried to imagine what he had planned.

After I was settled, he joined me on the bed, straddling my body. He started at my chest, unwinding the rope binding me as slowly as he had put it on. Maybe slower. When one coil of rope fell away, he did as he promised so many weeks before and trailed his finger along the marks left.

"Your skin has deep impressions," he said. "Do you feel?"

I did. My skin was hypersensitive where it had been covered for the last day. It felt like it did when I removed a Band-Aid, leaving the newly exposed skin new and almost raw. I shivered as his finger traced the indentations I could imagine in my mind.

More of the rope fell away and his lips joined his fingers in the exploration of my skin. I closed my eyes and felt. Warm breaths over my nipples. Sweet, tender kisses to my heightened and on-edge skin. Soft, soothing caresses to my backside, still prickly from the heat of his flogger.

His hands dropped to my waist to undo the ropes there.

"Come when you wish," he said, his voice husky and coarse.

The rope between my legs fell away, to be replaced by the warmth of his touch. I knew then what he was doing: he was making love to me as my master. One man. Two parts.

Nathaniel, my beloved. My gentle, considerate lover, who worshipped my body and captured my heart.

Master, also my beloved. My dominant, who commanded me with a look, controlled my body, and held my soul lovingly in his powerful hands.

In that moment, for that sliver of time, they combined together into one, and I opened my eyes to see him looking up at me from below my waist.

"Yes," I said, a soft almost whisper, even to my own ears.

"Yes?" he asked, turning his head to lightly kiss the inside of my thigh.

"Yes," I repeated. "Both. Now. Like this."

I knew it probably didn't make sense to him, but I couldn't help it. Whether he understood or not, he continued what he was doing, slowly removing the ropes. All the while making me feel as if he unraveled *me*.

I sighed when the last rope fell away. It was as if I was newly born in my own skin. Every touch, every breath, felt new and untested. My body trembled at the sensations he created in me. I turned my head and got lost in the dance of the candles' shadow flickering on the wall. Then I closed my eyes and let myself experience the delight of his touch as the soft music carried me away.

He chuckled against my skin. "You aren't falling asleep on me, are you?"

"No, Master. Just trying to savor it all."

He made his way up my body, stopping at my chest. His tongue gently circled my breast, and he blew warm breath across my nipple. "I want you to savor it all, too."

He sucked me into his mouth, swirling his tongue, his teeth scraping ever so softly. Repeated it on the other side.

"Do you feel me?" he asked, shifting his body so I felt his need, his desire.

I dropped my hand between our bodies and took him in my hand. "Yes, Master."

"Do you want me?" he asked, thrusting slightly.

I tightened my grip. "Yes, Master."

"Show me," he whispered.

I positioned my legs on either side of him and lifted my hips, aligning our bodies. I took him inside, feeling my body stretch as he filled me.

"Yes," I said again. *Yes*, I repeated in my head.

He slid his arm under my knee and lifted my leg high, slipping deeper inside.

"Oh, God," I said, as he hit a new spot.

"Like that?" he asked, punctuating his question with a thrust of his hips.

"Yes, Master." I moaned. "More. Please. Again."

He answered with another thrust, hitting the same spot. His other hand slid to my backside and pulled me close. I whimpered at the pleasure of his hand, *there*, right where my skin was still sensitive from the kiss of his flogger.

"Feel it?" he asked, and I felt everything: his ownership, his mastery, his protectiveness, his love. Him.

I couldn't form the words, so I answered with a moan.

"I love you," he said, in time with his next thrust. "I love you, Abigail."

He'd told me only once before on a weekend that he loved me, and that had been in response to my own declaration. After I spoke the words first, on the phone. However, at that moment, he was doing more than making love to Abigail, his submissive. He was showing me with his body, his words, and his actions that he'd conquered his fear of not being able to be both lover and dom to me.

I ran my hands up his back, not realizing until then that I'd shared some of those exact fears. That I'd feared one day he would discover he didn't want or need both sides. As he continued to move in me, I knew, in the deep recesses of my soul, that he would always need both sides of himself. Just as I needed both sides of myself. As we needed both sides of the other.

He thrust again, and I lifted my hips in answer.

Our bodies took over, speaking for us in ways words never could. As my climax approached, I wrapped my legs around him.

My release built slowly until he reached between us and gently rubbed my clit. I came with a short yelp and shudder that shook my body. He held still, deep inside, as his own release surged through him. I kept my legs tight around him, wanting to keep our physical connection for as long as possible.

Finally, he rolled us over so I rested on top, and he gathered me into his arms. I lifted my face and kissed along his jaw. He sighed.

"Master?" I said, wanting to make sure I had his attention.

"Hmm?"

"I love you."

His arms tightened around me. "I love you."

Chapter Twenty-eight

——ABBY——

The end of September found us in Florida. I'll admit my idea of a nice vacation was not being surrounded by screaming kids, overly tired families, and sweaty, sticky bodies. Unless, of course, you counted Nathaniel's sweaty, sticky body.

The resort we stayed at was very nice. From a distance it looked like a sprawling Victorian mansion and, if you ignored the constant traffic in the lobby, it was nicely decorated as well. Nathaniel had procured us a roomy suite, and it was relatively quiet on the upper floors.

When we arrived on Friday night, I had my collar on. At first I thought it would be like when we stayed in Tampa for the Super Bowl, but he was quick to tell me otherwise.

"I want you in my bed this weekend, Abigail," he said.

I wasn't about to argue with that.

His part in the conference didn't start until Sunday evening, so for the first part of our trip, our time was ours. Well, ours and the two hundred thousand people who happened to be visiting at the same time we were.

We tried the touristy thing on Saturday. I watched Nathaniel and enjoyed his almost childlike playfulness, realizing just how much of his childhood had been stolen from him with his parents' deaths. But a day was just about all we could take of the push and pull of the crowds. I supposed we were both relatively quiet people who enjoyed our privacy. This was just as well, considering his plans for Sunday morning. It had somehow escaped my attention that spreader bars, floggers, and paddles filled one of his suitcases.

On Monday, I spent the morning in the resort's spa, Nathaniel's reward for the day before. Afterward I lounged by the pool, watching little kids splash around the shallow end. Even though I was half reading, I noticed at once when Nathaniel entered the pool area.

For one, he still had his suit and tie on. Regardless of being in Florida for a conference, no one else I'd seen had visited the pool dressed in such a manner.

Second, he *was* Nathaniel and he *was* a sight to behold. As evidenced by the number of women who perked up or talked more animatedly when he showed up. I held my magazine up higher, hiding for just a second as I watched him.

He looked around the pool, eyes scanning faces as he tried to find me. I shot my gaze to the text before me when he started looking at the pool deck.

The ladies' voices to my right dropping to a low murmur was my only indication he'd found me. I strained to hear what they were saying as it became obvious he was walking toward me.

"There you are," he said, taking a seat in the empty lounge chair to my left.

I folded my magazine across my chest and smiled brightly at him. "How'd it go?"

"Eh," he said. "As well as can be expected. Talk, talk, and more talk. Boring as hell, actually."

"No receptions. No cocktail parties tonight?"

"Nope," he said. "Just you and me."

"Heaven," I said. The night before we'd attended a reception, and the never-ending smiles and introductions had just about done me in.

"It will be as soon as I get out of this suit."

I thought back to my comment to Elaina the month before about getting him out of his clothes. And our suite did have a private whirlpool. "How about I help you with that?" I asked. "Maybe order some wine from room service?"

He stood up. "Count me in."

I collected my things and draped my gauzy wrap across my shoulders. I didn't miss the viperlike stares of the women to my right as we left with Nathaniel's hand protectively settled around my waist.

Late Tuesday afternoon, he surprised me after he finished with his conference for the day.

"Pack an overnight bag," he said, finding me while I dug through my bag in search of a book to read. "I have a surprise for you."

"Overnight? Aren't we already doing that?" I waved my hand to an unpacked suitcase visible in the open closet.

His eyes were positively dancing with excitement. "Consider this an overnight overnight."

"Okay," I said, getting caught up in his playful mood and shoving my new book to the back of my mind. "What does one pack for an overnight overnight?"

"First"——he undid his tie as he talked, and I walked over to help him——"wear the dress Elaina gave you, and——"

"That one?" I asked, my hands stilling at his neck. I held his face, forcing him to meet my gaze. "Where are you taking me?"

His mouth curled up at one end. "It's not a surprise if I tell you."

I scowled at him, but he just kept on with the half smile.

"Okay. Fine," I said. "I'll wear the *gown*. There's no one on this planet who should be allowed to call it a *dress*. What else?"

"Casual for tomorrow."

Wednesday was his free day. I narrowed my eyes at him as if I could pick the information from his brain simply by the force of my will.

What is he planning?

"A bathing suit." He nodded toward the bathroom. "And I suppose you'll need to bring your two hundred bottles of face cream."

I laughed. "They aren't all face cream, and there aren't two hundred of them. I have only a cleanser, a toner, and a——"

"Yes, yes," he said, clearly enjoying himself. "All of them. Bring them all."

"You're impossible."

Again with the smile. "Not for you," he said. "Never impossible for you."

I huffed and crossed my arms in mock disgust. "How long do I have?"

He gave me a quick kiss on the cheek. "Two hours?"

Two hours later, I was dressed and packed. I'll admit I felt a bit silly wearing the gown Elaina gave me for my birthday. I still didn't quite understand why she'd felt the need to give me a gown, of all things. I supposed she knew I'd need several formal items, since Nathaniel attended various black tie events in any given year.

The gown was lovely: an elegant halter dress made of flowing chiffon and belted at the waist. The slate-gray color should have washed me out, but somehow Elaina had known how fabulous it'd look on me.

Still . . .

I'd be walking around a family resort in a formal gown, dragging an overnight bag behind me, for crying out loud. I was willing to bet everyone would look at me like I was two bricks short of a load.

I checked myself in the living room mirror to make sure I didn't have lipstick on my teeth. Wouldn't do to be all dressed up with someplace to go—*someplace secret*, I corrected myself—and to have lipstick on my teeth.

I gave my reflection a satisfied half nod. Not bad. Even for dragging around an overnight bag.

Then Nathaniel stepped out of the bathroom.

Now, I'd seen Nathaniel in a tux before, and it had always been enough to give me pause, but somehow he looked even more . . . *more*.

I looked him up and down. "Hello, handsome."

"Hello, beautiful," he said, planting a kiss on my forehead. "You look too perfect to touch."

This from the man who packed spreader bars and a wooden paddle for vacation?

"Don't be silly," I said, patting his chest.

He jumped backward as if I'd punched him, his face freezing in horror, but almost before I could register what happened, his expression returned to normal.

I blinked.

"You okay?" I asked.

"Oh, yes," he said. "Just thought I'd forgotten to pack a little something, something."

I tilted my head. "Did you?"

"Did I what?"

"Forget to pack a little something, something?"

"No. The something, something is perfectly safe."

I grabbed the handle to my bag. "Are we ready?"

He glanced at his watch. "Almost." He held up a finger. "Just need . . ."

Someone knocked at the door.

"That," he finished.

That?

"The bellboy to take our bags," he said.

Of course. Why did I ever think Nathaniel would have me drag an overnight bag while dressed to the nines?

He opened the door, handed the waiting gentleman our bags, and held out his arm to me. "Ready?"

We walked through endless hallways and corridors on our way outside. I knew we turned a few heads as we passed. From the corner of my eye, I even saw one lady take a picture of us with her cell phone. I chuckled before remembering my name had been in *People*. Matter of fact, my picture had been as well, thanks to being Felicia's maid of honor.

Still, that hardly warranted a hastily snapped picture.

I recalled Googling Nathaniel's name after meeting him in his office for the first time and how I'd found the picture with Melanie at his side. I wondered if that image was still the first to pop up, or if it had been replaced by one with me. I made a mental note to check on my laptop once we made it back to the room.

As we wove our way through the lobby, something interesting happened.

I walked straighter, my shoulders back and my head up. I realized on that walk that I was not merely Nathaniel's date, his submissive, or even his live-in girlfriend.

I was Nathaniel's equal.

In everything.

In the bedroom, out of the bedroom. In the playroom, out of the playroom. In the business world, out of the business world.

He was no better or worse than me, and I was no better or worse than him.

I was so caught up in that realization, we made it to the end of a dock before I comprehended where we were.

I looked in front of us.

"You're taking me on a boat?" I asked.

He leaned down and whispered to me, "Technically, it's a yacht, but yes, I am."

It was long and sleek, and looked like it should be gracing the cover of a boating magazine instead of being docked in south central Florida. Not that I was complaining about it being docked in south central Florida.

"I've never been on a boat before," I said, then hastily added, "Or a yacht."

"You haven't?"

"No," I said. "I never had much interest in fishing."

"Do you not want to sail?"

"Oh, no. I've always wanted to be on a boat, just not a fishing one."

"Yacht," he said, nodding toward the uniformed man approaching us. "He might take offense if you keep calling his baby a boat."

"Yacht," I said. "Always wanted to sail on one of those, too."

The captain welcomed us aboard and then left us alone to explore. There was a bedroom, a sitting room, and a well-appointed bathroom. I noted our bags had been stowed away in the bedroom closet.

Dusk was falling when we stepped back out on deck. I looked

around. The yacht had pulled away from the dock and resort and was making its way to the middle of the lake.

I watched the water for a few minutes, enjoying the soft breeze and the hum of the yacht's motor. Once we'd pulled away from the majority of the resort water traffic, we stopped.

"Dinner's ready," Nathaniel whispered, coming up behind me and taking my hand.

I nodded and turned. Someone had been busy. A candlelit table had been set up on deck with crisp white linens and delicate china.

"It's beautiful," I said.

He smiled. "I suppose beauty's relative. Come with me," he said. "I ordered your favorites."

He pulled a chair out for me and, once he took his own seat, poured us both some red wine. I took the glass he offered and looked up as I sipped. A thousand sparkling stars were visible, joining in to perfect the scene further.

A waiter appeared and set a bowl of soup in front of each of us.

"You know," I said, after I enjoyed a few spoonfuls of the delectable soup. "One of these days, I'm going to surprise you."

"You are?" he asked.

"Yes," I said. "First of all, I'll blindfold you."

"I like the sound of this."

I took another sip of soup. Butternut squash. The taste was a delicious combination of oaky sweetness. "Then I'll force you into the car and drive."

"Where will you take me?"

"Somewhere completely unexpected." His expression practically begged me to continue, so I did. "The grocery store."

He set his spoon down. "The grocery store?"

"Yes," I said. "And I'll drag you up and down aisles and show you how to properly choose your milk and bread."

"You're going to surprise me with a trip to the grocery store?"

I nodded. "Yes. Because I could never come up with anything as wonderful as all this." I waved my hand. "This is lovely. Thank you."

"You're thanking me, and we haven't even made it to our entrées yet."

"I don't need the entrées," I said. "Just being here with you. The thought, the planning you put in to all this. It's perfect. Thank you."

"Abby," he said. "I've lived the majority of my adult life alone. I thoroughly enjoyed planning this." His eyes still held the glow of excitement they had hours ago. "Besides. You, in the moonlight, with candles lighting your face. That gown." He shook his head. "It's all the thanks I need."

He hadn't exaggerated when he said he'd ordered my favorites. The soup was followed by braised lamb with roasted asparagus. A plate of cheeses came next.

"That was wonderful," I said, finally putting my napkin beside my empty plate. "I don't think I can eat another bite."

Nathaniel smiled at the waiter, who had appeared to remove our plates. "Nothing else for right now."

I wondered what else he had planned.

"Thank you, sir," the waiter said and left, hands full of empty plates.

Soft music had somehow been piped on deck and had played while we ate. Moments after the waiter left, the music changed and the familiar strains of a piano started to play.

Nathaniel stood, walked to my side, and held out a hand. "Dance with me?"

I took his hand and stood. "Always."

He drew me close and as we danced, I felt the warmth of his hand along my shoulders. I thought back, remembering, and sighed.

"Happy sigh?" he asked.

"Yes," I said. "Just remembering."

"Remembering what?"

"Our first dance." I pulled back and caught his eyes. "You re-member?"

"Of course," he said. "You made me want to dance. How could I forget that?"

"I think," I said, catching my bottom lip between my teeth. "I think that was the night I first realized I could fall in love with you."

"Really?"

"Mmm," I hummed as he spun me slowly around the deck. The waiter was nowhere in sight, and it felt as if we were the only people on Earth. Maybe we were. "It scared me, that real-ization. I still wasn't sure who you were, but it didn't matter. I knew I was in danger of falling in love with you." I squinted at him. "What were you thinking that night?"

He had a faraway expression in his eyes. "The night of our first dance, Linda's benefit, I was still in horrible denial. I couldn't admit to myself how much I felt for you."

Not surprising when you thought about it.

"Now," he said, hand slipping to my waist. "The night of our second dance—"

"Felicia and Jackson's engagement party?"

He nodded. "That night, I knew exactly how much I cared for you. How much I loved you. And *I* was the scared one. I was so afraid you'd never want anything to do with me again."

The night was too perfect to dwell on our past. We'd dis-cussed and talked about it so many times. I wanted to talk of our present, our future.

"But our third dance," I said. "When they got married . . ."

"That dance," he said, with a smile. "Was near perfect."

"Yes, but not nearly as perfect as this one."

We came to a stop in our dancing, and though the music continued, we simply stood with our arms around each other. I looked up into his face. My Nathaniel. My heart hurt just thinking about how I loved him. If I could just bottle the night to somehow breathe it in when things got difficult . . .

He swallowed several times.

"Abby," he started and then stopped.

Oh, fuck, is something wrong?

"Are you okay?" I asked.

He nodded, almost absentmindedly, before continuing. "I've, uh, thought about this so many times and came up with line, after line, after line. Somehow, though, I think the simple approach is best."

What the . . . ?

He moved a step back, took something from his jacket pocket, and dropped to one knee.

My hand flew to my mouth.

"Abby King," he said, his eyes filled with love and adoration. "I love you. Will you marry me?" He opened what I now saw was a ring box, exposing a stunning diamond solitaire inside. "Be my wife?"

It wasn't until he said, "Abby," again that I realized I was frozen with my hands covering my mouth.

Have I not answered?

"Yes," I said just in case, and his face erupted in an expression of joy, relief, and delight.

"Yes?" he asked, still not moving from kneeling on the deck.

"Yes. Yes. Yes," I said. The ring looked all blurry.

He stood to his feet. "You're crying."

"Sorry." I wiped the moisture from my eyes. "It's just you. There." I pointed to the ring. "And then . . ."

He very slowly slipped the ring from the box, and I saw it

clearer. The band was composed of a single row of diamonds and the center stone had to be at least three carats.

Making sure he kept his eyes locked on mine, he lifted my left hand and kissed my ring finger, right where it met my palm, before sliding the solitaire on.

"Perfect fit," I said, finally breaking eye contact to look at my hand. The moonlight bounced off the flawless stone, and my hand felt heavy and weightless at the same time.

"I cheated," he said. "Felicia helped with the ring size."

I laughed as I understood just how long he'd been planning the night. "And Elaina?"

"Actually," he said, "the gown was her idea."

"But she knew?" I asked. "About tonight?"

"Mmm." He nodded and lifted my left hand up once again. "I can't wait."

"Me either," I said, wiggling my fingers, knowing exactly what he was talking about. We'd be married before the year was out.

He drew me close, placing soft kisses along my cheekbone. I dug my fingers through his hair and lifted my chin to brush his lips with mine. The touch of his lips was so familiar, and yet somehow still so new. I parted my mouth and tasted him, taking his hands and pulling him closer, delighting in the knowledge that *this*, this man, his touch, would be mine forever.

And I would be his.

Eventually, he pulled back and kissed the inside of my hand, his lips brushing my ring finger once more. "Abby West," he said. "I like the sound of that."

"Abigail West," I said, testing the words on my tongue.

"Oh, yes," he said with a delighted smile. "That, too."

Epilogue

——SIX YEARS LATER——

It's Friday night and the house is quiet. Apollo sits in the upstairs hall, as usual, in between the two closed bedroom
doors. He sighs and places his head on his paws, knowing it
won't be too long before he can check on the baby again. Perhaps tomorrow they can all go outside and play under the shade
of the tree house again.

Henry is eight weeks old. His sister, Elizabeth, turns three
next month.

The door to the master bedroom opens and Abby steps out,
naked except for a bra, her steps light and quick. While her body
is still lithe, it has changed much in the last few years. And
though her nights are far from restful, she is not tired at the moment.

She was promoted to library director three years ago. In that
time, she has started a new literacy campaign, expanded the
high school tutoring program, and implemented a summer
camp for primary- and middle-school-aged children. She has en-

joyed the position, but will step down and turn in her resignation next week, as she wants to be at home with the children.

Tonight, though, her focus is on something else entirely, and she pauses briefly outside each of the two rooms, making sure there is no sound from within before turning and entering the playroom. She is both excited and tentative as she enters. Excited, because it is the first time in far too long since they have been in the playroom, and tentative, for the same reason.

She knows he will go easy on her tonight. He had the first time after Elizabeth was born. She doesn't care, though. After years of living, loving, fighting, and making up, she rests comfortably in the knowledge that in the playroom, he is her master.

She wants it no other way.

Moments after the playroom door closes behind her, the master bedroom door opens once more, and Nathaniel steps out into the hallway. He wears the black jeans he normally does for playroom time. His mind runs through the plans he has for the night, and he spends a few minutes trying to anticipate her reaction. She probably knows he won't push her too hard. This will just be a reacclimation for them both.

For a moment, he stands outside his children's doors and imagines them sleeping within. Elizabeth, so full of life, with inquisitive eyes and a curious mind so similar to her mother's. And Henry, already showing signs of a quiet, contemplative soul.

He glances down at his wedding band, his father's wedding band, and smiles before walking to the playroom. Inside is his wife, submissive, lover, the mother of his children, and his best friend. Tonight, he will once more command her body and soul, playing them both the way she craves, the way only he can.

When they are finished, he will carry her to their bedroom, where he will worship her with words and touches, wrapping her in the security and comfort of his love.

Tara Sue Me wrote her first novel at the age of twelve. It would be twenty years before she picked up her pen to write the second.

After completing several traditional romances, she decided to try her hand at something spicier and started work on *The Submissive*. What began as a writing exercise quickly took on a life of its own, and sequels *The Dominant* and *The Training* soon followed. Originally published online, the trilogy was a huge hit with readers around the world. Each of the books has now been read and reread more than a million times.

Tara kept her identity and her writing life secret, not even telling her husband what she was working on. To this day, only a handful of people know the truth (though she has told her husband). They live together in the southeastern United States with their two children.

According to Julie's best friend and business partner, Sasha, men only bought flowers for two reasons: to get in your pants or to get back in your pants. While Julie didn't think that to be an absolute truth, once Sasha made up her mind, she didn't often change it.

The front door of Petal Pushers, the floral shop they owned together, opened with a melodic ring. After seeing the two customers walk in, Julie decided to make her case once again.

"Look at those two," she said with a whisper, making sure the customers couldn't hear. "I highly doubt he's trying to get into *her* pants."

Sasha looked up from the computer where she was placing an order for next week's stock. The "he" in question was tall, with sculpted angular features and dirty blond hair, but the woman by his side wasn't the usual trophy girlfriend. She was an older woman, dressed for the chilly weather in Wilmington, Delaware, in a winter white coat that probably cost more than Julie made in a year.

"Never know these days." Sasha punched a few keys on the computer. "I need to make a few calls. Can you handle these two?"

Julie waved her to the back office and turned her attention to the couple still standing by the door. This time she noticed how expensive the guy's coat was while he talked on his cell phone. The woman with him admired a floral arrangement displayed for an upcoming wedding.

"Good afternoon," Julie said. "Welcome. Can I help you with something?"

The older lady smiled. "My great-granddaughter has a ballet recital tonight. I wanted to pick up some flowers." She turned to the guy, still on his phone. "Daniel, do put that away and come here."

The man at the door spoke a few more words before disconnecting. "Sorry, Grandma. It couldn't wait."

She rolled her eyes. "It never can."

"I heard that." His voice was low and deep, and as he approached, his gaze met Julie's. Blue steel was her first thought when she saw his eyes. Hard and immovable. She actually squirmed under their scrutiny.

For a second, she thought he realized the effect he had on her, because something in his expression flickered with understanding. Just as quickly, though, his mouth upturned into a soft smile. "We're looking for something to thrill the heart of a five-year-old ballerina."

Julie stood and told herself to focus on the sale, not on the customer's eyes. "Your daughter?"

The older lady laughed. "Heavens no, dear. Not Daniel," she said as if the idea of Daniel having a daughter was the most humorous thing in the world.

Daniel appeared unaffected by his grandmother's words. He

only raised an eyebrow to Julie and proceeded to take off his leather gloves.

He pulled one finger at a time free, and for whatever reason, Julie found herself unable to stop watching the mundane task. His fingers were long, and as he took the last glove off and kept it in his fist, she admired the elegant but subtle strength in the way he moved. Her mind drifted, imagining those fingers brushing her skin. Those hands on her . . .

How would his touch feel cupping her chin, trailing downward, across her breasts? Lower, brushing her hips, inching closer—

He smacked the gloves against his palm.

"The five-year-old in question," he said, eyes lighting at her startled expression, "loves ruffles, ponies, and all things princess."

Focus, she scolded herself. Flowers.

"Sounds like she would love pink roses."

"Pink roses. Excellent suggestion, Ms. Masterson," he answered with a whisper and a glance at her name tag. "That's exactly what I thought, but Grandma thought wildflowers."

"Based on what you said, the roses. Definitely pink roses."

"We'll take a dozen." His blue eyes were steady on hers and she leaned closer as his voice dropped further. "How about you, Ms. Masterson? What type flowers do you like?"

"I'm not really a flower-type girl."

"Really?"

She shrugged. "I guess it comes from working with them all day."

It wasn't that she didn't like flowers. She just didn't like getting them from men. In her opinion, there were plenty of other more romantic gifts.

"Daniel," his grandmother said, "have you decided on something?"

He winked at Julie. "We're going with pink roses. She's guaranteed to love them."

After they left with the roses, Julie tried to decide what it was about Daniel that made her react the way she had. He had a breezy confidence about him, but a lot of her male customers did. There was something, though, about the way he moved that seemed somehow *more*.

"They leave?" Sasha asked, returning from the back office and running her fingers through her dark spiky hair.

"Yeah. And you were wrong. He wasn't trying to get into anyone's pants. He was buying flowers for his niece."

Sasha flipped through the day's receipts. "Daniel Covington doesn't have to try to get into anyone's pants. Women just drop them at the mere sight of him."

Julie looked up from the new arrangement she had been working on. "You know him?"

It really shouldn't have surprised her. Sasha knew everyone. It was one of the reasons the shop had been so successful. Julie was the business-minded one; Sasha the people person.

Or maybe she had dated him. Sasha was known for her ability to run through men like tissue paper. Every other month, it seemed she was on the arm of a new guy. *New and improved. Highly disposable.* But certainly Julie would have remembered Daniel.

"I don't *know* him know him," she said. "But I know of him. He's the Senior Vice President of Weston Bank."

Second-largest bank in Delaware.

That certainly explains why he didn't blink at the cost of a dozen pink roses in January.

"Wealthy and good-looking," Julie said with a sigh. "The universe is so unfair."

Sasha's head snapped up. "Not you, too."

"Not me, too, what?"

"Wanting to drop your pants for Daniel."

Julie picked up the flower she'd been trimming and twirled it between her fingers, trying not to remember how she'd imagined Daniel's hands and what they'd feel like on her body. "I don't want to do any such thing. What's it to you, anyway? You're always telling me to get out more."

"I didn't mean with *him*."

"Are you telling me I'm not good enough for the Senior Vice President of Weston Bank?" Julie pointed the flower at her friend. "Don't make me come over there."

She added the last as a joke, but in reality she was just covering the hurt at the suggestion she wasn't good enough for someone like Daniel. Hurt, yes, but there was also anger at her friend. How dared she insinuate that Julie couldn't date an executive? Besides, who was Sasha to judge? It wasn't like she had a stellar record with the opposite sex.

"I'm just telling you, you're not compatible."

"And I thought you didn't know him."

"I don't," Sasha said in the tone of voice that told Julie the topic wasn't up for further discussion.

Julie tried to decide if she wanted to push it. What did Sasha know about Daniel that made her so certain Julie and he weren't compatible? She wondered again for just a second if they had dated.

"Doesn't matter anyway," Julie finally said. "He just came in to buy roses. It's not like I'll ever see him again." Because the universe really wasn't fair.

Sasha looked at her apologetically and nodded toward the trimmed flowers Julie was working with. "On the other hand, people we would be okay never seeing again always seem to pop up. I took a phone call in the back."

Julie dropped the flower. "Mrs. Grant? Again? She's already changed her order twice."

"She read an article."

"Of course she did."

Sasha dug in her pocket and pulled out a ten-dollar bill. "Why don't you go grab us some mochas? I'll handle her this time."

Julie took the cash. "You're the best."

"Don't you forget it!" her friend teased as she left.

The sound of flesh slapping flesh rang out in the otherwise silent room as Daniel watched the couple in his playroom. Ron was his new mentee, a highly coveted position in their local BDSM group. Daniel had held several conversations with the young man, but this was the first time he had watched him with a submissive.

Dena, the submissive, was an experienced sub in their group. A good choice for a Dom in training, which was why Daniel had asked her to join them for the afternoon.

Daniel walked to where Ron had her positioned over a padded table. "Nice location," he said, in response to the spanking the young man had just administered. "But do it again. Harder this time." He ran his hand over Dena's ass. Barely warm. "She's no masochist, but she needs to feel it."

Ron nodded and went back to spanking.

"Watch for signs," Daniel instructed. Dena hadn't been commanded to be still and she wasn't bound. "When she starts to get aroused, she'll lift up to you. Listen to her. If she's not required to be silent, you can judge her response by her moans." He lifted his voice for her benefit. "But I did command silence today, so if she gives so much as a whimper, you can watch me punish her."

He didn't miss the hitch in her breathing. He smiled in response and walked to stand by her head. "Don't get too excited, girl. I call it punishment for a reason. You won't like it."

Dena steeled her body, and if Daniel were a betting man, he'd guess there would be no disobedience today. He took a step back so he could keep both participants in his sight. Ron was putting more power into his strike and she loved it.

"Run your hand between her legs," Daniel instructed. "It'll allow you to see how wet she is and heighten her arousal."

Ron gave her one more slap on the backside and then slipped his hands between her legs. "She's soaked."

"Smack her pussy quick and hard a few times. Tell her she's been a good girl."

Ron continued with the lesson, following Daniel's advice, correcting himself when needed, and bringing Dena closer and closer to climax. While watching his mentee pleasure the submissive orally, he recognized his own need. It had been weeks since he'd played with anyone. Far too long since he'd held a woman's submission in his hands and showed her the pleasure he could bring her.

Without even thinking about why, his mind wandered back to the petite florist with the long dark hair he'd talked with days earlier. There had been an air about her. Something beyond her physical beauty drew him to her. Maybe the intelligent and self-confident look in her eyes or the unveiled way she'd sized him up. Certainly, there'd been some kind of sexual awareness between them. What would it be like to have her submission? To control her pleasure? It was far easier to picture her on her knees before him than it should be.

Forget it, he told himself. She's strictly vanilla.

Not that he knew it with any certainty, but he'd learned a long time ago, it was best to assume a woman was vanilla until proven otherwise.

He forced his attention back to the couple before him. Ron needed a lesson in how to care for a submissive after play ended. Any thoughts having to do with the beguiling florist would have to wait.

Because as much as Daniel tried to think otherwise, he knew it to be only a matter of time before she joined him in his fantasies.